HARD WHISPERS

PAMELA MARTIN

LIVE OAK
BOOK COMPANY

Published by Live Oak Book Company
Austin, TX
www.liveoakbookcompany.com

Distributed by Live Oak Book Company

For ordering information or special discounts for bulk purchases, please contact Live Oak Book Company at PO Box 91869, Austin, TX 78709, 512.891.6100.

Design and composition by Greenleaf Book Group LLC and Alex Head
Cover design by Greenleaf Book Group LLC

Publisher's Cataloging in Publication data is available from
Live Oak Book Company.

Print ISBN: 978-1-936909-63-6
eBook ISBN: 978-1-936909-65-0

Second Edition

PROLOGUE

Chevy Chase, Maryland
5:03 a.m.

Zia always hated the last two hours of her shift, but when she looked back at that particular morning, she would realize that she should have savored the last few moments when her life was normal. But for now, time seemed to slow to a crawl, and repetitive glances at her watch did nothing to speed the pace. *I have got to stop looking at the clock.* According to the local weather website, the murky overcast would soon burn away as the sun rose across Maryland. Zia was looking forward to some sunshine for a change.

But today, a different kind of cloud would remain in place. Typically, Zia's seven-to-seven shift at the Maxwell Morris Medical Institute was uneventful. This morning's shift would not be.

The multiline private phone rang. Zia stared at it for a second. *That's new; that phone never rings.* Located in the most secured room in the MMMI building, it was the only direct line to the particle-free clean room in which Zia worked. To get into the room, Zia had to pass her badge through a magnetic lock to enter the hallway that the room was on, and then she had to press her thumbprint to the scanner controlling the only door into the room. And that was just to gain access; next, she had to stand in the air shower and let it remove all traces of dust and microscopic fibers that might contaminate the absolutely sterile environment. As for communication, though, all incoming calls passed through the MMMI operator who in turn would direct the calls to the appropriate department. Calls forwarded to the clean room just did not happen. And yet the phone was ringing. Zia picked up the handset.

The caller's monotone voice captured her attention; his words were sectioned off in perfect pauses; he sounded almost like a computer.

"Put your boss on the phone now," the voice instructed.

Zia informed the caller that her boss would not be in for a few more hours.

"Get him on. I'll hold."

The appropriate response from Zia's training at MMMI automatically kicked in. *Remain vague but courteous* . . . "I am so sorry, sir, but there is absolutely no one available right now. Can I leave a message?" *Don't use anyone's name; stay general* . . .

"This is Zia Sudario, right? I am aware that you are anxious to get home to your dog, Paulo."

Zia's body tensed. *He knows my last name . . . and my dog?* Zia felt a chill creeping down her neck.

"I assure you that it will serve you well to *not* be privy to any message I would leave," the caller said. "Follow my guidelines, stay out of the loop, and you will not regret your actions. I could just as easily go to 3203 Coquelin and talk to Mr. Joseph Pierce personally. However, I think it would be much easier on everyone for you to just get him on the phone. After all, Ms. Sudario, it's not as though I'm asking you to do anything that would set you back from your usual 7:25 arrival at your rented home. And by the way . . . your Woodbrook address . . . " The man paused. "It's on a dead end . . . am I correct?"

"One moment please." Zia's hands trembled as she placed the call on hold and switched to the second line. Her fingers quivered in a rush to dial her boss's personal number. This stranger knew more about her than the people at MMMI who had been working with her every day for the past five years.

* * *

At 5:17 a.m. Joseph Pierce was jolted out of REM sleep by a persistent ringing that jangled his nerves like a splash of cold water. Instinctively he reached for the clock on the nightstand, but pressing the snooze button repeatedly yielded no results.

He growled, turning on his side, away from the noise. His large hands pressed the pillow over his head in an effort to block the disturbance. The ringing stopped, then it continued again, easily penetrating the thick padding of the cushion. His eyes fought against opening; he blinked rapidly to clear the blur of sleep so he could see the time. The glowing red numbers on the digital clock did not make any sense.

That can't be right. Five seventeen—what the hell? Is that my cell phone? An unintelligible mutter crossed his lips as he reached to the other side of the bed for his phone. The darkness would not allow him to make out the indistinct caller ID display.

No one—well, no one insignificant—even knew his cell number. He answered with deliberate dryness in his voice. "Yeah, this is Joseph." *Why am I taking this call? Should have just ignored it . . .*

"Mr. Pierce?"

"Yeah, who is this?" Joseph tried to clear his throat of the hoarse, prefunctional limitations of this ridiculous time of day.

"Sir, this is Zia. I really hate to wake you up, but we have a minor emergency here."

* * *

Zia began to feel stress twisting across her neck as she spoke to her boss. She wanted to be done with this as soon as possible. "There is a man on the line that insists on talking to you—now."

"Tell whoever it is that I will be in my office after seven."

"Exactly . . . I tried to tell him just that. But . . . "

"After seven!" And he was gone—just like that.

Zia bit her lip as she pressed the button for line one and the awaiting stranger who knew far too much. By now, she was feeling spasms in the muscles of her shoulders.

"I'm very sorry, sir, but Mr. Pierce will not be available until after seven this morning."

She listened to the monotone reply and felt her pulse nudge faster.

Fighting to keep down her rising panic, she switched to the second line, dialed Pierce's number again, and took a deep breath.

"You've got to be kidding me, Zia!"

"I'm so sorry, sir." She could hear her boss's frustrated breath-sounds.

"Did you tell them what I said?"

"Yes, sir, I did. The caller told me to tell you that he is about to call your home number. He also said if you don't answer, that although he is in Atlanta now, he will be at your door in two and a half hours."

More frustrated breathing. "This is a joke, right? Did you give him my home number?"

Zia rubbed the back of her neck, lifting her face to look up at the ceiling. "No sir, this is far from a joke. And I did not give him your home number."

* * *

Joseph Pierce sat up in bed, now fully awake. He attempted to make sense of what he had just been told. Calls to his unlisted home did not happen. The fact that someone would even suggest that he was going to call Pierce's home number balanced on the edge of insanity, because no one except his mother even knew it.

"Umm . . . Zia, just go ahead and take off, I'll handle this when I get in . . . Zia? Zia, you there?"

No answer.

* * *

Zia had already placed the phone back on the hook and left the clean room, hearing the computerized locks click into place behind her. She dropped her white smock in the bin outside the door. She went to the door and swept her badge through the magnetic reader to exit the secure area. She didn't bother removing her lab coat or her shoe covers as she made her way through the maze of almost-deserted hallways.

She reached the lobby just inside the main entrance. Zia looked in her purse. Yes, her passport was still there. Thank God she had visited the U.S. Immigration office earlier that week to extend her work visa. And, since yesterday was payday, there would be enough money in her account—especially now, since she wouldn't be paying any bills.

She called for a cab, and the yellow taxi arrived in less than five minutes. She had a momentary pang, thinking about her recently purchased late-model Ford Festiva, now sitting abandoned in the parking garage.

Just before getting into the taxi she looked back at the MMMI building for one last time. When she was hired here, she was certain that this would be her place of employment forever. The prestigious research facility had represented the epitome of her career, or so she thought. Not anymore. The faceless caller had changed all that. Zia thought about how excited she had been about being involved in the high-level research and development being done at MMMI. She had always known, somewhere in the back of her mind, that the powerful people involved with MMMI probably had powerful enemies. And now she had proof. Someone out there knew far too much about her. That, added to everything that had been going on lately, told her it was time to go back home to the Philippines . . . to walk away and never look back.

"BWI Airport," Zia said to the driver as he pulled away from the curb. She called her neighbor Barbara, who always turned her cell phone off at night. Zia left a voice mail message, telling Barbara that she had to make an emergency out-of-town trip for work; could she please check in on Paulo? Zia ended the call, wondering how long it would take Barbara to realize that Zia wasn't coming back.

How would anybody possibly know about Paulo? Zia had named her dog after her favorite author, Paulo Coelho. Since she had no relatives in the United States, Paulo was her family here—or had been, up until now.

Zia thought about some of the things she had been hearing. The information consisted mostly of rumor, but some of it was too feasible to dismiss, plausible enough to make Zia wish she'd never heard it.

The cab rolled through the quiet predawn streets on its way to the airport. Zia felt the cold track of a single tear on her cheek as she stared into emptiness. She would purchase a one-way ticket on the first flight leaving for Manila, and in twenty-six hours she would be home—and safe, she hoped.

I'm sorry, Mr. Pierce. And whatever is about to happen . . . God help you.

CHAPTER 1

Pamela Graham flipped a few more pages of the magazine and then checked her watch for about the millionth time in the last fifteen minutes. Where the hell was Roxy?

Actually, Pam knew exactly where Roxy was—she was late . . . unless, of course, she was a no-show. With Roxy Reynolds it was always one or the other, and it was usually impossible to tell which until you were already inconvenienced to the max.

As soon as Pam had told Roxy about her plans for going to Russia after graduation, Roxy had insisted on reserving the last night she would be in Dallas for, as Roxy phrased it, painting the town red. Of course, as Pam knew from experience, Roxy was more likely to smear the town than paint it. Pam recalled Roxy's words that morning, "Just be ready at seven thirty and let me handle all the details, okay?" Pam noted that the current time was well after eight. With the extra moments she was sure Roxy was going to allow, she went over her travel checklist again. Then, she picked up her pocket journal and started on the latest version of her will.

This was maybe the fifth will Pam had written for herself. It had started as an assignment in a high school English class: "Write your will, as if you were going to die tomorrow, and account for everything of value in your life." For some reason, Pam had taken the assignment to heart. She had gone through maybe a dozen of these small pocket journals, writing down ideas for the most valuable things in her life, then crossing them off and replacing them with others. In a box somewhere, Pam had all the journals she had ever written in. Now and then, it was interesting to read what she had written in her younger years.

Lately, Pam's wills had less to do with things and more to do with accomplishments. That was a good thing, she supposed. But her evolving consciousness was having the uncomfortable result of placing her more and more at odds with her father's plans for her life. She looked at her will, changed a couple of words in the last line, and sighed.

Pam had considered passing on the celebration with Roxy several times before she finally accepted. With an early morning flight the next day, partying with Roxy the night before smelled of disaster. In the end she surrendered to the idea more for Roxy and less for herself. Roxy had been a good friend for a long time—well before SMU. Even after they'd graduated and Roxy had gotten her dream job with the television station, she and Pam had stayed close. Roxy was an airhead and a little bit of a user, but she was Roxy, and Pam just couldn't bring herself to ditch her best friend's party plans.

The doorbell chimed. Pam checked the time again as she made her way to the front door of her penthouse apartment: a little past eight thirty. Pam opened the door and blocked the entry with her body, giving Roxy an annoyed stare. "Sooo . . . seven thirty, huh?"

Roxy gasped, tapping her watch. "Really? Am I late?"

As usual, Roxy wore an outfit suspiciously similar to the one Pam had had on the last time they went out. Pam had long ago taken a vow to stop telling Roxy the names of her favorite stores. She gave Roxy a once-over, twisting her mouth to one side. "Cute outfit."

If Roxy even noticed the sarcasm, she let it fly right over her hair extensions. She slid past Pam into the apartment. "Really? You like? Just picked it up today," she said, giving Pam a catwalk twirl.

"Nieman's?"

"Yes, how did you guess?"

"Psychic." Pamela shook her head and smiled.

Roxy, in her customary fashion, did not come empty-handed. She placed two bottles of champagne on the bar. If this evening went as others had, one of the bottles would be for Roxy and the other would be . . . for Roxy.

Pam remembered her resolve to brush aside any exasperation she might be feeling toward Roxy. As much as Roxy tended to either purposely or inadvertently irritate her—and Pam usually couldn't be sure which it was—it had to be forgiven; she was just being herself. Most of Pamela's friends had entered her life as compatible spirits; Roxy had sort of grown on her.

Roxy and Pam met in high school but had never really hung out until a couple of years after graduating. If anyone asked Roxy, she would say that she and Pam had been buddies since the tenth grade. In reality Pam befriended the adolescent Roxy, who sported thick glasses, frizzy hair, and braces, because no one else would. In those days, Roxy Reynolds was called "R Square." Unfortunately, the "square" part of the epithet referred to her peers' assessment of Roxy's lack of coolness rather than her double-R initials, as Roxy had led herself to believe. Pam never had the heart to tell her any differently.

As usual, Roxy made a beeline for the mirror. She teased her dark brown curls with a small comb, creating a difference that only she could see. The long curls fell past her shoulders, bouncing as she turned from one side to the other. Pam realized once again that her friend's outer appearance suited her occupation as an entertainment reporter. Her slim figure and semi-natural beauty complemented the guest stars instead of detracting from them. And, Pam had to admit, in a very short time Roxy had established herself as the go-to girl for numerous red carpet interviews. Production managers desired someone who was somewhat beautiful but would not overshadow the main subject; Roxy fit the bill to camera-ready perfection.

"I don't know about you, girl, but I needed this night," Roxy said over her shoulder, maintaining eye contact with herself in the mirror. She leaned toward the mirror, peering into her own eyes. "I have been feeling like shit the past few days."

"Really?"

"Yeah. I was fine till I took that damn flu shot. Hey, Pam, can I borrow some mascara? I can't find my purse that had my makeup in it."

Rolling her eyes, Pam retrieved an extra mascara from the bathroom and brought it to Roxy. "I never take those shots," she said. "Need anything else?"

"Yeah, some blush, if you don't mind. Well, I might have to stop taking them too. I don't have time to be sick."

Lecturing herself to not get angry with Roxy, Pam went back to her bathroom vanity and found a container of blush. "Was your ID in your purse, you doofus? What were you planning to use at the bars?"

"Oh, I just brought my passport," Roxy said. "Thanks," she said, grabbing the blush from Pam's open palm.

"No problem. What are friends for?" Pam went to her bedroom to retrieve from her half-packed luggage a Marc Jacobs purse she had purchased for the trip. Coming back out, she met Roxy in the hallway. Her eyes went directly to Pam's purse. She reached over and pulled it out of Pamela's hand. "Hey, nice purse! Where did you get it?"

Pamela pulled it back. "Walmart."

"Touchy, touchy! What the hell, you never put anything in your purse anyway."

"Yeah, I know, but I still like to carry one around."

"I would die without my purse. I keep everything in mine."

"Hope you survive the evening, then."

Roxy stuck her tongue out at Pam. Still, she could not take her eyes off the Marc Jacobs.

"Come on, Rox, let's get going before I change my mind. I still need to finish packing before I fly out in the morning."

"Oh God, Pamela, let's worry about that later. I'll help you pack and take you to the airport, so relax."

Pam looked back through her bedroom door at the large, open suitcase. "You may be on to something."

"Of course I am, dear. Might as well enjoy tonight before you go all save-the-world on me. I still don't know why you think you've got to go all the way to Russia to work with underprivileged kids. There are plenty of needy kids right here in Dallas, girl."

"Are we really going to go through all this again, Rox? First of all, it's only for three months, before I start with Formula 1. And second, not underprivileged—orphans. And if you could see some of the stuff I've seen on the Internet about how bad the Russian orphanages are—"

"Yeah, I know, I know. I get it, Pam. Don't start the sermon again."

"Okay. And besides, I've spent all that money on those Russian language CDs—"

"Enough, already! I give up. You're going halfway around the world, and I just want my bestest buddy to be safe!"

"Aww! That's so sweet of you to care, Roxy."

"Speaking of which, I heard on the news that some human rights guy just disappeared from Russia. I didn't catch the details, but they think that he was gotten rid of . . . you know, like Jimmy Hoffa. Some kind of activist."

"Yeah, I saw that too," Pam said. "Evidently he was kicking up a fuss about some kind of health-related plan the government had going. Immunization? Sterilization? I can't remember."

"So, anyway, just be careful over there, okay?"

"I will, I promise. And speaking of careful, please take care of my place when I am away, and don't forget to come and get my mail every week and forward it to me."

"How can I? This is only like the hundredth time you've reminded me," Roxy said, rolling her eyes. She went to the bar and began unwrapping the cork on one of the bottles of champagne. "Right now, let's get the party jump-started, what do you say?" Roxy popped the cork off the champagne bottle. The bubbly liquid flowed from the bottle onto Pam's thick white carpet. Giggling, Roxy covered the bottle's opening with her mouth to catch the excess.

God, I hate to think what this place is going to look like by the time I get back, Pam thought.

Roxy turned, holding out the bottle toward her. "Drink up, Pamela, my dear! Tonight, Pam and Roxy do Dallas as it has never been done before."

"Okay, but first, remember how we spent half the night trying to locate your ID last time we went out? So how about you give me your ID this time, and I'll keep it in my purse."

"Works for me, but I don't have it on me."

"You drove over here without your driver's license?"

"Nope, it's in the car, downstairs. Got a *man* driving us!" Roxy rotated her hips seductively.

Pam took the bottle from Roxy and took a long pull, figuring she was going to need all the fortification she could get.

After they had traded a few shots of Patrón and finished most of one bottle of champagne, they went downstairs. Their car, a sleek, silver BMW 750Li limo, was waiting by the front curb. As they came outside, Roxy's "man" jumped out and opened the rear passenger door for them. Judging by the bulge of his biceps against the tight black T-shirt he was wearing above his snugly fitting khakis, his driving ability wasn't all Roxy had been concerned about.

"Rox, how did you score a limo?" Pam said, genuinely surprised. "It's the height of prom season. Are you sure you can—"

"Not to worry, girlfriend," Roxy said. "I know the owner of the company . . . know him really well." she winked, giving Pam a knowing elbow. "Anyway, we've got the car—and Ricky, here—for as long as we want, no charge."

"I don't even want to know—"

"Sure you do!" Roxy was all too eager to brag about her accomplishment. "See, Beau—he's the owner of the company. Beau and I have a real good understanding, especially when it comes to his wife and her need-to-know status." Roxy pranced toward the driver, all smiles and flounce. "Thanks, Ricky," she said. "This is my friend Pam. You're going to take good care of us tonight, aren't you?"

Ricky grinned. Pam groaned inwardly. *Lord, save us . . .*

A few seconds later, they were headed toward the nightclubs in downtown Dallas. Roxy leaned toward Pam. "So, how did it go when you told dear old Dad about your save-the-planet plans, huh? Bet that went well."

"Well, Rox. First of all, taking on a temporary volunteer position at an orphanage hardly constitutes saving the planet. Second, it went okay . . . I mean, Dad is Dad; unlike the Texas weather, he ain't changing anytime soon."

"True that," Roxy said, pulling Pam's compact from the Marc Jacobs purse and flipping it open to check her makeup. "How long do you think you can put him off pressuring you to run the family biz before he pulls the drawstring on your trust fund?"

Sure, Rox, you can use my mirror. "Don't worry, Roxy. Dad isn't ruthless. Just . . . extremely persistent, that's all."

Roxy dropped the compact back into Pam's purse. Pam wasn't sure if Roxy was actually listening to the answer or not; most of the time there was only about a ten-second span before Roxy's mind drifted off. "Well, that's good. Oh, and here's my passport," she said, dropping it into Pam's purse on top of the compact. She slid forward to the front of the limo and draped a hand casually across Ricky's shoulder. "Take us to Hotel ZaZa first, Ricky, okay?"

"Yes, ma'am."

"Oh come on now, that's way too formal. Call me Roxy, rhymes with—"

"Don't even say it!" Pam interrupted. If she heard that corny-ass Roxy-Foxy line one more time, she was going to throw up.

This is gonna be a long night. Pam rolled her eyes at the back of Roxy's head.

* * *

Pam's last night in Dallas before leaving the country would be one to remember—or forget, depending on which part of the night was under consideration.

After a few tequila shots at the bar inside Hotel ZaZa, they headed for the Glass Cactus at the Gaylord resort. The Ghost Bar at the W Hotel followed, then a list of other hot spots filled in the rest of the night.

After the first five clubs, the remaining stops were a blur in Pam's mind—a hazy series of vignettes composed of thumping music, gyrating bodies, garish lighting, and far too many mixed drinks—all blended together with a liberal mixture of Roxy's uncontrolled giggling and shameless flirting with just about anything that moved.

The seesaw aspect of the night caused it to fade in and out of memory. Portions of the evening died away and then resurfaced in Pam's recollection as fast as they were created, while other parts of the night faded into obscurity, washed away on a tide of mimosas and Manhattans.

At one point, Pam realized that a truly accurate account of this night would never be fully known. It was forever lost in an alternate universe of Roxy's design. Sometime well after midnight, for reasons that probably made no sense at all to Roxy, Pam convinced Ricky to drive them home. Then she convinced Roxy to leave Ricky in the car, rather than dragging him up to the penthouse. Pam managed to get inside, walk to her room, and collapse across her bed.

And then . . . nothing.

CHAPTER 2

As soon as Pam's eyes opened the next morning, she knew that something was not right. Ignoring the questionable feeling in her stomach, she rolled over and managed to focus her eyes enough to see the red numbers on her bedside clock.

It was 8:45. Her flight left DFW International in just over two hours.

Shit, shit, shit!

She bolted from her bed and ran to the closet. *Who am I kidding? I don't have time for any more packing.* She went to the half-packed suitcase, still lying open on the floor where she had left it last night, and flung inside fistfuls of panties, bras, tops, and slacks, grabbed at random from her bureau drawers and various piles that were probably waiting to be laundered. She heaved the suitcase closed and then pushed one of the prepacked bags back inside the closet for Roxy to send later. She grabbed her carry-on bag and dashed to the bathroom, raking into the bag a random armload of cosmetics and personal-care items. Then she ran into the living room and froze in her tracks.

Dammit!

Roxy, Pam's designated driver, was passed out on her couch. Her body was slumped awkwardly, with one arm dangling to the floor and the other one twisted beneath her.

"This can't be happening!" Pam shouted, then immediately regretted it; the sound of her voice caused an even greater pounding in her head.

"Rox! Roxy!" Pam shook her. Roxy moaned and rolled away from Pam. *Well at least she's still alive.*

Time for plan B. One semipacked bag, her purse, and a carry-on had just become the only items she would take on the trip—for now, at least. She flipped open her cell phone and made a frantic call to the building concierge.

"Gabe, it's Pam Graham. Can you please be a sweetheart and call a cab for me? And is there any way you could help me get some luggage downstairs? I'm running kind of late for a flight . . . Thank you so much, Gabe, you've saved my life—again!"

Barely five minutes later, Gabe was slamming the cab's trunk and telling Pam—for the fifth time—not to worry, he would take care of everything and make sure Roxy was okay. Pressing a twenty into Gabe's palm, Pam hopped into the back of the cab and began applying light makeup. Her blurred image in the small compact mirror revealed red veins crisscrossing a pair of sleep-deprived light green eyes.

Pam snapped her compact closed, dropped it in her purse, and leaned back in the seat. This departure may not have been as smooth as she had planned, but she was at least on her way. The invitation to life, and whatever it might encompass, had been readily accepted. Pam could hardly believe she'd made it this far, and it felt good.

Pam thought about her father. Though she never would have admitted it to Roxy, there was a lot more involved in his reaction to Pam's going to Russia for volunteer work than the offhand reply she'd given Roxy last night. Roxy was always digging for dirt—even on her friends. It was just another of Roxy's annoying habits that Pam had learned to mostly ignore; it probably made her a good journalist, though maybe not always the best confidante.

But to say that Dad was persistent was the understatement of the century. To say that he was driven, focused, and wouldn't take "no" for an answer would be more accurate. And, on the few occasions when Pam had allowed herself to read some of the articles written about her father, many would broadly label him as ruthless, abrasive, and heartless. To be honest,

Pam found it hard to argue with most of the descriptions. Her edge was that, unlike the rest, she was fairly sure that Dad loved her.

Did he love her unconditionally? Well . . . the jury was still out on that one. But so far, though he had not exactly been thrilled about the prospects of his daughter, with her freshly minted bachelor's degree in international marketing from SMU, volunteering for three months in a Russian orphanage, he hadn't forbidden her from going. He'd even admitted that it would be good for her to "see how the other half lives." So, there was that, at least.

He was considerably less understanding about her having accepted the job with Formula 1. The fact was that the greater extent of Pam's relationship with her father dwelled somewhere between cigar puffs (his) and conversations about sports cars (definitely theirs). When the opportunity came up with Formula 1, Pam actually thought that perhaps the enthusiasm for high-performance cars that she and Dad had always shared would allow him to give some sort of reluctant blessing to her wish to forge her own path—at least for a while. So far, though, no blessing had been forthcoming. Her announcement of her first job—communicated with the maximum amount of excitement she had been able to fake—had been met, as she feared, with stony silence. No rage, no threats, and no demands for her to turn the job down . . . but nothing anywhere remotely close to approval.

Still, Pam was certain—on most days—that Dad meant well. And, after all, what father would not want his only child to enter into a business that had been owned and operated by the family for over a hundred years? Furthermore, Pam well understood that Graham Publishing and her father had afforded her the things that most would—and many had—died for. Yet she also knew that such privilege came with a cost that most only think that they are willing to pay.

And Dad was far from subtle about his intentions for Pam's career. He would voice the desire to whomever was in earshot, any time she visited him at the office. His rough voice would project across whatever room she entered, "There she is! Better start getting on her good side now, before she starts whipping you boys into shape!" The hangers-on and flunkies would laugh hysterically, as if it were the first time he had said it. Pam would roll her eyes toward the ceiling, *Oh, God . . .*

The cab pulled up in front of the international departure terminal at

DFW a minute or two less than two hours before takeoff—just enough time to make the flight, if she was lucky. As Pam tipped the driver and flagged a skycap, she wondered if she was about to take the first step toward a new life, or if she was about to step off of a ledge. Of course, free fall could be exhilarating; it could also be a drop of tremendous terror. She prayed for the former.

The nearly twenty hours she would spend en route looked to Pam like a passage to another world. Her first nine-hour leg was on KLM to Schiphol airport in Amsterdam, and then she had an Aeroflot flight of nearly equal length into Saint Petersburg.

She found her seat and grimaced when she realized she was in the center of the middle row. She stowed her carry-on, saving several brochures with information on Russian orphanages and some of the institutions she wanted to look at once she got to Saint Petersburg.

The Dutch announcements over the intercom were gibberish to Pam. She wondered if things would be any better when she boarded the Aeroflot plane. She was hoping that the hours she had spent with her Russian language CDs would at least enable her to tell if she should buckle her seat belt or start looking for her life vest. All around her, the quiet murmurs of boarding passengers came in a variety of languages; Pam had no idea of their origin. She settled into her seat, and two other passengers soon sat on either side of her. *Damn, I wish I'd had the sense to book an aisle seat!*

Time crawled past at a lethargic pace, and feeling fenced in by her seatmates didn't help. The overweight man on her right was a snorer, and the woman on her left was a gum smacker. Pam studied her brochures about Saint Petersburg apartments and hotels, and she read everything she had brought on orphanages in Russia. She had already seen every single one of the in-flight movie choices. Pam looked at the snoring man, wishing fervently that she, too, had been born with the ability to fall asleep on public transportation.

After what seemed a dark eternity, the sky began to turn pink and the aircraft began to near Schiphol. For Pam, the one-hour layover couldn't come soon enough. She decided to grab a cocktail and unwind in one of the airport bars. She was also hoping she would be luckier with her seating arrangements on the Saint Petersburg flight.

After going into the bar closest to her arrival gate at Schiphol and downing a whiskey—neat—she made a beeline for the nearest Aeroflot kiosk. Relief filled her soul when she showed the attendant her boarding pass and learned that she had a window seat. *Nothing to my left but the plane's wall—there is a God.*

At the appropriate time, she sauntered to her departure gate and waited until her section was called for boarding. As Pam neared her seat, she couldn't believe her eyes: the plus-sized snorer was plopped in the aisle seat of her row.

Why couldn't it have been the gum smacker? she demanded of an uncaring universe. But no, the hulking snorer formed a wall of flesh between Pam's seat and the aisle.

Pam normally prided herself on avoiding appearance-based judgments, but her corpulent seatmate severely tested her good intentions. His narrow glasses, which hadn't been stylish for years, balanced on the end of a bulbous nose. A coarse gray beard scattered across a weak chin and round face, growing unevenly in a minefield of acne scars and other indentations. His head rested on the absence of a neck, tilting to the side as it vibrated with a grinding snore that originated deep inside his thick throat.

Getting her body past him proved to be a daunting task. His trunk-like legs gapped open slightly, his knees touching the back of the seat in front of him. Pam calculated that it would be just possible to step between his thighs and get past him and into her seat without actually having to touch him, but the thought of stepping between his legs made her want to throw up.

Just as she passed by him, he shifted positions, closing his legs. Pam nearly felt weak with relief. If she had been sandwiched between his legs, she was sure she would have died on the spot.

Her plan for the rest of the trip involved remaining focused on the window and the wide-open possibilities for her future. But nine hours is a long time on any aircraft, even under the best of circumstances. Near the end of the flight, she could not hold it any longer; she had to get to the restroom.

Once again, she would have to squeeze past the sleeping giant. *I swear to God, next time I'll wear Depends.* She took a deep breath and stood. It was no use; in the position he was in now, she couldn't step past him. She would have to wake him up and get him to let her out.

She leaned over and began tapping the man on his bulky shoulder; it felt as if she were patting a gorilla.

"Prostite, ne mogli by vy menya vypustili?" she said, hoping that she had indeed asked him if he could let her into the aisle.

No reaction. She tapped a little harder, and then a little harder, but the man remained in a deep, gurgling sleep.

Another gentleman walked up from the rear of the plane. He pushed the man hard several times before saying a few words in Russian. Pamela's interpretation was too slow to catch every word, but she could make out some of it, and it didn't sound very polite. *I should have just held it.*

The oversized man grunted and his eyes flickered open behind the thick lenses of his glasses. He glared at Pam, his face wrinkled with disgust as he coughed, cleared his throat, and then turned to the man who shook him. The men exchanged more words.

Pamela was now certain that risking bladder damage might have been a better option. The large man maneuvered his round frame to the side. He mumbled to no one in particular as Pam squeezed past with an uncomfortable grin. "Spasibo," she said, and the large man gave her a grudging nod.

After returning to her seat, she discovered that the oversized man was now fully awake. He huffed impatiently as he saw her approaching, then he turned to the side again to allow her to pass. She could feel his eyes on her butt as she crawled past him and hated the thought of him looking at her as much as she hated the smell of cheap vodka that was secreted through his pores.

The red seat belt symbol illuminated for the passengers to fasten in for the final approach to Pulkovo-2 International. Pam adjusted her Movado watch, adding the nine-hour time difference. She was officially in sync with her new residence—well, at least her watch was.

After a relatively smooth landing and an interminable taxi, Pam deplaned with the rest of the passengers. When her single suitcase trundled out onto the luggage carousel, she realized once again that she was woefully underpacked for a three-month stay.

Her frustration faded, however, as she made her way out the revolving glass doors into the brisk air of a late spring evening in Saint Petersburg. *I'll be damned; I really did it!*

CHAPTER 3

Pam started walking toward the line of cabs. Most of them were Volgas or Ladas, with the odd Peugeot thrown into the mix. All looked pretty battered, but that was to be expected in any big city, Pam figured.

A cabbie was walking toward her, a big smile on his face as he reached for her suitcase. "You are American, yes? I speak ver' gud English, give you gud, cheap ride, yes?"

Pam's predeparture research kicked in. She knew she needed to nail down the price before she surrendered any personal belongings into Mr. Friendly's care. "Skol'ko Nevskii Ekspress Otel'?" she said, taking a firm grip on the handle of her suitcase.

"Don't worry, don't worry, gud price, gud safe ride, okay?" He was good, she thought, persisting in speaking English. And, she had to admit, it was working; Pam was tired, jet-lagged, and longing to stretch out to her full length in a reclining position. She stepped aside and let him take her suitcase. He pulled it over to a dented, dusty yellow Volga and opened the trunk.

"Nyet, nyet," she said. "V mesta, pozhaluista." She pointed at the backseat.

He gave her a puzzled look, shrugged, and slid her suitcase into the backseat. Pam got in and immediately noticed that the cab had no meter. *Time to ask again, I guess . . .* "Skol'ko Nevskii—"

"Yes, yes, I take you to Nevsky Express Hotel, no worry, okay? Gud price."

"But how much? You don't have a meter in your cab."

"I'm not big shot cab driver, okay? Just—how you say it—family man. I take gud care of you, okay?"

Yeah, Ivan, that's what I'm afraid of. What is this guy's name, anyway? "Kak tebya zovut?" she said.

He turned around and held out his hand. "I am Viktor Andreyev. And you are called how?"

"Pamela Graham." She shook his hand.

"Privet, Pamela Graham. Now you sit back and relax for gud ride, okay?"

The Volga coughed twice and started, and they pulled away from the curb, just as Pam realized she had scented vodka on Viktor's breath when he had shaken her hand. *Great. Killed in a car wreck on my first day in Russia . . .*

Viktor maneuvered the taxi onto Pulkovskoye Shosse and drove north toward the city through the evening traffic. For the first mile or two away from the airport, scantily clad saplings ran down the center of the median. Pam stared out the window at the drab, mostly featureless buildings marching past. This close to a major population center in the United States, the landscape would have looked very different, Pam thought. There would have been high-rise office buildings crowded along the shoulders of the highway, brightly colored billboards and storefronts competing eagerly for the attention of passing consumers. But here, the buildings lacked individuality, including an obvious absence of any form of advertising. The structures were strangely indistinguishable and unimpressive. Some even sat half-built, looking as if they had been abandoned for quite some time. Pam found the overall effect to be depressing.

Once they got in closer to the main metropolitan area, small blue signs with white arrows hung every few hundred meters and at the intersections, above the streets. The faded blue color reflected the down mood Pam suddenly felt. Every so often she saw locals making their way along the drab streets. Now and then she spotted a red-and-white tram with a few passengers aboard.

A few times Pam saw children, both alone and in small groups, who looked to her as if they had no place to go. They were dressed very shabbily—some in barely more than rags—and most of them seemed to be panhandling from passersby, who largely ignored them and their pleas.

The sight broke her heart. Pam knew that orphaned children lucky enough to be housed in one of the government-run shelters were often neglected and malnourished. Russian orphanages tended to be woefully understaffed, but still crowded with more children than they could adequately care for. Often, because of overcrowding and inadequate budgets, orphanages turned children out onto the street once they reached the age of ten to thirteen. Such kids—some of whom were likely those Pam saw as she passed—often turned to drugs, prostitution, or other types of criminal activity, just to survive. Many didn't survive.

Despite her weariness, Pam felt her resolve growing even firmer. Somebody had to care about these kids, and for at least the next three months, it was going to be her.

As they turned east on a thoroughfare called, as best as Pam could quickly translate the Cyrillic script on the sign, Ligovsky Prospekt, Viktor began going into his local guide mode, giving her a rundown, in his fair-to-middling English, of all the historic and artistic attractions in Saint Petersburg. "You like music, yes? We have here Mariinsky Opera House, where dances Kirov Ballet, very big deal, yes? And if you like art, you must go to Hermitage Museum, where they are having great paintings by Da Vinci, Titian, Monet, everybody, you know? Maybe you like me to take you to Summer Palace of Peter the Great? Not far, I can have you there very quick, very gud place to see."

Viktor, honey, I just spent the better part of twenty hours in an airplane seat, crammed up against Jabba the Russian. I just want to get to my hotel, get checked in, and lie down. "No, thank you," she said aloud. "Just take me to my hotel, please."

"You are tired, sure. Viktor understand. Just relax, have gud ride, and Viktor will tell you everything you need to know about Saint Petersburg."

He kept talking, but Pam tuned him out. She laid her head back on the seat and closed her eyes, allowing the droning sound of Viktor's voice and the hum and rattle of the road-worn taxi to rock her, if not to sleep, at least to a very relaxed form of wakefulness. For a while, time passed unnoticeably, punctuated only by Viktor's voice and the occasional sounds of surrounding traffic.

Eventually, though, Pam roused herself. Something wasn't right. Viktor had become very quiet, and as she looked out the window, she could swear that they were passing a large, columned building—apparently the Mariinsky Palace, according to the signs—for about the third time. Viktor was driving around in circles!

Pam sat up and leaned over the seat. "Umm, Viktor? Where are we going, exactly?"

"Sorry? Izvinite?"

Too late to fake not knowing English, tovarish. "I thought you were going to take me to the Nevsky Express Hotel?"

"I don't . . . Ya ne ponimayu?"

Oh, you damn sure do too understand, Viktor. You let me nod off in the backseat so you could rack up a nice expensive ride for the amerikanska. Probably going to charge me ten thousand rubles for driving me around the same block twenty times . . .

"Viktor, I'm very sorry, but . . . I feel sick. Bol'noi. I think . . . I'm going to throw up . . . " Pam leaned over in the backseat and started making loud, gagging noises.

Viktor started yelling in Russian. He slammed on the brakes and screeched to a halt in the middle of the wide plaza between the palace and a huge domed cathedral across the way, and a symphony of car horns erupted all around them.

Pam flung open the back door and dragged her suitcase out onto the pavement. Cars swerved around her, and she caught glimpses of angry Russians gesturing wildly as she dodged across the plaza to the nearest sidewalk. Meanwhile, Viktor had gotten out of his cab and was shouting at her, still in Russian.

By some miracle, Pam made it to relative safety. She watched as Viktor gestured in disgust, got back in his cab, and drove off, surrendering to the angry motorists stacked up behind him. By another miracle, she hailed a passing cab which, she noticed with relief, had a meter installed and apparently working. She ducked inside, gave the driver the name of her hotel, and got a prompt answer to her fare question.

She heaved a sigh of relief as the driver stowed her suitcase in the trunk and pulled back into traffic. A few minutes later, she was even more relieved to see the square, balconied façade of the Nevsky Express Hotel, so familiar to her from her Internet searches to make an online reservation.

Saying a little prayer of thanks, Pam paid the driver and then tossed in what she hoped was a generous tip. The grinning cabbie scooted out of the car, retrieved her suitcase from the trunk, and set it on the narrow sidewalk right beside the front door of the hotel.

"Bol'shoe spasibo," Pam said. "You probably saved my life, friend."

He smiled at her. "Dobro pozhalovat" he said as he got back in his cab. "You're welcome."

Pam looked up and down Nevsky Prospekt. The street was in the heart of Saint Petersburg's historic city center, and unlike the outlying areas near the airport, it was bustling with pedestrians. Pam could hear music thumping from a nearby nightclub, and people were smiling, laughing, and generally looking forward to the evening, from what she could tell. If she weren't jet-lagged out of her mind and still recovering from Viktor and the near-death experience he had instigated, she might have been tempted to walk up and down the street and sample some Russian nightlife.

But no. Pam was dog-tired. She needed to get some rest, because tomorrow she needed to be on her toes when she started her tour of the orphanages. She wanted to get a sense of how things were generally before she went to the Belarov Institute, the place where she planned to intern.

CHAPTER 4

For the next fifteen hours, Pam slept the sleep of the dead. Her internal clock was so out of sync that the few times she roused slightly in her slumber, she felt as if she had been tossed into another dimension. When she was finally able to keep her eyes open for longer than ten seconds, she looked at her watch, lying on the small table beside the narrow, hard bed. Almost noon here, three in the morning back home in Dallas. She took a deep breath and looked at her ceiling. Honestly, she felt as if she could still go back to sleep. But, she knew that she needed to get going on the reason she was in this country, and today was as good a day to start as any.

She rolled over and took from the nightstand her pocket journal. Before falling into bed the night before, she had made a few changes in her will. She read them over quickly, and to her surprise, they still made sense. Apparently, her fatigue had not rendered her mind completely incoherent.

Even though she hadn't brought her usual full complement of cosmetics and personal-care products, there wasn't nearly enough counter space in the tiny bathroom to hold her stuff. There was hot water, though, for which she was truly grateful. After a long shower, she felt much more ready to face the orphanages of Saint Petersburg.

Getting dressed was a little more of a challenge. Pawing through her hastily packed suitcase, Pam made a mental note to get in touch with Roxy and make arrangements to get the rest of the things that she would need sent over here. Maybe someone at the hotel front desk could give her some advice on the best way to ship it. She finally found enough pieces to put together a reasonable semblance of an outfit for the day.

Pam went downstairs, realizing she was really hungry. That made sense; she'd gone to sleep as soon as she walked into her room yesterday in the early evening and had slept through at least two mealtimes. Her first order of business was to find a cab that she could hire for the day, and her second agenda item was lunch. What was a typical Petrovite lunch? she wondered.

Pam walked outside and looked down the street. Almost immediately, a yellow Volga pulled to the curb right in front of her. Just as she was thinking that today was going to be her lucky day, the driver got out and came around toward her, his face looking everything but happy.

Oh, God. Viktor.

Not sure if he was going to start swearing at her in Russian or just shoot her, Pam started backing toward the hotel door. *Thank God there are people passing on the sidewalk. Surely, in front of witnesses, he wouldn't—*

"Pamela Graham, we need talk," he said.

"Look, Viktor, I'm sorry, but you never told me how much the ride was going to be, and you were driving me around in circles, and I was tired, and I don't speak much Russian, and—"

"Nyet, nyet," he said, shaking his head and pressing his palms toward her in a quieting motion. "Viktor doesn't care about cab fare. Well . . . I was mad yesterday, but now am okay."

"Really? You're not mad?"

"Well, little bit, maybe," he said. "Viktor need money like everybody else. But I want to tell you this." Victor looked around carefully before finishing his words. "We are being followed."

"What?" She stared up and down the street, again backing toward the hotel door.

"No, not now . . . yesterday, in my cab. We are being followed then. That is why I drive around in circles. Viktor not trying to—what is American word?—rip you off."

This was getting weirder and weirder. "What are you talking about?"

Viktor looked around suspiciously. "I don't like to say you this on street, Pamela Graham. Come get in cab, okay? You need to go somewhere, I take you. Then we can talk where nobody hears, yes?"

Do I really look that stupid? "Well, thanks, Viktor, I appreciate your concern and all, but . . . "

"Pamela Graham." He took a step closer to her, which probably wasn't the smartest thing he could have done, since now Pam could easily smell the vodka fumes on his breath. "You must listen to me. Government has taken away my brother. They are watching me. And now, because you are American, maybe they watch you, too. Please. Come with me. I swear on the grave of my mother, Viktor no hurt you."

Pam stared at him. She prided herself on having a pretty accurate bullshit detector, and right now, the only vibe she was getting from Viktor was dead-solid sincerity. "Why did the government take your brother?"

"Not here. In car. Okay?"

Still staring at him, Pam said, "How much to drive me around to some places I need to go today, Viktor?"

A grin slowly made its way across his face. "For you, Pamela Graham, very gud price."

She grinned back at him. "How good?"

"How about five thousand ruble?"

"How about four thousand, and I buy your lunch?"

"Is deal."

* * *

After a lunch of *croque monsieur* washed down with hundred-ruble bottles of Schweppes at a cute little French-style bistro just down the street from the hotel, they set off toward the first location on Pam's list. There were seven orphanages she planned to visit, in addition to the Belarov Institute. Sadly, due to the number of orphanages in St. Petersburg, she could have visited ten times that number of places, if she had the time.

Pam decided to sit in the front seat with Viktor. If nothing else, she reasoned, she'd be able to tell more easily if he was up to something. She noticed the flask lying on the seat beside him.

"Viktor, have you been drinking this morning?"

He looked at her, then away. "In Russia we have a saying, 'Call me whatever you like; just give me some vodka.' So maybe you don't judge me too quick, Pamela Graham?"

"Why would I judge you? I just don't want you to kill me because you're too drunk to be driving."

"Don't worry. Viktor must drink much more than little taste to be unable to drive."

Pam stared at him, trying to figure out if the vodka was supposed to insulate him from the loss of his brother, or something else. But Viktor had a point; he didn't seem impaired.

"So what happened with your brother, Viktor? Why did somebody take him?"

"Not somebody! Government!"

He glared at her long enough to make her nervous. "Eyes on the road, okay?" she said.

"My brother is good man," Viktor said, sounding like he was talking to himself as much as he was to her. "He tells people about vaccine." He glanced at her. "Do not take vaccine, Pamela Graham. Never take."

Pam thought about the hepatitis A and B immunizations she had taken prior to leaving on her trip. The Centers for Disease Control website had recommended them, citing an intermediate threat level existing in Russia. "Why not? I thought immunization was supposed to be a good thing. Keeps you from getting sick."

He gave a harsh laugh. "Just don't take vaccine, Pamela Graham. Not from my government, not from your government. My brother knows truth. And now he is gone." Viktor reached for the flask, thumbed open the lid, and took a quick gulp.

Okay, I'm riding with a vodka-swilling conspiracy theorist who is operating an unlicensed and probably illegal taxi service. Remind me why I shouldn't believe every word he's saying?

Then Viktor's words registered. "Viktor, your brother wouldn't be the fellow that was on the news in the U.S., would he? The activist who suddenly went missing?"

His look told her all she needed to know. No wonder he thought he was being followed. Pam really didn't relish the thought of being questioned by whatever organization had taken over for the KGB.

They were at her first destination. Viktor parked alongside the curb in front of a building that looked like its better days had been sometime in the ancient past. Pam took out her translation dictionary and told him she'd be gone about twenty or thirty minutes.

"No problem, I wait."

Conditions in this first orphanage were far worse then she expected. The "running" water was a mere trickle, and only some rooms had functioning electricity. The walls exhibited heavy signs of decay and mold. Nearly every ceiling bore water stains or missing tiles. The sickening smell of urine pervaded the rear nursery.

Viktor drove her to the next six orphanages on her list. At the first five of these she discovered similar or worse conditions than those she had seen at the initial location. However, the final facility was somewhat newer in construction and actually housed a staff large enough to accommodate the orphaned babies and children for whom they cared.

Once the tour of this last facility on her list was complete, the worker providing the tour had to leave Pamela by the front door to attend to an emergency. Pam nodded approvingly as she eyed the inside of the building, then she went outside.

She returned to her cab and sat down in the front seat, gazing thoughtfully at the relatively clean, reasonably well-run institution. "So what do you think, Viktor? The Belarov Institute has already approved me as a volunteer, but these guys look like they have it together and even said that they could actually pay me a salary."

Viktor looked at her for a few moments. "Viktor think you already know what you will do, Pamela Graham."

She turned and gave him a crooked smile. "Pamela Graham think Viktor know more English than he admits."

"Not really. But Viktor think you are not here to make a salary. Viktor think you are here to make, umm . . . difference."

"I like the way you think, Viktor," Pam said, nodding appreciatively. "How about taking me to the Belarov Institute so I can meet my new bosses?"

Viktor smiled and started the engine of the Volga. They drove to the Belarov Institute, located on Sadovaya Street. Pam realized, walking toward the front door, that she was actually only a few blocks down from her hotel on Nevsky Prospekt.

The Belarov Institute received funding from both governmental and private sources, like quite a number of orphanages in Russia, and from the literature she had acquired and the online research she had done, Pam expected it to be neither the best nor the worst of the lot in terms of its ability to take care of the children who lived there. However, walking toward the drab building with its cracked windowpanes and weather-beaten, chipped doors and woodwork, she began to wonder.

The challenge of working in an orphanage in another country did not frighten her. Though she had led a comfortable life—one, in fact, that would be described by many as opulent—Pam sensed that it was time to get out of her comfort zone and "take life by the longhorns," as some might say in Texas. Viktor was right; she wasn't here for a salary. She didn't really need one. What she did need was a sense that the direction of her life mattered, that something she was doing made a difference in some fundamental way.

She opened the stained and creaking front door and almost immediately spotted one of the children—a young boy who looked to be about ten or twelve, maybe older—watching her from a front window. She smiled and moved toward him, but he shied away and disappeared to another part of the building.

She finally located a staff member and introduced herself to the short, stout woman whose black hair was pinned into a tight bun. In fact, the bun was so immobile that Pam found herself thinking it was nailed into the woman's skull. That would also fit the unpleasant, unwavering expression on her face as she stood in front of Pam. "Da? Kak ya mogu pomoch' vam?"

"Privet. Menya zovut Pam Graham, iz Ameriki," Pam said in her best Russian. "Ya zdes', chtoby dobrovol'no."

The woman stared at her for so long that Pam was afraid she'd just unwittingly uttered an insult instead of saying that she was here as a volunteer worker.

"You wait here," the woman said finally. "I get director."

Guess my accent must have given me away, Pam thought, watching her stump away. Moments later, a middle-aged woman appeared, a weary smile on her face. "Hello, Miss Graham," she said, holding out her hands in greeting. "I am Sofia Lebedev, the director of the Belarov Institute. I am so very glad to meet you, at last. I cannot tell you how happy I am that you decided to assist us here."

Sofia's pleasant demeanor could not conceal her fatigue. The bags below her eyes accompanied a worn posture. The pressures of running an underfunded and understaffed facility had perceptibly taken their toll on her. Her gray hair lacked any real attention to style. Pam guessed that she was in her mid-fifties, although her clothes were those of a much older woman. Her well-worn brown cardigan hung unevenly atop a gray blouse. A wrinkled, dark wool skirt draped over down-at-the-heel black clogs. Her thin body revealed a curvature of her back that hinted at the imminent arrival of scoliosis. Pam wondered just how many hungry babies Sofia had carried and rocked to sleep.

Within moments, Sofia was giving Pam a litany of the challenges she faced, any one of which seemed to Pam to be sufficient grounds for waving the white flag and changing careers. Some of what Sofia told her Pam had already surmised from her quick tour of other facilities—Russian orphanages were critically understaffed and underfunded, with physical facilities far below anything that would be considered acceptable in most developed countries. "Our private donations have all but dried up," Sofia went on, citing the worldwide economic downturn and the subsequent scarcity of corporate and foundation underwriting. "And, to make things even worse, last week the Russian foreign ministry announced a freeze on all U.S. adoptions. So, even though we have several adoptions pending with American families, those children will now have to remain with us until the government permits U.S. adoptions to continue . . . or for as long as we are able to continue caring for them."

Just when Pam was wondering how Sofia managed to drag herself to work each day, the director began talking about the children. Her face changed. She didn't look any less tired, but Pam could easily sense the unflagging love that enabled this woman to keep doing what she did, day after day, even in the face of such impossible odds. Despite her worn and fragile outward appearance, Pam sensed that Sofia had a core of deep strength. She rose very high in Pam's estimation.

When she had finished her orientation presentation, Sofia led Pamela along the main hallway toward Sofia's sparsely furnished office. The little boy she had seen when she came in peeked around the corner right before Sofia pulled the door closed behind them. Soon, a rough voice came from the other side of the door. "What are you doing snooping around? Run along now!"

The voice then called through the closed door, "Miss Sofia, we will need more disposable diapers by the end of the day."

The unmistakable tone told Pam exactly who the speaker was: the less-than-accommodating woman she had met when she came in.

Do I really want to work in a place with that meat cleaver of a woman? From their short interaction, Pam guessed the other woman was younger than Sofia, but it was hard to tell.

Sofia shouted back at the door from her desk. "Please come in, Yuliya, I want you to meet someone!"

Oh, hell.

After an introduction that consisted of Sofia giving the dour Yuliya Pam's name and receiving a curt nod in return, Sofia walked Pam back down the hallway toward the front entrance. They agreed that since today was Saturday, Pam should come back the following Monday to begin her duties.

As she was heading down the front walk toward Viktor and his waiting taxi, Pam glanced back at the building for a final look. There, in a window by the front door, was the face of the young boy that she had glimpsed twice while touring the facility.

She got in the cab and Viktor drove her back toward her hotel. Pam pondered what she had seen at the Belarov Institute. The outdated facility needed a lot of work, the staff was rude—well one of them, anyway—and there were far too many children for the number of workers on hand. She could easily enough call Sofia back and tell her that she had decided to accept the offer of the new facility and the modest salary it had available. Still, something drew her back, and Pam had the sense that it had something to do with the face of that small, shy boy.

Pam had the feeling that her life was about to change, and that nothing would ever be the same again.

CHAPTER 5

Zia Sudario pulled the window shade aside just enough to give her a view up and down the section of Paros Alley that ran in front of her Caloocan City hotel. She didn't really know what she was looking for, and that was both scary and frustrating. Scary, because it was possible that she had been followed here to Manila, despite all her precautions, and she might not realize it until it was too late. Frustrating, because she longed more than anything to get on a bus headed north into the mountainous countryside around Baguio City, where she had grown up and where her family waited, still unaware that Zia was even back in the Philippines.

But how could she go home now? Until she knew whether the people behind the terrifying caller who had known everything about her had followed her here, she couldn't risk endangering her family by going back to Baguio City. No, she needed to stay here in the anonymity of the big city until she knew it was safe for her to resurface.

The more Zia thought about it, though, the more she despaired. For one thing, these people were ruthless. If only half of what Zia suspected about the real purpose behind the latest batch of H1N1 vaccine was true, then they were capable of anything. They certainly wouldn't blink at wiping out an entire Baguio City family—or neighborhood, for that matter—in order to keep their horrible plot secret.

And not only were they ruthless, they were apparently connected at some very high levels. Zia couldn't imagine how many federal statutes had been violated in order to provide the nameless caller with so much of her personal information. For all she knew, she had been under electronic surveillance for weeks or even months. To know what they knew and to keep secret what they were apparently planning, there must be people involved who had tremendous authority and reach. Zia tried to imagine how far up the conspiracy might go, but her mind shied away; it was too disturbing to contemplate.

She peered carefully up and down the street one more time and then picked up her journal. Since she had no idea what she should be looking for, Zia had decided to try to watch everything. Since checking into this hotel in a not-so-desirable district north of downtown Manila, she had been keeping journal entries on everything that happened around her. She ran her finger down the entries of vehicles parked along the street in front of the hotel for the last few days—no matches with any of the vehicles she had observed just now. The seedy Italian restaurant across the street from the hotel had received its deliveries at the usual time from the usual delivery truck, and the truck had departed at the same time it did every morning.

Zia varied her routine daily; she never went out to eat at the same time two days in a row, and when she did, she always picked a different café or restaurant than the day before. She bought as many groceries as she could from the street vendors and small storefronts and prepared food in her room whenever possible, to avoid having to go out more than was strictly necessary. She had paid cash when checking into the hotel, and she continued to pay in cash a week at a time for her small room. She kept track of the people she saw in the stairwells and lobby. So far, most of her fellow tenants had been transients; there were only a few people that had been here when Zia arrived who were still at the hotel. One of them was an old man who seemed to be retired and living alone, and another was a young woman from the countryside who always had a backpack of textbooks when Zia saw her—probably a student at one of the universities or technical institutes.

Zia tossed her journal onto the dingy table beside the window, sat down on the edge of her bed, and sighed. The constant vigilance and low-level anxiety were wearing her down; she didn't know how much longer she could live this way without at least trying to contact her family.

Beyond that, though, the sense was growing within her that she had a responsibility that extended further than just trying to stay alive and avoid endangering her kin. If the vaccine plot involved all that she feared and if it was carried out successfully, the results would be truly horrific, potentially on a worldwide scale. Even if she was able to avoid detection by the conspirators, they might still be moving forward with their plan. Shouldn't she try to stop them? But how? What could she possibly do against a scheme so entrenched and pervasive?

Zia was terrified about being so isolated and vulnerable, yet something within her knew also that she couldn't simply remain passive. She had to do something. If she could only figure out what that might be . . .

* * *

Pam straightened, her palms in the small of her back, then she arched backward slightly, wincing as she felt her vertebrae protesting. She had spent most of her first day as a volunteer at Belarov doing various odd jobs dispensed by Yuliya.

In less than eight hours, Pam had learned to despise the very sound of Yuliya's footsteps. The harsh, joyless woman seemed to be doing all she could to make jobs like scrubbing toilets and carrying out pails of soiled diapers even more unpleasant than they already were. "Sleduyushchii chistyi tualet," she would command, jabbing her finger at the dank, smelly communal showers, perhaps tossing a scrub brush and a pail to the floor at Pam's feet. Then she would turn and stomp off, usually sending a few angry syllables at any children who might be in the vicinity.

About midmorning, though, Pam had noticed that some of the tasks were started or even finished before she could get to them. Before long, she discovered that she had a guardian angel—the little boy she had seen on her first visit had been overhearing Yuliya's harsh instructions and trying to perform some of the tasks for her. He was still shy, though; the harder Pam tried to catch him in the act of helping her, the scarcer he seemed to make himself. It was almost as if he were some kind of elf or perhaps a Russian leprechaun; he seemed exceptionally talented at vanishing into thin air.

Pam managed to find out from Sofia that despite his small build, he was presently the oldest child at the Institute. He had lived at the orphanage for some time, and even amid the grim surroundings, he had a beautiful aura about him. Sofia told Pam that his birth certificate had never been received, so no one was sure of his exact age.

"So," she had said, smiling at Pam, "with you on board, we have five-point-five employees." At the time, Pam was slightly confused; she had seen two other women besides herself, Sofia, and Yuliya at the orphanage, but couldn't figure out who the "point-five" was. Now it was clear that the young boy was her silent helper, the other half.

Even from the brief glances she had gotten, Pam thought that he was the most beautiful child that she had ever seen. As she performed the grunt work Yuliya prescribed, Pam daydreamed about eventually having a relationship with him—perhaps even becoming a mentor for the boy, inspiring him to do great things. Then again, maybe she was getting way ahead of herself.

In the dreary, bare-walled dormitory wing, several cribs lined one wall of the children's sleeping area. Each of the outdated baby beds stood just far enough apart for Pam to slide between them. At the opposite end of the room, five twin beds ranged along the far wall. None of the twin beds appeared to be in use, except for what Pam assumed was the boy's bed, located on the very end of the row.

Judging by the general condition of the building, Pam could easily imagine that the sub-zero temperatures of the Russian winter readily seeped into the building. Still, her anticipation of seeing her new friend appear from his various hiding places lent her a persistent inner warmth. She would catch glimpses of him standing nearby, watching her throughout the day. And by the end of the day, he was slowly losing his shyness. When she would have to carry large items, he might even appear out of nowhere to assist her.

As she worked in the dormitory, Pam felt as if every crib and especially the one twin bed held a special little angel. She found it difficult to look at the four empty beds; they inevitably drew her mind to the children who had "outgrown" the orphanage. Due to limitations of funding, facilities, and personnel, the four who had previously slept in these meager beds had probably been released to fend for themselves on the streets of Saint Petersburg. When Pam thought about it, she felt her throat closing with anguish.

By the end of that day, Pam and the boy had formed a silent but tangible connection. Pam did her best to avoid contemplating the fact that his age threatened his time to remain at the facility. He had already beaten the odds for orphans in Russia, since most of the children never made it to their first birthday. On the other hand, the ones who got past the age of ten were almost never adopted.

The beginning of Pam's second day proved to be even less enjoyable than her first, primarily because the boy had apparently vanished and was nowhere to be found. By the time Pamela took her short lunch break she had not seen him at all during the morning and was too afraid to ask, fearing what she was going to hear. The fifth bed now sat like the other four, empty.

Even in her short time there, Pam knew that children frequently were removed or left the orphanage—some because of adoption, and, all too often, some because they simply no longer had a place. Her new little friend may have fallen into that second distressing category.

For about the tenth time since her arrival that morning, Pamela gaped blankly at the empty twin bed. Her eyes watered with the blurred visions of the beautiful little boy who was never given a chance. How many more were there; how many would follow the same lost destiny?

"Are you work, or just stand there, Miss Graham?" Yuliya's familiar heavy accent and sour tone snapped Pam out of her desolate reverie.

Damn, I hate that woman. "Da, Yuliya. Ya budu gotovit'oobed syeichas—"

"Never mind children's lunches," Yuliya snapped. She hauled the boy out from behind her, holding him tightly by his upper arm. "Clean this one up. He is filthy."

Doing her best to cover her delight at seeing him, Pam said, "Da, Yuliya. Nemedlenno." *Oh, yeah. I'll get on it right now, if it'll get him out of your clutches.*

Yuliya scowled at him, then shoved him toward her. "This one always a mess, always trouble." Yuliya stomped toward the kitchen. "I go prepare lunches. You can do this, I think. Is not missile science."

The phrase is rocket science, dumb shit. Pam spared a few seconds for sending hateful glances at Yuliya's departing back, then she turned toward the boy with a smile and bent down to his eye level.

He was covered in cold mud and his eyes begged for forgiveness. The sight of him made her discard her lingering thoughts of strangling Yuliya. "So, my handsome young man, what did you get yourself into?"

He stared at her curiously.

"Umm . . . Kak ty gryaznyi?"

He pointed at the window. "Out . . . out*side*," he said with an uncertain expression.

"You know English? You must be really smart," Pam said, her eyes wide with surprise.

He made a pinching motion with his thumb and forefinger. "Little bit. Ma— Madame Sofia teach me."

From an earlier conversation Pam had learned that Sofia had spent some time in the United States—Minnesota, maybe? "Well, you must be a really good student." He was looking at her blankly again. "Horoshii student," Pam said.

He grinned at her. "You say wrong."

"Is that so? Well, how do you say it?"

He pronounced the phrase for her, putting the little "y" lift before the accented second syllable of "student."

"Oh. So that's how it's supposed to sound," Pam said, her smile getting bigger by the second as his face lost its pallor and fear from earlier. "Tell you what. I have an extra set of clothes in the laundry room—ah, prachechnaya?"

He nodded his understanding.

"Okay, so run and change—naden'te chistuyu odezhdu—then you can bring me the dirty ones. I'll take care of them, deal?" She gave him a thumbs-up and a questioning look.

He grinned and matched her hand gesture. "Okay—deal."

A few minutes later, he came trotting back and gave the dirty clothes to Pam. Just as he handed them over, he sneezed violently and began to cough.

"Bless you!" Pam said. "I sure hope you're not getting sick, umm . . . ?"

"His name is Alexander," a soft voice said.

Pamela turned just in time for a camera to flash in her eyes. Sofia stood just a few feet away from them, wearing her signature tattered sweater and a warm smile.

"I like to get pictures of our new volunteers with the children before the craziness of this place drives them away," she said.

CHAPTER 6

Joseph Pierce stared at the phone ringing on his desk. The caller ID displayed "Centers for Disease Control."

More than anything in the world at this moment, he wanted to not take this call. Thoughts flashed through his mind: the phone call to his unlisted home number, a week ago . . . Zia Sudario, gone with no warning . . . the test he had personally conducted on the last batch of vaccine—the results he couldn't allow himself to believe, even though he ran the cultures twice and recalibrated the equipment with his own hands . . .

Joseph picked up the handset and placed it to his ear but said nothing. He closed his eyes.

The voice that rattled in his ear had a blunt sound. *Military?* "Pierce, you just gonna sit there and hold the phone or are you actually gonna say something, son?"

"Who the hell is this?" In his thirteen years at MMMI, the only orders he had known were the ones he issued. Who was this, anyway?

"Listen, Pierce, time is short, so I am going to get straight to the point here. I want—"

"Hold it a second. *You* want? Really? Hell, I don't even know who you are, and I'm having a damned hard time giving a shit, right about now. And the first words out of your mouth are about what *you* want? I don't know who the hell you think you're talking to, but—"

"Pierce, right now you need to focus every fiber of your being on shutting the fuck up and listening. And if you hang up on me, son, I give you my most solemn goddamn promise that you will replay that mistake for the rest of your drastically shortened life."

Joseph held the phone in shock, uncertain that he had actually heard what he thought he heard. The caller paused before continuing, allowing the words to soak in.

Joseph's mind ran back through everything he knew, everything he suspected, everything he feared. For a while now, he'd had a bad feeling in his gut about the irregularities with the H1N1 vaccine program. Now, hearing the blatant threat in the caller's voice—disturbingly enough, from the CDC—he was seriously rethinking what he wanted to say to the person on the other end of the line. He really had no idea who he was dealing with, but he was rapidly becoming fearful about what they were capable of.

"Pierce, I have gotten word that you guys are dragging your asses on the distribution of the H1N1 vaccine."

"I wouldn't say we're dragging our asses."

"Really? Then what the fuck *would* you say? You had this for four fucking months now, and we got word that since the first shipment, nothing else has been sent. Explain that to me."

"After the first shipment we decided to run some tests."

"Hold on right there, hero. *We* decided? Meaning, you and I? Because I don't recall a goddamn thing about agreeing to run any test on the vaccine."

"I meant my staff and I decided."

"I thought so. I am not going to play grab-ass with this, so listen very carefully. We authorized the vaccine to be shipped nationwide from your facility. We allowed your facility to do the mass production. We want it shipped now. If MMMI cannot handle the job, we will get someone who can. As far as I have seen, it didn't look like you guys dragged your ass on cashing the check we gave you. Your little test will stop immediately and your shipping docks will be loaded with the vaccine that was supposed to be disseminated months ago." There was a silent pause. "Are we on the same page here, Pierce?"

"Yes we are, but . . . what is the rush? I mean, there's a public safety issue here; surely you understand that?"

Joseph's question fell onto a silence that lasted maybe seven seconds. "There are no questions here," the caller said, finally. "And just so we're clear . . . Don't think that the fourteen billion dollars the Morris Foundation left MMMI makes you immortal, son. On this matter, you answer to me, and I answer to only one person. We are not people you want as enemies."

"Who said anything about enemies?" Joseph said, playing desperately for more time. "MMMI just has a policy to test everything we distribute before—"

"Send it out, goddamn it! And send it out now. Just for the record, I said 'enemies,' and I am not in the habit of bullshitting."

In the background on the other end of the call, Joseph could hear a voice coming over an intercom, "Dr. Jones, you have a call holding on line three."

The caller went on, "I think we are clear here, Pierce. I will follow up next week. For your sake, I hope it doesn't entail a personal trip to your office." The voice was replaced with a dial tone.

Joseph set the phone back in the cradle, his hands shaking. He ran his fingers through his steel-gray hair. He wiped his damp forehead with one hand. *Shit! This can't be happening.*

The background intercom said the name Dr. Jones, and there was only one person with serious authority by that name at the CDC. Why in the hell did Dr. Lee Jones, the head of the CDC, feel a need to call him personally about shipping out a vaccine?

Though he had never personally met the man, Joseph knew all about Dr. Jones. Rumors collected about the former U.S. Army general like maggots collected on rotten meat. Joseph Pierce wasn't the only CEO in the health care industry who had been surprised when Jones was appointed head of the Centers for Disease Control.

Jones's words hovered in Joseph's mind like a murky cloud, "You answer to me, and I answer to only one person." This was not just a nudge to do what they wanted; this was the threat of what could happen if he didn't. Joseph thought about Zia Sudario. As far as he knew, she was the only other person at MMMI who had spoken with Jones. Did she possibly speak to someone at the CDC regarding the delayed shipments? In any case, now she was gone. He was also positive that if Dr. Jones spoke to her the same way that he spoke to him, then Zia might very well be considering another line of work. *Hell, I am considering another line of work myself, right about now.* He thought about how much Zia may have been exposed to. If she came across some of the findings that he stumbled on, then he would need to talk to her. Had the abrupt end to the call been the cue for Zia's exit?

It was clear to Joseph that there was a lot more going on here than the CDC's impatience with a shipment delay. MMMI—or rather he—had obviously dug too far into certain matters linked to concerns consequential enough to instigate a call to his unlisted home number. Joseph knew that he was quickly running out of time to find out what was going on; he had unwittingly stepped on some very important toes.

No matter how he sliced it, Joseph Pierce was completely lucid about one fact: Jones was right about the inadvisability of having him as an enemy. If you crossed Lee Jones, you crossed his boss, and his boss did not get crossed by any rational entities.

Solid proof of the truth of Joseph's unsettling suspicions required a little more time. The dilemma dwelled in deciding if digging further was really worth the risk. Dr. Jones's words came back to Joseph's mind: *Fourteen billion dollars doesn't make you immortal . . .*

No, not by a long shot.

* * *

Lee Jones hung up his phone and stared at it for a few seconds. The light for line three was still blinking, and Jones knew there was only one reason why—just as there was only one reason Carol would dare to page him for a holding call when she could see he was already on the phone. He sighed and picked up the handset, then he punched the blinking line. "Jones."

"Did you talk to him?"

"Yes, sir."

"When does the vaccine ship?"

"Soon."

"I didn't ask for an opinion, Doctor. I asked for a date."

Jones clenched his teeth to keep from saying what he was thinking. He took a deep breath. "I gave him an ultimatum. He'll ship it quickly—" *Should I say it?* "—as soon as the batch is ready."

"What the hell is that supposed to mean? I thought they already had it finished."

"They've been doing some . . . testing."

The silence that followed seemed a lot longer to Jones than it probably was.

"What kind of testing, Jones?"

"I have no idea," Jones said. "I didn't want to play Twenty Questions with him, Director. If he gets too riled up, he may begin talking to others. I told him to get his ass in gear, to stop testing, and to start shipping immediately. I said what I needed to say, and all that I could say."

"Okay, General. This is not the way we planned, of course, but keep a close eye on Pierce. He's smart, and that's not necessarily good for what . . . what people a lot higher than you and I want done. And keep me informed."

"Always have, always will," Jones growled.

The line went dead. Jones slammed the handset into its cradle. He flung himself up from the desk and paced rapidly to the window of his office, then back—then he did another lap. He rubbed a hand through his salt-and-pepper, close-cropped hair. He needed a smoke badly, but he didn't feel like walking all the way down to the courtyard.

Jones was caught in the middle of something very big, and he wasn't sure he wanted to know all there was to know. When the director of the CIA first came to him with talk about some top-secret national security initiative involving the CDC and the H1N1 vaccine, he had been all too eager to salute the flag and follow orders. But the further this thing went, the less certain Jones became that he wanted to stay involved.

Who am I kidding? Jones had been around the higher circles of the military and the government long enough to know that at a certain point, you were in, no matter what. You couldn't walk away—you could only be carried away, packed inside a box accompanied by pallbearers. He was perilously close to that point with this thing, maybe already on the other side of the line.

Lee Jones was a man accustomed to keeping the walls in his mind intact. He'd heard the whispers, the hard whispers—the secret knowledge that was only entrusted to the elite few who had an absolute need to know. He had given orders to faithful subordinates, knowing that their obedience guaranteed their harm—or worse—and still he expected them to obey. They did. And the hard whispers make sure they kept their grim promises. Jones had climbed the long ladder with rungs made of the bones of those lower in the hierarchy, those who didn't have the need to know—those who would never hear the hard whispers, who would only reap their consequences.

Jones wasn't sure anymore. He had made it this far, had climbed on a lot of other people's bones. But there was a whole other level still above him, one where the air was thin and the hard whispers were constant. Once you reached that level, you weren't your own anymore. There, the hard whispers owned you, and you did whatever was asked, without questioning. It was the only way. And Lee Jones wasn't sure he wanted to go there.

So, for now, he was taking orders from the director, doing as he was told, and not asking any questions for which he didn't want to know the answers.

But he wasn't sure how much longer not knowing would remain an option.

CHAPTER 7

Pam's first weeks at the orphanage were filled with hard but fulfilling work. Yuliya still acted like she would have enjoyed nothing more than clubbing Pam over the head and leaving her body in a dark alley, but Pam's enjoyment and satisfaction at getting to interact with the children was more than enough to balance her coworker's sour attitude. She spent most of her eight-hour daily shift pondering the incredible number of homeless children in Russia and how she could make a greater impact in a deeper way.

As the summer began slipping toward the cooler nights of fall, an idea began growing in Pam's mind. When it first took shape in her imagination, she realized that actually, it had been in her thoughts all along; she just wasn't consciously aware of it. It occurred to her that she could do something much more than just volunteering at the orphanage: What if she actually adopted a child on her own? As soon as she verbalized the notion to herself, the prospect warmed her body.

Yuliya apparently delighted in adding tasks to Pam's routine every few days. Pam, however, had decided early on that Yuliya couldn't break her. Pam would show her scowling tovarischka that she wasn't some Southern sorority girl who was just trying to soothe her conscience about spending Daddy's money. Each time Yuliya would give her a smirking order, Pam would smile and nod, all the while thinking, *bring it on, bitch.*

Somehow, Pam would get it all done. After the laundry was processed, after the sheets and blankets were changed, after the infants were fed and changed, after the toilets were scrubbed and the dining area was wiped down and sanitized, she always found her way to Alexander—Alex, as she had come to think of him. She never wanted to leave his side; Pam regarded her time with Alex as her own personal reward for holding out against Yuliya for one more day.

Today, as she approached his twin bed he looked up displaying wide eyes and an even wider smile. "Hey, Miss Pam!"

His English was getting better every day. "Hey, you! I told you, just say Pam; Pam is fine."

"Okay," he grinned. "You are going back to hotel now?" She was wearing her coat, with her purse over her shoulder.

She nodded. "Pretty soon, but I had to stop by and see you, first. So what have you been doing all day?"

"I read one of the books you give me."

"Really now? Are you liking it? Can you understand the words?"

"Most of them. I like read about Bree and Aravis and the stuff they get into. I don't get to the end yet. I like Aravis's talking horse Bree—sometimes."

"Sometimes?"

"Yeah, sometimes Bree act like he is better than other horses because can talk. Is crazy, huh?"

"I'd have to agree with you, sport," Pam smiled.

"I bet I know what is happens."

"You mean 'what will happen.'"

"What will happen," he corrected himself.

"Really now. So tell me, what will happen?"

"I bet that something will happen that show him that makes him see that he is not better than rest of horses."

"Alexander, you're a very bright kid. I'll bet you could have given C. S. Lewis some good ideas, if you'd been around when he was writing this book. And I'm very proud of you for understanding so many of the words."

"Since I am oldest one here I help Miss Sofia a lot. She and Yuliya teach me a few words, then more and more every day. I still cannot read English so good, but I will . . . one day."

"I bet you will, too. You are the smartest kid I have ever met."

"Really?" he said. His eyes lit with a combination of surprise and delight.

"Yes indeed, Alex. That is a fact. You don't mind if I call you Alex, do you?"

He shook his head. He paused, a thoughtful expression on his face. "Miss Pam?"

Pam gave him a playful frown. He laughed. "I mean Pam! Pam, you think that kids have it easier in the United States?"

"Well, Alex, some do."

He thought for a minute. "That's where I am going to go."

"Is that right?"

He nodded, then he sneezed hard.

"Okay, my man, but get some rest for now so we can get rid of that cold."

Pam worried about all of the children, and especially about Alex. Years of living in the orphanage had taken a toll on him. Inadequate heating and lack of proper nutrition made it hard for him to fight off anything that might invade his system. According to Sofia, getting the kids vaccinated was next to impossible. But that reality seemed to have no effect on their spirits, and Alex was the best example; every time Pam saw him, his eyes were bright with optimism.

More and more, Pam sensed the bond between herself and Alex. Their relationship carried a special link. He would stare at her in wonderment then ask a barrage of questions, most of which surrounded the topic of America and the world beyond Russia.

Sofia entered from the hallway. She was holding a piece of paper. "Pamela, good, you are here. I was hoping to catch you before you left. We have a slight problem."

Pam looked up at Sofia. "Problem?"

"Yes, it appears that when we did your paperwork, we failed to place a copy of your passport with it. Do you have your identification with you? I could make a copy right now."

"Sure." Pam reached into her purse and felt around until her fingers traced the outlines of her passport. She pulled it out and handed it to Sofia. "Here you go."

"Thank you, I'll just . . . " Sofia opened the passport and paused. A confused look appeared on her face.

"Something wrong?" Pam said. She got up and walked toward Sofia with Alex close behind.

Sofia held the passport out toward her, and Pam took it.

Roxy's face grinned back at her from the passport.

Dammit! I forgot to give Rox her ID back the night we went out.

"I'm so sorry, Sofia! Here, just a second . . . " Pam opened her purse again, peering carefully inside this time as she retrieved the correct passport and handed it to Sofia. Laughing, she explained about her frenzied going-away party in Dallas and about her even more frenzied departure for the airport the next morning, as Roxy lay on the couch, sleeping off the previous night's activities. "I guess I've had both passports with me all this time, but I haven't carried this purse in a while, and . . . "

"It's all right, Pamela, I am certain that you are not trying to use a fake ID to work here." Sofia smiled. "I'll make a copy and place it in your file." She walked away.

Alex looked up at Pam. "You took your friend's ID? That's funny. I accidentally put on my friend's hat one time and wore it all day."

"Did you, now? Well, my friend Roxy likes to wear my stuff, too. But it is never an accident. I will be surprised if she even notices that her ID is missing; she is just dingy like that."

"Dingy? What is dingy?" Alex said.

"Oh, you know . . . " Pam looked around before she whispered into Alex's ear. "Like Yuliya."

Alex fell to the floor in laughter. After catching his breath he looked at Pam.

"Miss Pam?"

Pam playfully raised a fist at him.

"I mean, Pam."

"Yes?"

"Never mind . . . "

"Oh come on now, Alex, you can tell me anything. What's on your mind?"

"Not gonna get mad at me?"

"Oh, honey, I could never get mad at you."

"Promise?"

Pam placed a hand over her heart. "Promise!"

"Okay . . . Anyone ever tell you that you talk funny?"

This time it was Pam who fell over laughing hysterically. "Yeah, I have to say that I have heard that a time or two! Oh my God, Alex, that is hilarious!"

Alex eventually joined in the laughter, but his was laced with nervousness. He was positive that he had insulted her but appeared so relieved that she found the question funny.

Coming back into the room, Sofia watched the unfolding of the shared moment between the boy and Pam. She hesitated before she handed Pam's passport back to her. She smiled, hating to disrupt the bond that continued to build between them. "Pam, excuse me. I won't be in until late tomorrow. After you are done with most of your work, would you be a dear and file the paperwork on my desk before you leave for the day? I have two stacks of files I have been putting off forever. I placed notes on all the files to help you. A couple of the files may not be complete. If so, just leave them on my desk and I'll tackle them when I get a chance."

Sofia moved over to Alex. She smiled and pinched him softly on his cheek. "Don't worry, Alexander, I won't keep your new friend away from you for too long."

Alex's face turned bright red. "Oh my God, Miss Sofia! I am too old for that now, huh?"

"Never," Sofia said.

Sofia squeezed Pamela's arm lightly as she turned to leave. "You are going to do just fine here."

Pamela sighed. "Well, I guess I better head home, big guy." She bumped her fist against Alex's. This made him laugh every time they did it. She had taught him the greeting a few days before, and when he questioned the gesture's meaning, she simply said, "It's a Texas thang."

* * *

The next morning, Pam entered Sofia's office, feeling a certain level of trepidation. She could not avoid the sense that she was invading Sofia's personal space. The office smelled slightly of mildew but was very neat. A rusty file cabinet sat next to Sofia's brown wooden desk. The worn, time-stained wooden floor creaked with each step Pam took across it.

Just as Sofia had said, two stacks of files were piled on the top of her desk. Post-its attached to each folder indicated where they needed to be filed. Atop one stack was a sheet of paper bearing the Russian letters "PBP." The other, larger stack also had a sheet of paper on top of it, labeled with the letters "PA." All of the files contained a red label that read "Confidential." Beginning with the larger stack of files, Pamela placed the records on the gray metal file cabinet. The rusted metal emitted a screeching sound as she pulled the sliding file drawer out of its enclosure.

Sofia had said she'd been putting off this filing forever, and Pam observed that "forever" may have been a drastic underestimation of the amount of time since this particular file cabinet had been utilized. Sofia had organized the files alphabetically, however, which simplified the task. Pam completed the first stack about an hour after starting the job.

Halfway through the second stack a name caught her attention; "Юров, Александр" appeared across the upper left-hand side of the file. Pam translated the characters: "Yurov, Alexander." Her first inclination was to just place the file with the rest. However, after listening for a few seconds and hearing no approaching footsteps, she slowly opened the file and began to read its contents.

CHAPTER 8

Giles Girard drove slowly along the narrow street, peering closely at the buildings while trying to avoid colliding with the handcarts that crowded the street and the sidewalk. He'd never been in this part of Caloocan City, and he had tried to get Zia to meet him somewhere else, but she had insisted not only on this neighborhood, but also on having him come on a market day, when the vendors were swarming and the air was clogged with the smell of everything from fish to *balut*. How he was supposed to find her in this melee was beyond him. But Zia said it had to be this way and when he tried to find out why, she wouldn't say anything else.

As he was creeping along near the intersection of Paros Alley and Halaan, she stepped from behind a street vendor's stall, opened the passenger-side door of his car, got in, shut the door, and ducked as low in the seat as she could.

"Hello, Zia. Long time since we—What are you doing?"

"Just keep driving. And don't look at me."

"Okay . . . sure. Can I ask what's going on?"

"Not yet. Just drive, and if you notice anybody following us, tell me."

"Zia, what the hell? What have you got me into? First time I've seen you since college, and this is how we meet?"

"Giles, you always said you were a journalist because you wanted to know what was really going on, right?"

"Right."

"Do you still feel that way?"

"Well, sure, but—"

"Okay, then. I'm going to tell you something that is going to turn your whole world upside down. But first I have to know that we haven't been seen, and second, I have to know that you'll follow this wherever it leads."

He stared at her.

"Stop looking at me!"

"Oh, yeah, sorry." He weaved back and forth across the narrow street. "I was really surprised to get your call the other day, Zia," he said, his eyes on the road as he searched for a path through the thronging market-goers. "I thought you were in the U.S. for good. Nice job at an important research institution, interesting work . . . "

"Yeah, me too," she said in a flat voice. "But things changed. Very unexpectedly."

"Is there anywhere in particular we're supposed to be going, so you can stop being so cryptic?" Giles said.

"No, just keep driving. When we get out of the market area, keep going. Turn pretty often, and notice if any cars are staying behind you. Once we know we're in the clear, I'll tell you what I know."

"Can you at least tell me who's after you?"

"I wish I knew for sure," she said. "Maybe nobody. But we have to be careful."

Giles shook his head, feeling mildly exasperated. "Okay, fine. This seems a little beyond careful, but fine."

Giles had met Zia when they were both students at the University of the Philippines at Baguio. Zia was a hometown girl and Giles was on an Australian student visa, figuring it would be easier to get into the graduate program at the Asian Institute of Journalism if he had an undergrad degree from another school in the Philippines.

Giles and Zia had dated for a few weeks, and they had remained friends after the romance faded. He remembered her as an intelligent, disciplined student who still knew how to have fun on weekends.

Trying to keep his face turned straight ahead, Giles stole glances at her as he drove. When Zia had called him, she had sounded like someone in one of those Cold War–era spy movies: talking in hushed tones and short, cryptic sentences. A part of him knew that Zia was given to neither paranoia nor half-baked conspiracy theories, but receiving her call out of the blue as he had, combined with the way she was acting right now, was making him feel irrationally nervous. Still, it was Zia, so he owed her a full hearing, at least.

They drove northwest on Paros, and by the time they were nearing Lapu-Lapu Avenue, the market traffic was thinning. Giles turned left onto Lapu-Lapu and drove across the barge canal, all the way to Marcos Highway. He drove south on Marcos for a mile or two, then turned back east into the streets of downtown Manila. After cruising back and forth aimlessly for a while, he said, "Okay. I haven't seen anybody staying with us, Zia. I really think we're okay. What do you want to do now?"

"How far are we from Malacanang Hospital?"

"Not too far."

"Let's go there. It's always crowded. Right now, I think crowds are the safest place to be."

"Whatever you say." Giles drove across the southern end of downtown Manila on Paz Mendoza Guazon and turned into the hospital grounds. They found a parking place near the main entrance.

"You know that MMMI, the place I worked, was under contract from the U.S. government to produce and ship the H1N1 flu vaccine, right?" Zia said without preamble as they got out of the car and began walking toward the hospital entrance.

"No, but I do now," Giles said. "Does all this secrecy have something to do with that?"

"A few weeks ago," Zia said, "I got a phone call at my work, at just after five in the morning."

"Pretty early, I guess."

"The call came from outside, and it came in on a line that nobody except the MMMI staff is even supposed to know about." She gave him a careful look. "I think the call originated from somebody in the government, maybe the Centers for Disease Control."

Giles gave her a confused look. "That's who you're making the vaccine for, right?"

"Right. The caller knew everything about me, Giles. Where I live, when I leave work—even my dog's name."

Giles's eyes widened.

"But that's not even the worst part," Zia went on. "There's something going on with the vaccine, Giles. Something really bad. My boss, Joseph Pierce, had a feeling about it. He never said anything to me directly, but I saw him run some tests on the early batches of the vaccine that we made, using the cultures the CDC sent us."

"What did he find?"

"I'm not sure."

They were at the front door. Zia waited as a large family went inside. After peering around for a few seconds, she grabbed the handle and tugged open the door; Giles followed her into the lobby of the hospital.

"Mr. Pierce wouldn't tell anybody what he found or suspected. But he ran all the tests himself, wouldn't let anyone else do any of it."

There were some padded benches in an alcove of the lobby, and Zia moved toward them. They sat, and she faced him, speaking in a low, urgent voice.

"Giles, I think the government is doing something to the vaccine—something really bad. Maybe something that could affect thousands of people. You've got to find out, Giles. The only thing that can stop them is for people to know—for everybody to know."

Giles stared at her, still trying to pin down a few coherent thoughts as the information Zia was giving him swirled around his brain. "You think there's some kind of plot—conspiracy—to spike the vaccine, somehow? For what purpose? Why would the government do that?"

"I don't know, Giles. When I got the call, I got scared. With all the rumors that were going around, and with the hints I'd managed to pick up from Mr. Pierce, I knew something was weird about the vaccine. And when that person called and practically threatened me . . . " She swallowed several times and looked away, tears bulging along her lower eyelids. "I came back here, but I've been hiding out in my hotel all this time, Giles. I didn't know what to do. What if they were watching me? What if they followed me to my family? There's no telling what they might do, Giles."

She turned toward him again. "But I can't just sit on this. I can't risk that by doing nothing I make it easy for them to do something awful. That's why I called you."

"Yeah, great," Giles said weakly. "Nothing like handing old Giles the red-hot baton and telling him to run with it."

"Giles, you're a journalist. You believe in the truth, in shining light into the dark corners. That's what you always said."

It was true. A part of Giles's mind already knew that he had to act on what Zia knew or suspected. She wasn't the type to make up stuff like this. But if her suspicions were correct, things could get interesting in a hurry, couldn't they?

"Zia, what can I do for you? Want me to figure out a way to at least let your family know you're here?"

She shook her head. "I don't want them to know—not yet. They'll try to contact me, and I can't risk that right now. What you can do for me, Giles," she said, putting a hand on his arm and giving him an intent gaze, "is to swear to me that you'll find out what's going on with this. I don't know how high it goes or how wide it reaches, but the only way to stop this is to make sure it's outed. Can I count on you, Giles? If you do that, I'll figure what to do about my situation."

Her dark eyes burned into his. Giles had to admit: Zia was still one very smart, very beautiful, and—it would seem—very brave lady. He nodded and put his hand on top of hers. "I'll figure out a way, Zia. If something's going on, I'll find out and I'll make sure the whole world knows."

She closed her eyes; a few tears strayed down her cheeks. "Thank you," she whispered. Then she leaned over quickly and brushed his cheek with her lips. She got up and strode briskly toward a group of people who were headed for the main doorway. And she was gone.

Giles had a few hours before he needed to check in for his return flight to Melbourne. He left the hospital and drove until he spotted the nearest Internet café, then he parked and went inside.

As he sat in front of the terminal, he thought about all the predicaments he had landed himself in by virtue of his penchant for uncovering facts that other people were trying to conceal. There were several major international corporations and even one or two third-world governments that wouldn't be inviting him to any banquets in this lifetime. But as the Web browser launched and he began keying in search terms on Google, he quickly surmised that if Zia's lead was anywhere close to on-target, he might need to look into some real estate that came with a bombproof shelter.

By using conventional sources he learned that the president of the United States personally selects the head of the Centers for Disease Control, which was based in Atlanta, Georgia. The president's appointee did not have to be approved by Congress, and the president was the sole person who could dissolve the position.

He then did a quick background fact scan of Maxwell Morris Medical Institute. As he finished each article, he saved the files to a format that he could attach to e-mail. He then sent the documents to his cell phone, so he could review everything on the flight back to Australia.

Next, he logged into a site that very few people even knew existed, basically an online data bank that was a hodgepodge of rumors, conspiracy theories, partially documented allegations, and a few articles that looked as if they'd been pasted together by out-and-out whackos. Though he would never directly cite this resource in any article that would see the light of day, Giles had often found it to be an interesting source of leads, if one was prepared to sift through the abundant chaff to find the occasional kernel of truth. He found a few passing mentions of under-the-table linkages between the CDC and certain private-sector research groups, though MMMI was not specifically mentioned. He copied the articles and sent them to his phone. Right now, everything he could find, documented or not, was grist for the investigative mill. Later, he would start weeding out the half-truths and innuendo. When he next looked at his watch, he realized it was time to head for the airport.

Two hours later, as the 747 reached cruising altitude and the seat belt lights dinged and switched off, Giles powered up his phone and began skimming through the information he had gathered so far, trying to absorb it in toto, trying to see any patterns that might be emerging. One thing that occurred to him with disquieting suddenness was the fact of the CDC's central location in Atlanta. *An international airport, a rail hub, intersections of several U.S. interstate highways . . . how morbidly convenient.*

As the aircraft winged south over New Guinea, Giles reflected on the chain of events that had led him to the information Zia had provided, information that could potentially indicate the tip of an iceberg that would have otherwise lain undetected. What if he and Zia had never met? What if the person who had uncovered the first bit of information had not happened to have a friend who was an investigative journalist?

What was needed, Giles thought, was a way to open more lines of communication in a multitude of different directions—just as he did with Zia, but on a wider scale—a worldwide scale, in fact. What if there were a way to provide an anonymous outlet to any whistle-blower, any person with secret and potentially damaging or dangerous information? All he needed to do was create the same situation for others that his relationship with Zia had provided for her. And of one thing Giles was certain: there were others. He was more than positive of that.

What if there was a way to allow anyone anywhere to leak information—securely and anonymously? Something like the rumor site he used, but outgoing, not incoming. The operation would need to be as simple as looking up a definition on the Internet, and its central clearinghouse function would have to be beyond reproach. By offering professionally vetted documents to be disseminated widely and almost instantly, such an enterprise would provide the leaks heard round the world.

It also would gain some unwanted attention. If Giles's idea actually worked, he would create nervous governments across the planet—possibly a few death squads, even. He had already had a taste of the lengths powerful people would go to in order to keep him quiet. This new idea—it needed a catchy name, didn't it? Something that flowed trippingly from the tongue—could easily become tenfold more explosive than the most headline-grabbing story Giles had ever written to this point. Conservative thinking told him that he was onto something very big. Deductive thinking told him to be prepared to expect ten times the pressure to silence him.

The name, the name . . . Something that implied speed, the Internet, the reach and anonymity of the World Wide Web . . .

WebLeaks.

Giles smiled. He scribbled the name on a Philippine Airlines cocktail napkin. He liked it. He had a concept, and he had a worthy project in view for it. All he needed now was a little seed capital to get the network launched.

There was only one name on Giles's potential donors list, but he knew it was the only name he would need.

CHAPTER 9

As far as Pam could tell, Alex's folder contained only general information about him, for the most part. Very little information existed about his birth parents. His mother was just seventeen, also an orphan. Nothing was available on the father. According to the files, the mother stopped visiting Alex a few years after bringing him to the facility; apparently, she had never resurfaced.

Pam's discovery about Alex's background saddened her, but something else in the file suddenly caught her interest: Alex was up for adoption. The lettering on top of the files now had significance: "ПВП" was an acronym for the Russian phrase "prinyatie v protsesse": "adoption in process."

A family with a Florida address was listed. The file indicated that they had obtained approval for a scheduled pickup of Alex that very week. The family had two other children—a thirteen-year-old boy and a six-year-old girl. Alex's adoption would have given the children a new brother. An attachment, handwritten by Sofia, was clipped on to the last page of the file. Sofia's note expressed very high hopes for Alex with his new family. In her words, the father was a pleasant man with a big heart and the mother nearly burst with joy whenever she came to visit Alex.

But a second sheet, a preprinted memo, was stapled to the file, and

Pam soon realized that a copy of this attachment was added to the other eleven "ПВП" folders as well. The sheet noted the foreign ministry's suspension of all U.S. adoptions, along with the effective date, not long before Pam had arrived at the orphanage in late May. Adoptions in process during that time period were placed on an indefinite hold, according to the stapled memo. The adoption of "Yurov, Alexander"—along with the hopes of his intended new family—fell into that category. *No wonder he keeps asking me so many questions about America. Sofia hasn't told him that the government won't let his new family have him.*

Pamela closed Alex's file and leaned back in the chair, her heart sinking. Due to Alex's age, the suspended adoption may have been his last hope. She tried to imagine him at one of the horrible state-run facilities she had seen in her tour, but her mind rebelled. And even that was better than imagining what might happen to him on the streets.

Pam opened one of the other files in the "adoption pending" stack. The spaces on the form, where the final approval was indicated along with the name of the adopting family, were left blank. She took another quick look at Alex's file. It was the same; all twelve files lacked the final information needed to officially complete the adoption.

She stared at the blank lines on Alex's form as it lay on Sofia's desk. A thought was forming in her mind, an idea so extreme that Pam instinctively tried to dismiss it. And then she noticed Sofia's computer.

The device was so outdated that Pam couldn't remember ever using a similar one. However, when she toggled the power switch, the monochrome monitor hummed to life as the sound of loud internal electronics flowed through the aged circuitry. Pam had a fleeting memory of visits to her grandmother's house, where an old black-and-white floor-model television had sat in her small living room.

Once the screen illuminated, she clicked on the file tab indicating new adoptions. The computer responded sluggishly, and Pam was afraid she'd misread the Russian characters. Then, bingo! Fifteen names appeared in a list on the screen. Near the bottom of the list she saw Alex's name.

Pushing her Russian reading skills to the maximum, Pam raced to review the online document. Several times she heard sounds that caused her to look up at the closed office door. Once, she lost her place and had to start over with the visual scan of the document. Pam shuddered to think what might happen if Yuliya came through the door and caught her using Sofia's computer. Despite her heavyset build, Yuliya still had a way of sneaking silently.

Pam keyed a few changes into the document. Her hand trembled as her fingers moved across the keyboard. Beads of sweat formed on the back of her neck and her heart raced. She paused briefly and then clicked on a final command: Send.

Pamela, girl, you have done it now.

An electronic copy of the document would now be transmitted directly to the offices of the Russian adoption agency, verifying that everything was approved. She pressed another button to print out a copy to keep with her. It had taken less than ten minutes. Pam altered the effective dates on the hard-copy file to indicate that the approval had come before the implementation of the freeze on U.S. adoptions. The online approval reflected that it was electronically signed by Sofia as director of the orphanage. Pam thumbed off the power switch and stood, gathering the other eleven "in process" files and moving toward the ancient file cabinet.

"Why are you in Sofia's office?" Yuliya's rough voice roared across the room from the suddenly open door, causing Pamela's body to quiver.

Damn. Ten seconds earlier, and I'd have still been sitting behind the computer.

Pamela regrouped quickly. "Because Sofia asked me to do some filing for her. Is that a problem?"

Yuliya narrowed her eyes. Pam prayed that the ancient computer didn't make any sounds that would give away the fact that she had just powered it off. Yuliya's eyes flickered toward the open file cabinet. The sight of the open drawer seemed to ease her stance. "When you are finish piddling around I could use some help back here!" she said, finally.

"Okay, sure. I'll tell you what; you finish the filing while I go take care of the babies?"

Yuliya sneered at Pamela. "I no finish your damn work! I take care of children, been doing it before you are here and will long after you go back to America!" Yuliya wheeled around and was gone.

As she put the rest of the files in the cabinet, Pam considered her next steps. Now that she had a document approving her "adoption" of Alex, it was just a matter of setting a plan in motion to get him out of the country with her. She would take him home with her, and Alex would never have to be hungry, cold, lonely, or facing an uncertain future, ever again.

A small part of her mind was still asking if there wasn't another way. Her father could write a check big enough to remodel this place, top to bottom. Hell, he could do it out of petty cash.

No! I came here to prove to myself and Dad that I can set my own course and stick with it. And anyway, even if I did ask him to help, he'd probably just use that as leverage to get me on the payroll at Graham Publishing.

She would get Sofia's approval to take Alex on an outing . . . from which they wouldn't return. By the time Sofia missed them, they'd be eating Texas barbecue on the balcony of her condo. Pam just needed to figure out how to get some identification for Alex that would match up with the paperwork she had just created. And she might have an idea for that, too, come to think of it . . .

Five minutes later Sofia walked into the office. Pamela placed the last file in the cabinet and pushed it shut. The rusty file drawer screeched a complaint.

"So you have been hard at work I see," Sofia smiled.

"No, it wasn't bad at all. You had everything in order, so it went fast."

Sofia made her way over to the chair at her desk. Her body dropped into the worn leather. "My, my, what a day! I could fall asleep right in this chair."

"Well, I'd better go and help Yuliya. I don't think she was too happy with me, in here filing for the past couple of hours."

"Oh, don't mind her. She is all bark. Also she knows that filing is not her thing. Give her some time and she'll get closer to you."

"Yeah, like a python at night, right?"

Sofia laughed lightly. "Oh dear, I wouldn't say that. Certainly Yuliya is just not what we call a people person. But she is very loyal to those she likes."

"I'll take your word for it. Well, I guess I'll be leaving after I finish with Yuliya. Good night, Sofia."

"Good night, dear."

Pamela left the office, closing the door behind her. And then she heard a sound that stopped her in her tracks.

On the other side of the door, inside Sofia's office, the printer connected to Sofia's computer had come to life.

Shit!

With no plausible explanation for reentering the office, and knowing that the printer was likely creating either a copy of the form she had printed or an automatic acknowledgment of the file she had transmitted to the adoption agency, Pam panicked.

She dashed to the dormitory and saw Alex, sitting in his bed, reading the book she had given him. He looked up and smiled when he saw her. Behind her, she could hear the door to Sofia's office crashing against the wall as it was flung open . . .

CHAPTER 10

The ticketing machine clicked and whirred as Joseph Pierce put his credit card back in his wallet. His boarding pass for American Airlines Flight 504—Washington-Dulles to Tokyo, with a short layover at LAX, returning in four days—whisked quietly into the dispensing tray, along with a copy of his ticket and itinerary. He picked up the documents, looked at them carefully, and then walked away from the ticketing kiosk, methodically shredding the travel documents into very small pieces. He threw the handful of paper into a trash can and then walked across the crowded concourse toward the British Airways ticketing counter.

The smiling agent gave him an inquiring look. "Good morning," Joseph said. "I'd like to book a ticket to Barcelona, please."

"Yes, sir. When will you be returning?"

"I won't. One-way, please."

"Of course. Departing today?"

"As soon as possible, yes."

The agent's eyes flickered toward him and then back to the terminal as his fingers clicked away at the keyboard.

Damn. Don't be memorable, Pierce. Say only what you have to; keep it light.

"I have a flight leaving in just under two hours, but I believe I can still get you on. Do you have much luggage?"

"No, just a carry-on." *Shit! Did it again. You don't take just a carry-on when you're going to Europe one-way . . .*

"Great. That'll save you some time. Okay, let's see, that's . . . Five hundred twenty-seven dollars. Which card will you be using for payment, sir?"

"Cash, please," Joseph said, pulling five crisp hundred-dollar bills and two twenties from his wallet. *Oh, well . . . so much for not standing out. I'm probably the only traveler in the past year who has paid for a ticket in cash . . .*

If the agent was surprised, he did a good job of hiding it. He scooped up the cash and gave Joseph his change. He dispensed the ticket and boarding pass and handed them over with another big smile. "Enjoy your flight, sir. The departure concourse is to your left, and you'll need to clear security right away."

"Thanks very much." Joseph grabbed his valise and walked quickly toward the security gate. He wasn't sure exactly how long it would take before someone in some nameless government office alerted Lee Jones at the CDC that instead of being in the office at MMMI, hastening the release of the new H1N1 vaccine, Joseph Pierce had dropped out of sight. At the moment, he was just hoping that he could get to Spain before they figured out he wasn't really headed for Tokyo to attend the nonexistent conference that he had told his administrative assistant about.

Joseph's eighty-year-old mother lived in Barcelona. Mom had taken her Spanish second husband's name and she lived pretty much off the grid; Joseph was hoping that would make him hard enough to find that it would give him time to figure out what his next moves should be.

He hoped he got a brainstorm pretty soon; he was too damned old to live long as an international fugitive.

Then again . . . living too long may not be my biggest problem . . .

* * *

"Miss—I mean, Pam? We're not going back, are we?" Alex said, looking up at her.

Pam quickly studied the area around them; as far as she could see, all the other people in the department store were bored, tired shoppers—what she hoped they all thought she and Alex were. She squatted down in front of him, placing her hands on his shoulders.

"No, sweetheart. I can't go back to the Institute but I will make sure you get back there if you want. But if you want to stay with me I've got a plan in mind, and I hope you'll like it."

His eyes opened a little wider. "What is it?"

"How would you like to come live with me, in the United States?"

The sudden bloom of excitement nearly burst her heart with gratification. And then, he looked worried. "But . . . I am supposed to go to Florida?"

This is the tricky part, Pamela. Don't screw it up.

"Honey, I'm so sorry, but you're not. I saw the files in Miss Sofia's office. The government says you can't."

His brow wrinkled deeper. "Cannot?"

She nodded. "But I don't agree with the government, and if you'll let me, I'll take you to live with me. I really want you to stay with me, Alex. I promise to take the very best care of you, buy you all the books you want to read, take you to school and pick you up every day—whatever you want. But I want to know that's okay with you. And if you say so, I promise that I'll take you back to Miss Sofia right now, and we'll pretend I never said anything."

Pam was praying harder than she had ever prayed that Alex would say yes. She knew that the future awaiting him at the Belarov Institute was not bright. But how could she tell him that right now? She had just flipped his world upside down; she didn't think he could handle any more big news.

So she watched his face, watched his eyes as they stared intently into hers. And when he smiled and held out his arms to her, it took every ounce of self-control that she had to keep from melting down in tears.

"Okay, buddy. It's you and me, then," she said, gripping him tight. "And now, we've got to find a place to stay."

She still had the dog-eared business card that Viktor had given her at the end of that first day. "If you ever need help, Pamela Graham," he had said, "please to call me. Whatever you need, no questions." Well, she needed help in the worst way, right now, and if Viktor was resourceful enough to operate an illegal cab business and not get caught, she had a list of a few other things that he might be able to assist with.

Pam was relieved a few minutes later to see that the yellow Volga had been replaced by a blue Lada. This car looked just as beat-up and abused as the Volga had, but she supposed that Viktor, realizing he had been "made" in the other car, had changed his camouflage. Right now, that seemed like a good thing.

He leaned across and opened the passenger door from inside. "Privet, Pamela Graham. You say you need ride?"

Despite being scared and tired, Pam had to smile. She scooted from the doorway where she and Alex had waited, crossing the sidewalk and bundling them both into the front seat, beside Viktor.

"Spasibo, Viktor. I really appreciate this."

"Is no problem, Pamela Graham. And who is nice young man?"

"Alex, this is my friend Viktor. Viktor, Alex."

"Privet, Alex." Viktor nodded gravely as he shook the boy's hand.

"Privet," Alex replied.

"We need a place to stay for a couple of nights, Viktor. Preferably, a place in a different part of town where people aren't very curious, if you know what I mean?"

Viktor smiled and nodded. "I know perfect place, Pamela Graham. Do you need to get anything?"

"No, let's just go. I'll find what we need a little later."

Viktor nodded, and off they went, into the evening traffic of Saint Petersburg.

* * *

Sofia sat in her chair, staring at the form that had come from her printer. She wrestled with her options, none of them good. The longer she waited to call the officials, the more difficult it would be to find Pamela and Alexander. And yet . . . did she really want to bring Alexander back here—especially now? Pamela clearly loved the boy; it was so easy to see why she had done what she had done. And what sort of future could the Belarov Institute offer poor Alexander?

But not making the call had its own potential for disaster. Officials would come in and focus on the facts, and one of those facts was that volunteers were not supposed to handle the confidential adoption paperwork. To allow any such worker complete access to her office, computer, and files was a direct violation. Yet Sofia had permitted it to happen—requested it, even! It was so clear how much Pamela loved the children, and Sofia had thought that just this once . . .

And the repercussions of the security breach traveled far past the single missing child. This situation could potentially dry up the already fragile outside funding, likely closing the orphanage forever. The government investigators would go through her documents with a fine-toothed comb.

Sofia stared at the printout. It felt heavy in her hands, too heavy to even hold. Her eyes focused on the space indicating the current "legal" guardian of Alexander Yurov: Pamela Graham.

Sofia held the phone in her hand before she even realized that she had picked it up. In her other hand was the form Pamela had forged. As illegal as Sofia knew it to be, everything appeared in order. From an outside perspective it would be regarded as a legal adoption. Sofia's instincts about Pamela were that she would be a kind and considerate caretaker for Alexander.

Sofia dropped the receiver back into its cradle. She allowed the adoption form to fall from her hand to the floor and massaged her temples with her fingertips. What to do?

There were voices in the hallway. One of them was Yuliya's, but she did not recognize the others. Yuilya's voice dominated the others, and the indistinguishable syllables overflowed with excitement. "Thank God!" Sofia said softly. "They are found."

The door to her office burst open and Yuliya stomped in without knocking.

"Miss Sofia! I got them! They were passing by, but I got them!" Yuliya said.

"Very well, Yuliya. Just calm down; we can sort this all out. The main thing is that everyone is safe," Sofia said.

"Safe? That is not what we were told." A uniformed officer stepped through the door, flanked by another.

"This woman told us that there has been a child abduction here at your facility. I have already notified the other agencies and they are on the way. This is a big problem, so let's just start from the beginning," he said.

Sofia took a deep breath. *So much for indecision. The die is cast. Pamela, may God help you; I cannot, now.*

* * *

Special Agent Novikov looked up as the junior investigator came into his office. "Sir, I thought you would want to see this. It just came across the interservice notification site."

Novikov picked up the document, feeling slightly annoyed that the junior officer had interrupted his reading of the morning newspaper. He had few rituals, but his morning paper was one of them, and he considered saying something sharp to his younger colleague.

But then he read farther down the document and realized the junior investigator had been right to bring this to him straightaway. The American woman's name meant nothing to him, of course, nor did the fact that she had apparently snatched some brat from an orphanage and vanished into the night. But the name of one of her known associates in Saint Petersburg was of great interest to Novikov: Viktor Andreyev—the brother of Boris Andreyev.

The Graham woman had been observed getting into Andreyev's vehicle while he was under observation at Pulkovo International Airport. The surveillance detail had lost Andreyev sometime afterward, but it was clear that the woman had been in contact with him for some period of time, or at least had had the opportunity.

Novikov sat back and scratched his chin. Boris Andreyev, of course, was not going to be a problem anymore. He was under lock and key, unable to continue spewing the loudmouthed accusations that the bigwigs in Moscow had been so anxious to silence. And it was not clear that the activist's ne'er-do-well brother had any credible knowledge of the vaccination program that Boris had been so worked up over. To Novikov, it all seemed a little silly, but as long as the brass in Moscow wanted Andreyev silenced, who was he to think otherwise?

And now, this Graham woman. Maybe it was just a coincidence. After all, if she was in the country to make contact with someone suspected of subversive activity, it made little sense to get herself mixed up in something as stupid as a child abduction. One would think she would be more interested in avoiding notice altogether.

And yet . . . Novikov was younger than most of the special agents in the Federal Security Service, and he hadn't achieved that by being lazy or making unfounded assumptions. If this Graham woman had possibly obtained information from Viktor Andreyev that Moscow wanted kept quiet, then it seemed irresponsible to not bring her in for questioning. Plus, rescuing some kid from an Amerikanska child-snatcher wouldn't do the Service any harm in the public relations department, either.

Still staring at the printout, Novikov reached for his telephone. He dialed a number and waited. "Customs," said the voice at the other end.

"This is Special Agent Novikov with the Federal Security Service. I am requesting an all-points alert for a person of interest in a . . . in a child abduction case . . . Yes, all airports, train stations, all public transportation, in fact. Yes, the name is Pamela Graham. She is a citizen of the United States."

CHAPTER 11

Pam stared at Roxy's passport photo and then studied herself in the mirror of the small, dark bathroom. Even with every light in the room switched on, the view was a far cry from that provided by her makeup mirror at home in Dallas. Oh, well . . . she was just going to have to make the best of it. Nadia, Viktor's lady friend, was kind enough to allow two fugitives to stay in her spare room, so Pam really didn't have much reason to complain.

Roxy, for once your airheadedness has paid off. It may just get me out of Russia alive.

Pam studied the bottle of hair color she had purchased from the shop around the corner. She had no clue on earth how different product in Russia was to what she was accustomed to in the United States, but she was going to have to make do. And it didn't have to be perfect, just good enough to get her through customs with Roxy's passport as her ID. Exchanging her blonde color for something approximating Roxy's brunette was the first step. Then, she'd employ the curling iron she'd borrowed from Nadia to go from Pam-straight to Roxy-curly. That plus a little creative makeup should do the trick. At least, Pam was praying it would.

Daddy, look at your little Pamela—disguising herself so she can escape Russia using a false identity, and taking along a kid who is techni-cally kidnapped. What would the Graham Publishing board of directors have to say about this, I wonder? Not to mention the women at the Dallas Country Club.

So far, Viktor was the best ally she could have hoped for. Given his brother's situation, he wasn't a fan of the Russian government, so that put him pretty much in her corner right off the bat. And he seemed to have many friends in low places. When Pam had told him she needed identifica-tion for Alexander that would show him to be a boy named Ryan Reynolds, the son of Roxy Reynolds, Viktor never batted an eye. And when she had asked him if there was a way to get rubles with her credit card without leav-ing a trace back to her, he just laughed and shook his head. "I have friends who make industry of this," he said. "No problem, Pamela Graham. How much you are needing?"

An hour later, she stared into the mirror at her handiwork. Staring back at her was a face framed by brown curls, a face that, if the customs official wasn't on red alert, had a chance of passing for the face in the pass-port photo.

I wonder what the chances are that they won't be on red alert, with a missing orphan snatched by a woman with a U.S. passport.

Oh, well. There wasn't anything she could do about that. This was her best shot. Either this succeeded, or Alex would be back at the Belarov Institute . . . until they put him out on the street. Any risk seemed better to Pam than the dark certainty that awaited Alex if she couldn't get him out of the country.

Pam had toyed, off and on, with the thought of calling her father. I'll bet he could make a few phone calls and all this would go away, she thought. Alex and I could fly home first-class—or in the Graham Publish-ing Learjet . . .

No. She wouldn't allow herself to go there. She'd had enough of her dad's stubbornness and drive to prefer spectacular failure on her own power to meek victory with the aid of his influence.

Benjamin Graham III relished the perks of his elite lifestyle—the cars, the jets, the houses, the weekends he spent at Bonham Grove with his rich and powerful friends—and a big part of the reason, Pam knew, was the sheer, heady satisfaction of having succeeded because of his own ambition, vision, drive, and determination. The kind of power and confidence that came from winning the sort of battles her dad had won as he had built and maintained the worldwide influence of Graham Publishing made him a person who didn't have to shout to command the attention of a roomful of people—even the kind of people who gathered at Bonham Grove. Once you had breathed that rarefied air, you never came all the way back down.

Well, this situation, Pam had decided, was the first battle she would fight, the first rung on her ladder to . . . wherever it was she was headed. This mattered—Alex mattered. And winning this fight was the initial step in defining the person Pamela Graham was going to be . . . whether Daddy liked it or not.

Alex stepped into the doorway of the bathroom. He stared at her, a curious look on his face. "Why you must do this, Pam? Change the way you look?"

She turned around and kneeled down to put herself at his eye level. "Sweetie, there are some people who really don't want me to take you to America with me. I'm going to have to tell a little lie so we can go home—and I need you to help me. I know it might seem wrong, but it's the only way I can think of to keep you with me. Can you still trust me?"

He immediately nodded vigorously. "I trust you, Pam. I do whatever you say."

She hugged him. Good Lord, I love this kid! "That's what I'm talking about, buddy boy!"

"Pam, I am little bit tired of being in house so long. Can we go out? Take walk, maybe?"

Pam thought for a few seconds. She had been trying to watch the news and had asked Viktor and Nadia to keep an ear to the ground for her. There had been one or two news stories, and the first time she had seen her face next to Alex's on the television screen with the big red Russian letters underneath, she had started to freak out just a little bit.

But Saint Petersburg was a big city, Viktor assured her, and the street kids and orphans were not at the top of most people's list of concerns. If she laid low for a few days, he said, things would probably quiet down.

She stood up and studied the Roxy disguise she'd just completed.

Giving Alex a long, thoughtful look, she came to a decision. "Sure, buddy. Let's go get a bite to eat, okay? There's a restaurant around the corner, and you can wear that hat Viktor got for you, pulled way down. I bet we'll be fine. And to tell you the truth, I'm getting a little bit of cabin fever, myself."

He pulled a puzzled face. "What is . . . cabin fever? You are sick, Pam?"

She laughed. "No, not sick, not like I need medicine. Cabin fever means . . . well, go get your coat and your hat and I'll explain . . . "

A few minutes later, they walked into the small, dingy eatery. A few people huddled in the single row of booths lining the wall; none of them looked up when Pam and Alex entered. That suited Pam just fine.

She was also pleased that the booth in the far back corner was empty. She and Alex moved toward it, and she seated Alex with his back to the door and herself leaning against the back wall of the restaurant. She would be able to see anyone who came in, and no passersby would be able to see Alex's face. She let her brown curls bob in her face, further obscuring her features from anyone who might be at all curious—which would be nobody, at this particular moment.

A sleepy-looking girl who looked about sixteen shuffled over and slid a couple of well-worn menus onto their table. Pam studied the offerings, which mostly consisted of sandwiches on various types of breads, a couple of varieties of soup, and anything you wanted to drink, as long as it was coffee or hot tea.

Alex told her he wanted something called an obzhorchiki. From the little that Pam could read the menu, it seemed to be made on black bread with some kind of nasty-sounding cheese and slathered with olive oil, garlic, and salad dressing.

She leaned toward him and spoke in a low voice. "Are you sure, Al— Are you sure that's what you want?" Dammit, Pam! You nearly said his name out loud!

He nodded. "Obzhorchiki is very good. You should try."

"Well, thanks, but maybe some other time, okay?" She opted for something that, as best as she could tell, had nothing more exotic than fried ham as an ingredient. When the sleepy girl came back, Pam ordered for them in her best Russian—which probably still wasn't good enough to fool anyone much. If she could just pass for a foreigner of indeterminate origin, that would have to be good enough.

After they had finished eating, they stepped back into the cold night. Alex turned toward the apartment, but Pam put her hand on his shoulder. "Let's take a little walk, okay, bud? Get a little more fresh air before we go back?"

Alex shrugged and nodded. Pam led the way along the sidewalk toward a section of shops just ahead that showed light and evidence of activity.

As they neared the shops, Pam saw some men mingling among the shoppers. Now and then they would show something on a piece of paper to one or two of the people standing about. They would look at the paper a few seconds, then shake their heads or just shrug and turn away.

Pam felt her pulse accelerating. These were police, and they were canvassing the area to see if anyone had seen Alex or her. She was about to spin around and head back to the safety of the apartment when one of the men looked at her.

Willing herself to appear just as bored, tired, or inattentive as the people around her, Pam continued walking, with Alex trailing behind her. She resisted the urge to turn and grab his hand. The officer's eyes slid past her and he turned to someone standing near him to show the picture.

Pam and Alex walked past the people and on toward the concealing darkness, past the reach of the shop lights. Just keep walking, Pam . . . blend in . . . no reason they should notice you . . .

An alley opened to her right, and Pam quickly ducked into it, pulling Alex with her. From the corner of her eye as she turned, she could have sworn that she saw one of the officers staring in the direction she and Alex had just taken. She quickened her pace down the alley, hoping to find a concealed corner in which the two of them could evade any unwelcome attention. "Come on, honey," she whispered to Alex. "Let's go down this way, okay?"

After she had gone maybe thirty strides down the alley, she heard a voice behind her. "Izvinite? Mogu li ya pogovorit's vami syeichas?"

Hell, no, you can't speak to me. I don't exist, and I don't hear you. She kept walking, praying that either he wasn't talking to her or that he would decide she wasn't worth the trouble of chasing. The alley curved gradually to the left, and Pam calculated that the opening they had entered was no longer visible. Maybe they were hidden in the dark—

"Izvinite! Prihodite syuda, pozhaluista!"

So much for not being noticed. Resisting the urge to break into a run—that would only transform their pursuer's doubt into certainty—Pam went a few more paces and flattened herself against the wall of a building, pressing Alex close beside her. Maybe if he thinks we're gone . . .

Then, to her horror, she heard quick footsteps coming down the alley toward them. A flashlight beam played faintly back and forth across the bricks of the building on the other side of the alley.

There was a small, sudden movement in the dark across the way. Pam's heart leaped the rest of the way into her throat, and then she realized a child was standing across from them, beckoning to them. Then the small form leaned over and tugged at something on the ground. Pam heard the sound of a heavy piece of metal scraping across pavement. The child's legs disappeared into what Pam guessed must be a manhole. Again the child waved at them.

The footsteps were getting closer; the flashlight beam was getting brighter.

"Quick, honey. Down the hole!"

She and Alex scurried across the alley. The child had gone down, and now Alex followed. "There is a ladder, Pam," he said in a loud whisper, just before his head vanished into the dark, vertical tunnel.

Pam stepped into the hole, her foot waving about in the void for a second or two before finding the rung of a ladder. She climbed down as quickly as she could, and as soon as her head was below street level, the child who had beckoned them scurried up the ladder and shifted the manhole cover back into place.

The three of them stood silently in absolute darkness, listening as the sound of footsteps got louder and louder, now coming from directly over their heads . . . now fading into the distance.

A weak beam of light appeared then; the child had switched on a rusty flashlight. "On ushel," the child said. "He is gone."

Pam shivered with cold and the aftermath of her adrenaline rush. She looked at their small deliverer, then at as much of their surroundings as she could see in the weak illumination of the child's flashlight.

What in the hell have I gotten us into now?

CHAPTER 12

As her eyes adjusted to the dark, Pam could make out the shadowed outline of several children huddling together in the sewer. Her eyes widened then softened as she gained a mental grasp on what she saw. Living here, below the rest of the world, were the forgotten, the discarded, the bottom feeders . . . the street children of Russia.

The young girl who had first beckoned to Pam in the alley stood near Alex. She said something to him in Russian, but the words were so quiet Pam couldn't make them out. Alex looked at her. "She says, 'I wouldn't stick around here if you don't have to.'"

"Ne volnuiutes'. My ne budem delat' nepriyatnosti," Pam said, assuring them she meant them no harm.

"I don't worry about me," the girl said, giving Pam a cold stare. "You are the one who is not belong here."

Pam looked over at Alex, then back toward the children. "Yeah, I know. We, umm . . . are just avoiding a problem for now. What are your names?" Pam fought back the tears that were quickly forming in her eyes.

"They don't speak English, just me," the girl said. "Is better to get money from Americans." The girl gave a short, harsh laugh that came from a life where infancy was never experienced. It was not a child's laugh.

One of the younger boys approached Pam, and the smell coming from his small, unwashed body made her instinctively want to move away. But on her immediate right was a puddle of sewage water. It was too dark to move with confidence, so she remained still, fighting with her discomfort. Her unease was heightened by the quick, scratching sounds she heard, coming from the surrounding dark. Then the faint glow of the girl's flashlight picked up the form of a scurrying rodent.

It was too much for Pam. She felt her breath becoming shallower, faster, and more labored; she began to feel faint. Alex moved in beside her and put an arm around her waist. "Pam, you are okay?"

"Yeah, sweetie, I will be fine. We just need to get you somewhere safe. I should have never brought you into all of this."

"Why you say this? I choose, remember? I go with you because I want to, and I stay with you, Pam. Is better for me with you than waiting at orphanage for something that never happens."

Pam stared at him. "You knew that your adoption was suspended?"

He nodded and looked down, appearing slightly ashamed. "Am listening at Miss Sofia's door when news report is on television. I hope is not true, but when we are in store and you tell me, I know."

"I am so sorry, honey."

Alex shrugged. "Is okay."

The other children had stood silently, listening to this exchange. Of course, only the girl holding the flashlight could understand them, presumably. If any of them had any reaction, it was hidden behind impassive faces, locked inside motionless forms.

As she and Alex moved to one side, Pam's foot pressed against something soft. Pam gave a quick gasp. The girl with the flashlight gave a mirthless giggle. "Is okay. That one is already dead. When rats are alive they have nasty bite." She said something in Russian and the other children laughed quietly.

Pam was still fighting to keep her composure. She decided to focus on the girl who spoke English, since she appeared to be the leader of the band.

"What is your name, honey?"

The girl looked to the others then back at Pam. "What do you care? No names." She was no more than twelve, Pam guessed, but she was certain that this little girl had seen more than had any adult Pam knew. Her layers of tattered clothing hung like dirty laundry on her frail body. Her hair was lank and matted; Pam wondered how many months it had been since the girl had held a brush in her hand.

"No family to go to?" Pam asked.

"Sure, if I want beating from drunken father, or to watch mother pass out." She stared at Pam. "Down here, wind doesn't blow; no one hit us."

Pam said nothing. She had never walked in their worn-out shoes. She had grown up in a world with more abundance than these poor children could possibly imagine. For these kids, childhood dwelled in some vague dimension, written in the pages of a lost fairy tale. Pam tried to imagine Alex, instead of standing at her side with his arm wrapped protectively around her waist, huddled with the children in the fading glow of the girl's flashlight. Pam could feel the cold tears slide down her face.

A young boy no more than seven or eight walked over and stared at Alex but did not say anything. The girl with the flashlight barked a few harsh syllables and he moved away. The children stared at Pam and Alex as if they were objects from another world; there was nothing as human as even mere curiosity in their eyes. Pam understood; how could they embrace emotions that they had never seen or experienced? In their simple, harsh world, everything was either food, an advantage, or a threat. She and Alex were none of the three. They were objects of little interest.

The girl darted back up the ladder. Pam heard the sound of the heavy manhole cover sliding across the pavement of the alley above. Her agile, small body scurried back down. "Is nobody there," she said. "You should leave." She stood to one side, a hand gripping the rusted rail.

A final question formed in Pam's mind. "Why did you help us, up there?"

The girl shrugged. "I am coming back here when I hear them chasing you. If they find you, maybe they find us. We don't like police."

Pam nodded. *Well, I guess we've about used up what little welcome we had.*

They moved toward the ladder. Before they went up, Alex stood in front of the girl. He took off his coat, handing it to Pam. Then he peeled off the sweater he was wearing and handed it to the girl. He retrieved his coat from Pam and put it back on.

The young girl stroked the sweater tenderly, staring at it in wonderment. It was the first emotional response Pam had seen from her.

They climbed up to the alley. As they made their way back toward the street, Pam listened intently to the surrounding sounds. The sounds of traffic, the low voices of pedestrians on the sidewalks . . . she heard nothing that indicated threat or pursuit. Good.

At the alley opening, before they stepped onto the sidewalk, Pam leaned from the shadows and studied as much of the street as she could see. Cars passed; a few cabs were parked along the curb. A family of four walked past on the other side of the street. The way was clear.

They walked toward the cluster of shops, and just on the other side, someone stepped up beside Pam.

"Miss Graham, you must come with me," the woman said. Pam swung her head around to see who was speaking. It was Nadia.

"Nadia! You scared me to—"

"Come with me quickly, Miss Graham. We cannot go back to apartment. They have taken Viktor."

* * *

Special Agent Novikov held up a hand, and the burly officer stepped back from Viktor's doubled-over form. Novikov kneeled down beside the chair in which Viktor was bound. Andreyev's panting breaths were mixed with quiet groans.

"Now, then, Mr. Andreyev. Perhaps you remember where Pamela Graham has taken the young child she stole?"

"Go to hell," Viktor grunted. "I don't know anyone by that name, I already told you."

Novikov gave a sad little chuckle. "Ah, but Vitya, we have pictures of the two of you together. How can you possibly lie to me about this?"

"She was a cab fare. I picked her up at the airport, like I do hundreds of people per week. I don't know their names."

"Yes, your illegal taxi business. We'll have to discuss that a bit later, as well, I'm afraid. But right now I am very anxious to know what you discussed with the American woman and where she has taken the orphan. Please say you'll help me?"

"Like you helped my brother?" Viktor spat. Blood, mixed with mucus, spattered from his lips onto Novikov's shirt. The special agent recoiled, making a disgusted sound. He took a handkerchief from his pocket and daubed at his clothing.

"Your brother is a subversive and a liar," Novikov said. "I had hoped that you would make better decisions than he chose to make." He nodded at the officer and turned away as the dull thump of leather on flesh resumed, along with tortured gasps from Viktor Andreyev.

A minute or two later Novikov motioned at the officer. "Viktor, one of our investigators saw the woman with the child in an alley around the corner from your girlfriend's apartment. Why are you hiding a foreign criminal, a kidnapper?"

Viktor took several ragged, gurgling breaths before responding. "I don't know what you are talking about. I have not seen the person you are looking for."

"When I have spoken with Nadia—that's her name, yes?—I will probably learn that you are lying," Novikov said. "I also know that you are lying about talking to the American woman. Isn't it true that you told her about your brother and his misguided notions of the government's immunization program? Aren't you trying to spread malicious gossip about your country's leaders to the West, so that they can publish it on their foolish websites and blogs? Why are you doing this, Viktor? Why are you following your brother into lunacy?"

"My brother is the only person whose sanity is beyond question," Viktor said. "You are the crazy ones. You and the murderers in the Kremlin who want to kill everyone who—"

The officer's cudgel smashed into Viktor's cheek, fracturing his left maxilla and zygomatic bones. The officer raised the club again, but paused, peering at Viktor's unmoving form. "He is unconscious, Special Agent."

"Very well," Novikov said. "Take him back to the cell. When he wakes, we'll try again." Novikov pulled a cell phone from his pocket and pressed a single button. "Yes, Novikov. Any word from the airports or train stations? I see . . . Well, I think we should increase the media exposure. Someone somewhere must have seen her. And let's bring in the orphanage director, also. Perhaps she can tell us something. Yes, that's all for now."

Novikov snapped his phone shut and watched absently as two

uniformed officers unstrapped Andreyev and roughly hoisted his inert form. His instinct told him that the Andreyev brothers were fanatics, and fanatics always sought converts. Whether the Graham woman came to this country specifically to make contact with Boris Andreyev or for some other reason, Novikov could not afford to risk that she was ignorant of the brothers' foolish suspicions.

He had to find her, and he had to know what the rogue cab driver had told her. And, depending on the outcome of that line of inquiry, it might be necessary to ensure that she never returned to the United States.

CHAPTER 13

John David Boone took a long sip from his tumbler, allowing the dark, peaty taste of the single malt to work its way under his tongue and along the sides of his mouth. His square build reminded Giles of an American football player. Boone—known as J.D. to anyone close to him—stared across the harbor at the distinctive, sail-like outline of the Sydney Opera House. "So what you're telling me, Giles, is that the CDC and this Maxwell Morris outfit are in some kinda cahoots to spread a bogus vaccine? And the feds are mixed up in it somehow?"

"Not mixed up in it, J. D.," Giles said, appreciatively eyeing the bottle of Aberfeldy 21 as he swallowed his first mouthful of the drink. "Running it. I don't know how far up it goes, but it's damned high. And the people at the Morris Institute are being played for saps, as best I can tell. The director, a guy named Joseph Pierce, is the one who smelled a rat in the first place."

Boone's snow-white hair blew gently in the harbor breeze as he leaned back against the railing of his yacht and studied Giles Girard's face. "I like you, Giles, you know I do. The way you took on them fat-ass pansies that were dumping their skim water into the lagoons up at East Timor . . . Shit fire, I woulda bought twice that many lawyers if I'd known how much fun it was gonna be to watch those old boys squirm."

Giles gave the older man a weak grin. "Yeah, well, there were some tense moments."

"Ah, hell, son. You wasn't ever in serious trouble. All it took was money. Thanks to the old family gusher I got plenty of that. Didn't even have to bring in my ass-kickers."

"Yes, well, I think we're still at the money-only stage with this situation," Giles said. "If I can get this thing out in the open—"

"Well, now, that's just it, ain't it?" Boone said, walking over and sitting in the lounge chair across the low table from Giles. "Now you know that I don't like these sunglasses-wearing, hidden-camera, no-name pricks any better than any freedom-loving American. Hell, they work for the people that look down their damn noses at anybody that ain't afraid to admit it when there's a turd in the punchbowl, you know what I mean? That's the people that have lined up against me all my life, would've just as soon let me and my family starve as say 'good morning.' Shit, I take a special joy in kicking that kind of ass.

"But it sounds like you might be talking about something that involves the highest levels of the government. Hell, maybe the president, I don't know. Now, I've got some pretty solid resources, don't get me wrong. But I ain't got shit if they start tossing air-to-ground missiles at me, boy, you hear what I'm saying? I don't mind giving some well-deserved hell to those cocksucking political bastards, but I ain't real keen on dying to get 'er done, see? I've still got some whiskey I need to drink." Boone drained his tumbler and poured himself another two fingers of Aberfeldy 21. He offered the bottle to Giles with a questioning expression.

Giles shook his head, holding up his still-full glass. "J. D., I completely understand. And you're right, of course. One hundred percent. We can't fight this with muscle—never could have."

"I'm listening," Boone said.

"I didn't come here to ask you for some kind of militia, or even a legal team. What I need is equipment and bandwidth."

"Come again?"

"The only thing these people fear is exposure, J. D. I figured this out a long time ago. They can lock their money in a safe, and they can hire people with guns to get rid of someone they don't like. But they have to live in the same world as you and me, J. D., and once the world turns on them, all their money and all their power don't mean a damned thing. They're just like cockroaches in the middle of the kitchen floor when you turn the light on; they can't stand it, and they'll run for the nearest dark corner. What I want to do is keep the light on them the whole way."

Boone, looking thoughtful, took a sip of scotch. He swallowed, nodded, and smiled. "I like the way you think, boy, always have. You're right; that's how you have to handle these high-and-mighty assholes. If you keep quiet and ease out info, they see the spark before the barn fire and snuff you out before you get too big. But if you shove all their secret shit right up their ass and out in the open . . . then you got 'em. And if you think this Internet idea of yours is the way to skin the cat, I'll buy you a shitload of computers and the people to run 'em. Just don't get any sniper rifles pointed in my direction, savvy?"

"Savvy," Giles said. He picked up his glass and gave Boone a small salute. "To WebLeaks and its founder and benefactor, John David Boone."

Boone made a scoffing sound. "Don't waste my good liquor drinking to shit like that. And you might better see about finding you a couple of stainless steel leisure suits too, I reckon, once the shit hits the fan."

* * *

Nadia shoved the envelope into Pam's hand. "This is money and documents you request from Viktor. Our friend Maxim will drive you to airport. After that, is up to you. And now I must go, before they come for me, too."

Pam put a hand on Nadia's shoulder as she turned away. The Russian woman turned back, and Pam wrapped her in a hug. "Thank you so much, Nadia," Pam said. "I don't know what I'd have done without Viktor—and you."

Nadia looked at her with frightened, tear-stained eyes. "Take boy to America. Give him better life. That will be enough."

"I'll do my best," Pam said, emotion choking her voice.

Nadia gave her a tight nod and left.

"Come on, buddy," Pam said, taking Alex's hand. "We've got a ride to catch."

They went downstairs and waited in the small foyer of the tenement. In a few minutes, as Nadia had promised, a battered brown car creaked to a halt beside the curb. Pam and Alex hurried out and got inside as quickly as possible.

Maxim, the driver, looked over his shoulder at the two of them in the backseat. "Hello," he said in a guttural, slurred accent. "I tack you to airpor', jes?"

"Da, spasibo," Pam said. She fished in the envelope and retrieved two hundred-ruble notes, proffering them to Maxim.

He looked at the money and shook his head. "No pay. I Viktor friend. I do for heem, jes?"

"Jes," Pam said, her throat tightening with emotion. Poor Viktor. She hoped to God he would be okay.

They drove through the early morning traffic. Maxim's radio played static-laden operatic music, and he hummed along, generally drifting somewhere south of the correct tune. From what Pam could tell, they weren't being tailed. Maybe, just maybe, she would be able to get out of this country.

She opened the envelope and looked at its contents. There was a bundle of rubles and a much larger bundle of euros. An official-looking U.S. passport identified Alex as Ryan Reynolds, son of Roxy Reynolds. Despite her anxiety, Pam had to smile. Roxy would turn inside out at the thought that she had a preadolescent son—and a Russian one, at that.

"When we get there, just let me do the talking, okay, honey?" she told Alex. "Right now, you're supposed to be American, but you don't really sound that way, right? So just smile sweetly and nod if anybody says anything to you, got it?"

Alex gave her a sweet smile and nodded. Pam had to laugh. "Good boy."

"Besides, Pam, is truth—I am to be American, yes?"

She hugged him. "Yes."

Also in the envelope was the credit card that she had given Viktor to use for the currency purchase. She started to crease the card and dispose of it, but then she had an idea.

She put the card, the cash, and Alex's passport in her bag. For maybe the twentieth time that morning, she got out her compact and flipped open the mirror, studying her appearance and comparing it with Roxy's passport photo. *Please, God, let it work . . . please let it work . . .*

She got out her pocket journal and flipped to a blank page. "I, Pamela Graham, being of sound mind," she wrote, "do hereby declare this to be my last will and testament . . . "

* * *

Novikov stared at the monitor in the central security office at Pulkovo Airport. Steven Shew, the newly hired head of airport security, stood next to him. Shew, a former U.S. military police officer, hailed from Toledo, Ohio. While stationed in Germany on his last tour, he had fallen in love with Europe and had resolved to return there to live. After making himself fluent in Russian, German, and French, he had been overjoyed to successfully apply for the position as head of security for Pulkovo Airport. He was very proud of his job and, at the moment, very annoyed by the Federal Security Service special agent who had barged in moments ago, demanding to hold all international flights and to see the recordings from all the surveillance cameras in the international terminal. He overheard Novikov swearing softly. "Special Agent Novikov," Shew said in Russian, "if you will tell me exactly what you are looking for, perhaps I can more quickly—"

"What you can do," Novikov said in English, "is move away from me with your bad American accent and allow me to do my job. I do not trust a former American military officer to help me find an American kidnapper. When I require your assistance I will ask for it."

Shew felt his blood pressure spiraling upward. This was typical behavior from these neo-apparatchiks who thought they still worked for the KGB. *Fucking asshole.* "Listen, Novikov, we can't hold all the flights any longer without a valid reason. Just let me know what you are looking for and then I can take over and get this done."

Novikov rotated his head toward the doors that led outside of the security room. He placed an arm over Shew's shoulders. He casually guided the security chief away, out of the others' earshot.

"Mr. Shew, I am not leaving here without the person I am looking for. So either you work with me or you may find yourself and your family watching over your backs more than you desire. Do you really want to jeopardize the good life you have here in Russia? Trust me, your disappearance would merit no more than a one-line mention in the back section of our newspapers."

"Special Agent, I think we have something!" one of Novikov's investigators called out, pointing at a computer screen.

Novikov hurried over. He stared at the screen where his assistant was pointing. "The stupid bitch," he said, smiling. "Using her credit card to buy her ticket. Splendid."

He whirled around. "Mr. Shew, you will tell me which gate is scheduled for the use of—" he glanced back at the screen—"Swiss Air Flight 2016. And you will immediately instruct your agents to hold the flight and secure the area. Then, and only then, you may release the other flights."

Shew entered a few keystrokes on a nearby monitor. "Swiss Air 2016 is at gate thirty-seven."

Novikov whirled and raced from the room, followed by his assistants. Shew stared after them for a few seconds, shaking his head. Then he picked up his phone. "All flights except Swiss Air 2016 are released for normal boarding and departure," he said in Russian.

CHAPTER 14

Alex and Pamela sat in separate areas in the terminal as they waited for their flight. She would occasionally smile at him from across the seating area, and she kept her eyes on him constantly. Since the news media were instructing the public to watch for a woman and a boy traveling together, she figured that sitting apart would not draw as much attention. She remained on the lookout, expecting that at any minute her plan would disintegrate, but still determined to see it through.

As her eyes drifted back toward the television monitors in the waiting area for the flight, she suddenly felt her breath catch. On the screen was an image of Sofia Lebedev, the director of the Belarov Institute, being led away in handcuffs. The caption crawl at the bottom of the screen, from what Pam could understand, indicated that she was being questioned in connection to Alex's disappearance.

Oh, my God. Viktor, and now Sofia! How many more people are going to suffer because of me? Next, pictures of herself and Alex flashed onto the screen, accompanied by the usual admonition to viewers to report any suspicious woman who was accompanied by a young boy.

How am I going to get out of this? I'm Public Enemy Number One at the moment. She felt as if every eye in the terminal was upon her, every passenger and airport worker reaching for the nearest phone to report her to the authorities.

"Terrible, isn't it?" said the man next to her, in Russian-accented English. Pam looked at him, doing her best to keep the terror out of her eyes. Hesitant to allow her accent to reveal her nationality, she simply gave him a puzzled look and shook her head.

"Oh, I thought you were American or British," he said, switching to Russian. "The American woman and the boy." He gestured toward the television with his head. "Terrible."

Pam shrugged. "I don't know about it," she said, praying that her accent was good enough.

"Oh, I don't blame the Amerikanska," he went on. "The situation in our orphanages is what I'm talking about. A national disgrace. That someone could so easily walk into a place with the responsibility of caring for children, then walk out with a child and not be caught immediately . . . deplorable." He peered closely at her. "Don't you agree?"

Pam adopted what she hoped was a thoughtful expression, rather than the sheer terror she was feeling. The sense of being discovered, of being caught, was so powerful in her that it was all she could do to keep from leaping out of her seat, grabbing Alex, and sprinting for the nearest exit.

The boarding announcement for her flight came over the intercom, sounding like a message from heaven. "Izvinite. Moi polet." She stood, gathering her things.

He nodded. "Schastlivogo puti."

You have a good trip too, buddy. Hope I never see you again—in this country, at least.

She signaled Alex, then she followed him up to the boarding gate. The agent taking boarding passes beamed as she watched Alex walk up to her. She took the boarding pass, looked at it, and held it as she struck up a conversation with a coworker. Pam handed her Alex's passport. The agent looked at it, leaned over, and said to Alex, "Nichego sebe Vy—krasivyi molodoi chelovek!" Alex blushed, but said in English, "Excuse me? Sorry, I don't understand."

Good boy! "Thank you, ma'am," Pam said, smiling. "I think he's a very handsome young man, indeed."

The agent took Pam's passport and boarding pass, examined them, then handed them back to Pam. "Have a good flight, Ms. Reynolds. And you too, Ryan," she added, giving Alex another big smile.

Pam smiled and herded Alex toward the entrance to the jetway. An elderly man, accompanied by a younger man and woman, was very slowly and hesitantly trying to get his walker folded up for the flight. *Come on . . . come on!* Pam looked around nervously, expecting at any moment to hear shouting and the sounds of pursuit coming up behind her.

The young woman with the old man looked at Pam and shrugged apologetically. Pam did her best imitation of an understanding smile in return. The woman looked at Alex, then back at Pam. "Oh, you are both American?" she said in English.

"Yes, I am from Texas!" Alex responded.

Good job again, Alex!

"How did you like Russia?"

"We had a great time; we're just ready to get going, aren't we, Ryan?" Pam said. She was wishing fervently that more travelers would step up to enter the jetway, giving them an opportunity to slip out of the spotlight; she felt as if everyone in the waiting area was staring at her. And still, no one else approached the gate.

Finally, the younger man was able to help the old gentleman get his walker folded. He took one arm and the young woman took the other. "Poidem, Dedushka," he said as they started down the jetway. He looked over his shoulder at Pam. "Sorry for the delay. This is my grandfather's first time to travel by jet. Takes a little longer for him."

Pam smiled. "No problem. I just hope we can get boarded before my little man here has to go to the restroom again." Alex gave her a sour look that almost made her laugh, despite her anxiety.

The short distance seemed to take an eternity. They controlled their walk to a pace that was hurried but not too fast to draw attention. She gave Alex the ticket stub for his seat. "Honey, go on ahead of me, okay? I will be right there."

Alex moved along and entered the plane. The flight attendant held him up at the door before Alex pointed back to Pam. This relaxed the attendant's concerns and she let him enter the plane. Pam stalled, pretending to adjust her carry-on bag. As she did, she peered back down the jetway and into the waiting area to see if they were being followed or pursued. Nothing. She moved on down the jetway to board the plane. She didn't look back, afraid of what might appear behind her. Every instinct within her screamed that this was not over yet.

Pam's seating choice had put them as close to the rear of the plane as possible, with Alex's seat directly in front of her. Pam watched the other passengers trickling down the aisle, wishing desperately for the plane to push back from the gate and get airborne.

Alex leaned his chair back; she could see the smile of pleasure on his face. He had told her he had never been on an aircraft before. She envied his ability to find calm in the midst of chaos. The last time she had allowed herself to relax, she had almost missed her flight to Russia. As she thought about her current circumstances, missing that flight might have been an unknown blessing. But no . . . Alex was more than worth the stress. *As long as this works. Please, God, let this work . . .*

Alex peeked back at her through the small opening that separated the seats. "This plane is so cool!" he said. He turned back around. Pam watched him put the disposable earphones on, watched him switching among the channels available on the aircraft's music system. She could hear him humming and see the top of his head moving in rhythm.

Just as the intercom dinged and the standard preflight announcements began—first in Russian, then in Spanish—there was a commotion noticeable through the windows of the terminal. People scattered in all directions as a group of officers ran through the waiting area, headed toward the boarding gates. Pam felt her heart speeding up, but she could not turn away.

The disorder inside the terminal intensified as another large group of police made their way past the glass walls through the terminal. In front of the group a man in a dark overcoat appeared to be giving orders.

Pam closed her eyes and began praying harder than she had ever prayed in her life.

* * *

"Special Agent Novikov, here is the passenger manifest. Pamela Graham is listed here; this is her seat number." The assistant gave Novikov a worried look. "Sir, I am afraid that there was not a seat purchased next to her for the boy."

Novikov smiled. "She probably just purchased a seat in a different location on the plane. Trying to avoid being obvious." *But too stupid to avoid using her credit card.* He gestured to the police and other security officers who had gathered with him, beside the entry to the jetway. A crowd of onlookers was swelling rapidly behind them. *Good. It will do them good to see that the Federal Security Service has not been sleeping.*

"Here is the situation," Novikov said in a voice calculated to carry all the way across the waiting area. "We have a woman on this flight who has violated our adoption laws. We have reason to believe that she is on this plane traveling with a boy abducted from an orphanage against his will. I want this done peacefully. We don't want any harm to come to the child. Are there any questions?" Novikov took a dramatic pause, staring pointedly around at the officers. No one spoke. "Very well. You, you, and you," he said, pointing to his assistant investigators, "come with me. You five, secure the jetway and the gate area. The rest of you, reinforce those who are securing the plane from the outside. All right, let's go."

Novikov, followed by his three deputies, entered the jetway. He strode toward the aircraft's open doorway, passing the flight attendant without so much as a glance. He looked at the passenger manifest. "Seat forty-seven B," he read aloud.

He strode through the first-class area, then, pausing in the center aisle of the main cabin, held his badge high. "I am Special Agent Nikolai Novikov of the Russian Federal Security Service," he announced. "Please remain seated. This will only take a moment, and then you will be on your way to your destination." He nodded to his men, then he strode down the aisle, scanning the faces peering helplessly up at him.

Row ten . . . twenty . . . twenty-five . . . Novikov could feel his pulse accelerating, anticipating the capture. Row thirty . . . thirty-five . . .

Novikov arrived at row forty-seven and peered down at the window seat indicated for Pamela Graham on the passenger manifest. The seat was empty. The other two seats next to it were occupied by a skinny, bespectacled male and a woman who looked old enough to be his grandmother.

None of the other passengers in the row came anywhere close to matching Pamela Graham's passport photo. What was going on?

Novikov spun toward his assistants. They stared back at him, lost for words. Novikov slammed his fist into the ceiling of the cabin. "Search the plane, including all baggage compartments! No one leaves! You will all immediately produce your identification papers for inspection—including the flight crew."

For a few seconds, every eye on Swiss Air Flight 2016 stared at Special Agent Nikolai Novikov as if he had just uttered gibberish. "Now!" he screamed, and there was a sudden flurry of reaching in pockets and digging in purses.

"I don't understand, Special Agent," one of his assistants said meekly. "Where can she be?"

"Shut up, you moron," Novikov snapped. "Go outside and tell the officers to open the cargo bays."

* * *

A few yards away, Alitalia Flight 2147 pushed back from its gate and began taxiing toward an on-schedule takeoff for its flight from Saint Petersburg to Barcelona. Pam's body relaxed as the plane rolled unimpeded down the taxiway. She pulled out her ticket and Roxy's passport, looking at them one more time. She crumpled up the receipt to the decoy ticket she had purchased with her credit card. Thank God she had asked Viktor to get plenty of cash. She had enough rubles for her and Alex's one-way tickets, and she still had plenty of euros to use in Spain.

The jet accelerated for takeoff, pressing Pam into her seat. No takeoff had ever been more welcome. She closed her eyes as the plane's wheels left the runway, thinking about Pilar and Javier Garcin and their beautiful little house on the outskirts of Barcelona, where she had spent a year as an exchange student.

CHAPTER 15

As the euphoria of her escape from Russia gradually gave way to a post-adrenaline sag, Pam realized that her mind, recently preoccupied with avoiding capture and making good her getaway with Alex, now had leisure to consider a longer-term future—one full of problems. First of all, for all she knew the Russian authorities might have someone with handcuffs waiting at her arrival gate in Barcelona. All they had to do was spend some time studying the passenger manifests for departing flights long enough to notice that Roxy Reynolds, who had cleared customs and headed for Spain, had never actually entered Russia in the first place. Viktor's forger friend had faked the incoming customs stamp on Roxy's passport well enough to fool the bored official at the airport this morning, but that wouldn't stand up to a prolonged investigation.

Damn. I hope Roxy wasn't planning to travel to Russia anytime soon . . .

But even if Russia didn't think a single orphan boy was worth mounting an international search over, Pam still had the puzzle of what to do with Alex until she found a place to settle down. Once again, she realized she had been so focused on rescuing Alex from the immediate future of a life on the streets that she had failed to consider the long-term consequences of providing care for a young boy. Hell, I'm only twenty-three, myself! What was I thinking?

Daddy used to lecture her—on the few occasions when they were together long enough to permit conversation—about the dangers of making hasty decisions. Pam would usually roll her eyes, hearing only the irony of such advice being delivered by a man who had just decided, on the spur of the moment, to fly them both to Monaco for a weekend of watching very fast cars go around very tight turns. Since those last-minute decisions marked some of the best times in her life, quick decisions had always seemed to Pam like the way to go.

But now, as she studied the top of Alex's head while he slept in the seat in front of her, she was wishing she'd paid a bit more heed. It was one thing to get a wild hair and go out for a night of clubbing instead of studying for midterms. Even delaying her employment at Formula 1 for a three-month internship at a Russian orphanage could be written off as youthful exuberance mixed with a heavy dose of naive altruism. But abducting a child—yes, Pamela, call it what it is, girl—from legal authorities and taking responsibility for where he would live, what he would do, for everything about his future life . . . The sudden sense of the responsibility she had taken on nearly made Pam dizzy. Alex wasn't some puppy she had adopted from the pound; he was a human being who was now in her care and under her protection. The very last thing this little boy needed was to be dragged all over Europe while Pam tried to figure out what she was going to do for a place to live. Above all, Alex needed stability and a nurturing environment. Pam could see herself providing the second, but the first, right now, was going to pose a bigger challenge.

Pam took a deep breath and stared out the airplane window at the featureless cloudscape passing below. Think, Pam, think . . . It was still a couple of weeks before she was due to start working for Formula 1. Originally, going to Pilar and Javier's home in Spain had been an intermediate step in her plan, since Pam figured that trying to fly directly to the United States would subject her to greater scrutiny and a higher likelihood of being caught by Russian authorities. She had intended to fly to Barcelona, then to secure passage home to Dallas with Alex.

But now . . . Maybe Pilar and Javier would be willing to play a slightly larger role in this bit of improvisational theater that Pam called her life. Pilar and Javier were beautiful, giving people. Pam would talk to them. Maybe, just maybe . . .

The arrival in Barcelona renewed Pamela's spirit. Just breathing the warmer, less tainted air of the city on the Mediterranean coast felt like a rebirth. Spain had never failed to create pleasure inside her, and never more so than now, when Russia lay behind her like a dreary memory.

Spain, on the other hand, felt like home. The country effortlessly pulled Pam into its rich heritage. The ageless architecture appeared in postcard perfection, exactly the way she remembered it, as the aircraft circled Barcelona on its final approach.

Pam had been hypersensitive to the actions and reactions of the cabin crew during the flight from Saint Petersburg; surely, if the Russian authorities had informed them that they had a fugitive kidnapper on board, it would show up just a little bit in their faces. But the Alitalia flight attendants were unfailingly polite and solicitous, and the flight would have been boring in its routine, under any other circumstances. Likewise, as they now opened the aircraft door to allow the passengers to deplane, Pam half-expected police to burst through, overpower her, and lead her away in handcuffs.

But none of that happened. Instead, Pam and Alex strolled off the Alitalia Airbus, walked up the jetway, and arrived in the terminal of Barcelona's El Prat airport amid a crowd of people, none of whom gave the slightest evidence of interest in either Alex or herself. The weight of the world had lifted from her shoulders.

Even though they were still inside the airport, Pam imagined that she could detect the refined smell of grilled delicacies filling the air. The deep desire to stay in Spain forever had never wavered in Pam since the first time she visited, three years ago, when she was a sophomore at SMU. Now, of course, there was much more at stake than Pam's romantic feelings about a beautiful country and its people; from now on Alex's well-being would figure large in any decision she made—starting with her upcoming conversation with Pilar and Javier. Like Alex, Spain had captured Pam's heart with very little effort. Pilar and Javier Garcin had been her host parents, and Pam had maintained frequent contact with them in the years since.

Twenty minutes after leaving the airport, the taxi pulled up to their modest home, just outside the city. Pam got out and stood still for a moment, allowing her mind to revel in pleasant memories of her Spanish stomping grounds. Less than ten miles away was the international study center, established in 1990, where she had taken her courses. Now she stood in front of the home she had shared for an entire year with Pilar and Javier Garcin; they had occupied the home for well over four decades.

Pam paid the cabbie. She shouldered her bag and swung open the gate that admitted them to the small front yard. Asking Alex to wait at the bottom of the front steps, Pam approached the front door. She saw the curtains of the window beside the door twitch aside. Pam could picture Pilar—whom Pam called Mama Pili—peering through the small opening, likely wearing her signature flowered apron.

The front door opened, but Pilar remained behind the locked screen. Her short gray hair was loose and combed to the back, in the style Pam remembered. From the way Mama Pili was squinting, her silver, wire-rimmed glasses had long lost their ability to function properly. Pam guessed that Mama Pili's cataracts were probably getting worse.

Pam walked right up to the screen. "Hi, Mama Pili, it's me—Pamela."

Pilar frowned for a few seconds, then her eyes flew wide and a look of delight unfurled on her face. "Pamela!" Her fingers scrambled to unlock the screen door and fling it open. She hugged Pam tightly, dancing her back and forth a little, then she eased her embrace. She held Pam away from her. "What have you done with your hair? No wonder I didn't recognize you, Pamela!"

"It's kind of a long story," Pam said, glancing toward Alex.

Pilar, following Pam's gaze, noticed Alex. Her face took on a puzzled expression as she looked back and forth from Pam to Alex. Pam could almost hear her doing the mental math.

"It has been a long time but not that long, okay, Mama Pili? This is not what you are thinking."

Pilar took a few steps toward Alex. She smiled at him. "Hmm . . . could have fooled me. Looks just like a real child!"

Pam laughed. "Oh yeah, he's real, all right. His name is Alex, but . . . " Pam paused, looking around nervously.

Pilar gave Pam an odd look, then went to Alex and kneeled in front of him. "You are a very handsome young man, Alex. I am pleased to meet you. You may call me Mama Pili, okay?"

Alex smiled. "Thank you. I am happy to meet you . . . Mama Pili."

Pam felt her heart bursting with love—for both of them.

"Come inside," Pilar said, taking Alex's hand. "You too, my dear Pamela. Stop acting like a stranger."

They went in. Pam set her bag down and rushed to the kitchen, then returned. "So, where is Javier?"

Pilar made a dismissive gesture toward the rear of the home. "Oh, he is out back trying to start a garden."

"A garden? I didn't know he liked to work in a garden."

"He doesn't, but, well . . . "

Pam gave Pilar a questioning look.

"It is a matter of survival, Pamela. When Javier retired, I told him that I did not expect to share my house with a meddling, bored old man. I told him that he would either find a hobby that kept him out from underfoot, or I would leave him. Gardening is his latest attempt."

Pam burst out laughing. "Mama Pili, I'm ashamed of you! And I can't believe Papa Javier would ever swallow such a crazy threat."

Pilar smiled. "But never mind that; let's talk about this young handsome gentleman with you." Pili went to the kitchen and then approached Alex, offering him a plate of cookies. When Pam took one from the plate, she realized that the cookies were still warm.

"Mama Pili, you baked today? But you didn't know we were coming."

Pilar gave her a guilty look. "Baking keeps me out of the garden."

Pam laughed again.

"Thank you for the cookie," Alex said. "May I have another?"

"Of course. The old man and I have no real use for them; I'm glad someone will enjoy them." She offered Alex the plate. He took another cookie, then, after a quick look at Pam and Pilar, quickly took two more.

"So, how did this lovely young man enter your life?" Pilar said. Pam stared at Pilar for a few seconds and had opened her mouth to reply when a voice rang from the kitchen entryway. "Pam! Oh my God, is that you? What on earth are you doing here?"

Pam ran over to Javier and hugged him warmly. She realized that she could feel the bones of his back and shoulders; he was far frailer than she remembered. She stood back and looked at him; his lean body tilted much farther than before. His white hair, now missing even the few strands of black he had had when Pam had lived with them, thinly covered his head.

Pam loved them both dearly, but she and Javier had something special. A daddy-daughter relationship had developed upon her arrival and had never wavered. The twinkle in Javier's eye always made Pam want to kiss him on the face even if she had seen him only minutes before.

But a difference now sat heavily on the man she called her other dad. It appeared difficult for him to stand for very long at a time. Now in his mid-seventies, Javier's body had begun to show signs of deterioration. The twinkle still gleamed in his eyes, but the eyes were those of a much wearier man.

Still, he wore the same red suspenders on top of his favorite blue-and-black flannel shirt. The white canvas loafers looked like the same ones she had bought him several years ago.

"So, Mr. Rogers, how are you?" Pam said, using her favorite pet name for Papa Javier. She raised her voice, recalling that his hearing had begun to fade when she was still living with them.

"Oh, I'm fine." Javier puffed his chest slightly. "I'm starting a garden, you know!"

"Yeah, so I have heard." Pam winked at Pilar.

He gave her a curious look. "Your hair . . . "

"Never mind, it's a long story," Pilar said.

"Yeah, and I think it's time to tell it. A little of it, at least," Pam said. She wanted nothing more than to spend the next hour reminiscing, but time was short and she needed to find out if they could help as she hoped they would. Pam took Alex to the kitchen and seated him at the table with the cookie plate right in front of him, then went back into the living room where Pilar and Javier waited, both with curious expressions.

"Mama Pili, Papa Javier . . . I need a very big favor. I can't go into details, but Alex is . . . adopted under some very unusual circumstances. He has no one in the world except me, and I'm just going to have to ask the two of you to trust me when I say that. I'm about to start a job in Brussels, and the timing is terrible, but suffice it to say that I just couldn't leave him in the situation he was in.

"To complicate matters further, I can't stay long because I need to start my job, find a place to live that will work for Alex and me, and . . . make some other arrangements."

She asked them if they could look after Alex until she was able to set up a stable home in the United States for the two of them. She could see the hesitation in the glances exchanged by the old couple. "It won't be for long, I promise, and I will send money every month to cover the expenses. Plus, Alex is very accustomed to taking care of himself. If you can just feed him and give him a place to sleep, I promise you, he won't be any trouble."

There was a knock at the front door. Javier pushed himself out of his chair and went to the door. He glanced outside and then opened the door. "Oh, hello, Mr. Pierce. Please, come in."

A man with graying hair—but not nearly as old as Javier—entered the room. He greeted Pilar, then he looked inquisitively at Pam.

"Mr. Pierce, this is our young American friend, Pamela Graham," Pilar said. "She has just surprised us with a visit. Pamela, this is Mr. Joseph Pierce. He is also from your country, and he is here visiting his mother, who lives next door."

Pierce offered his hand. "Well, what a coincidence! Two American visitors in one Barcelona neighborhood," he said. "Where are you from, Pamela?"

"Dallas, originally. I've just finished a three-month internship in Russia, and I'm on my way to Brussels to go to work for Formula 1."

Pierce's eyes opened wide. "Formula 1? Really?"

"I've always loved race cars," Pam said. "My dream job, really."

"Well, good for you." Pierce turned toward Javier and Pilar. "I was just coming over to let you know that Mom would like the two of you to come to dinner this evening. If you're free, of course."

"Well, I don't know, I'll have to check with my social secretary," Pilar said.

"Of course we'll come," Javier said, smiling. "What time is convenient?"

"Around nine. Mom is planning some appetizers, then dinner. Awfully late for a boy raised in the Midwest, but when in Spain . . . "

"Exactly," Javier said. "A late dinner is the only civilized way."

"We'd be delighted for you to join us, Miss Graham," Pierce said.

"Oh, well . . . "

"You should come, Pamela," Pilar said.

The four of them walked toward the front door and stepped outside. Pam allowed herself to be persuaded. After all, it would be good to relax for a few hours and give Pilar and Javier a bit more time to consider her plea. It would also be great to eat something that hadn't been prepared in an institutional kitchen and that didn't contain beets. She agreed, and the four of them stood outside on the front doorstep, talking agreeably for a few more minutes before Pierce left them and walked back to his mother's house, next door.

* * *

On a rooftop fifty meters away, behind a low stone balustrade encircling a balcony, a man focused a camera through a telephoto lens. As the subject stood and talked with the two older people and the young woman, he snapped a dozen or so photographs. The subject walked back to the house next door, and everyone went inside.

The man peered at the last image he had snapped, displayed on the small digital screen of his camera. He compared the face of the subject to the photograph in the dossier he had received from Langley. No doubt about it; Joseph Pierce was in Barcelona.

CHAPTER 16

The flight from Barcelona to Brussels lifted off the tarmac. Pam watched the Spanish coastline vanish behind the aircraft as it climbed out over the Mediterranean, in preparation for its long bank back to the north. As Pam mentally said goodbye to Barcelona, she felt her throat tightening with emotion; she was also saying good-bye to Alex.

When they had gone back inside after seeing Mr. Pierce back to his mother's house, she had quietly restated her request and her need for their help.

"Why do you not just send the boy to your father?" Javier said quietly. It was a reasonable question, and for a few seconds Pam struggled with how to answer. Javier and Pilar had never met Daddy, of course; they had only heard about him from Pam and overheard a few of her Skyped conversations with him during her year in Barcelona. Pam had never felt it proper to share with them anything of her relationship with her father other than the affection expected from a child for a parent. After all, it was obvious that she was anything but neglected. Why should Pilar and Javier think her relationship with her obviously well-to-do father was other than peachy?

Pam took a deep breath. She tried to explain that adopting Alex (she didn't have the guts to say "abducting") was a decision she had made very suddenly, for reasons that she didn't believe her father would understand. She had done this on her own, she told them, neither wanting nor expecting his approval. It was her responsibility, she said, and one that she felt she had to see through on her own. She took another deep breath. "Papa Javier and Mama Pili, if you don't feel you are able to help me with this, I completely understand. It is a lot to ask, I guess, in all fairness. But if you could see your way clear to watch after Alex for just a few weeks, that should give me time to get set up and send for him. And I would be so grateful—more than I could ever express."

Pili and Javier looked toward one another, and there was something in their glance that Pam almost caught, but didn't, quite. They looked back at Pam and nodded with acceptance. For now anyway, her only friends in Spain seemed to accept the idea with partially open arms. They agreed to help her in any way they could. Neither of them ever pried for details, for which Pam said a silent prayer of thanks.

Next, Pam took a walk outside with Alex and explained her plans. At first, his face fell, but when Pam gave him the time frame and stressed in every way she could that the separation was only temporary, until she had a place where they could live together, he nodded and said that he understood. "So, you think you will be back before my next birthday?" he asked.

Alex's question caught Pam off guard. She remembered his file; it had no birth certificate. "Your next birthday? So . . . you know when your birthday is?"

Alex lowered his eyes again. "No, not really. But I just say that it is in November. On the twenty-eighth, like Friedrich Engels."

Pam smiled and ruffled his hair. "Same day as Karl Marx's business partner, huh? Well, November sounds just about right to me, buddy. Yeah, and you can bet that you have a party coming. So . . . November twenty-eighth?"

"Yeah, yeah, that is it, November twenty-eighth!" Alex grinned then, and Pam wondered if it was because he now had a "real" birthday, or because he knew when she would be back. She hoped it was a little of both. She kneeled down and wrapped him in a big hug, hoping he hadn't seen the tears streaking down her cheeks while she tried to ignore his sniffles and keep from feeling like she was abandoning him.

The flight reached cruising altitude and Pam got up to get some chewing gum from her carry-on. She sat back down, contemplating the fact that the contents of the bag in the overhead compartment above her were the only physical possessions she had remaining to her on the continent of Europe. She couldn't very well go back to the hotel on Nevsky Prospekt in Saint Petersburg and collect her things. In all likelihood, some law-enforcement person was probably pawing through her personal stuff right now, looking for clues to her whereabouts. The thought totally creeped Pam out.

When she got settled in Brussels, she'd get hold of Roxy and have a few more of her things sent over. And now that she didn't have to worry about alerting the authorities to her location, she could use her credit cards to do a little shopping. That thought cheered her up considerably.

As her aircraft taxied to its arrival gate, Pam admired the modern architectural structure of Brussels National Airport. Everything in sight looked new and fresh to Pam; maybe it was because her arrival here symbolized a new start in life for her.

She didn't know much about Belgium, other than that it lay fairly close to Paris. Whatever happened, Pam had decided that she was going to be open to new beginnings. After all, this city, or a European city very much like it, was going to be her home as long as she worked for Formula 1. Her home—and Alex's.

She emerged from the jetway into the hustle and bustle of the arrival terminal. As she followed the line of her fellow passengers to the customs area, she saw the small crowd gathered just outside, waiting to greet the arriving passengers. Some went out and embraced waiting friends and family members; some even wept with joy under the futuristic skylights of the terminal. Watching them, Pam felt saddened, isolated among the gathering as a stranger in a strange land.

One good thing about having few earthly possessions was that Pam had leapfrogged the need for waiting on luggage. She cleared customs relatively quickly, even though the immigrations clerk looked a bit strangely at her hair, by now not quite brown and also not quite blonde.

Her eye caught a sign bearing her name. Holding the sign was a casually dressed man who looked to be in his early to mid-twenties. He leaned against the railing, his gaze drifting back and forth among the short skirts that would pass by him. His dark, curly hair framed a face that, in Pam's opinion, deserved a few lingering looks of its own.

So far, I have to say Belgium is making a favorable impression. Staring directly into his eyes, Pam made her way straight to him. The closer she got, the more the view improved; his olive skin and the lazy lids of his smouldering eyes gave him a dark sex appeal that was impossible to overlook.

When she was standing right in front of him, he looked at her. She smiled and pointed to the sign he was holding, and a look of understanding bloomed, closely followed by one of appreciation as his eyes drifted over her form.

He lowered the sign and extended his hand. "Hello, my name is Lorenzo Gatti. I am here on behalf of Formula 1 and will be your escort for the day. They have made arrangements for you to stay at the Warwick Barsey Hotel."

"Well, very nice to meet you, Lorenzo." She offered her hand and Lorenzo kissed it softly. Belgium was officially growing on her—quite rapidly.

"You have no luggage?" he said, his thick eyebrows lifting in surprise.

Pam shrugged and let her arms fall. "What you see is what you get, Lorenzo."

He nodded and smiled. He gestured with a little bow, and they started walking toward the short-term parking. Pam could feel Lorenzo's eyes on her as they walked, and she was a long way from minding the attention.

"So have you been to Brussels before?" Lorenzo said.

"No, this would be a first."

"Ah! A virgin. Well, allow me to show you the beautiful city of Brussels."

"Your choice of words is a little suspect, Lorenzo," she said, grinning at him. "But I guess that's how they do it in Brussels, maybe?"

He gave her an easy smile. "Trust me, you are in good hands, lovely lady."

"I'll be the judge of that, Lorenzo."

They reached the parking lot, and when Pam saw which waiting car chirped in response to Lorenzo thumbing his key, her breath caught in mid-inhalation. The headlights had flashed on a silver Ferrari 458 Italia. *Be calm, my heart.* Brussels was starting to kick some serious ass! "You have just earned yourself some major points, friend. That is a beautiful car."

"Beautiful, yes, but I am afraid it is a loaner. My baby is at my home in Monaco."

"Is that right? Well, I love this car."

Lorenzo took her carry-on bag and placed it in the small trunk compartment. He opened the passenger-side door, allowing her access into the low seat. Pam ran her hand across the smooth, tan interior, inhaling the pleasing, pungent smell of the full-grain leather.

Lorenzo got into the driver's seat and noticed her admiring the car. "So, you like the sports cars, huh?"

"Oh, hon, this is more than a sports car."

"Is it now?" Lorenzo smiled and shrugged. "I guess I've quit noticing. I mean, if you have seen one Porsche, you have seen them all."

Pam gave him a quizzical look. "Are you trying to challenge my knowledge, friend? Is it the blonde hair?"

Lorenzo laughed again, but gave her a look that intimated a challenge. He backed the car out and coasted slowly down the covered drive from the parking area, allowing the convertible top to retract and vanish into the rear compartment.

"How about you give me a quick tour of Brussels and I'll fill you in on what you are driving here. Sound good, Lorenzo?"

He pointed to himself with a mocking half smile. "Fill *me* in?"

"Unless you have someone listening in the trunk, yes, you."

"Okay, sure. What do you know about this car?" he said.

"Well, for starters, this is a Ferrari 458 Italia. That's Ferrari—F-E-R-R-A-R-I—as in built in Modena, a city in your home country, Lorenzo. You are Italian, right?"

He nodded, chuckling.

"So, *not* a Porsche, okay? These cars were made from about 1999 to 2004. I am thinking this is one of the later models, so an '03 or an '04 would be my guess. There is a 3.6 V8 mid-engine in here that absolutely kicks ass, with about 400 horsepower. So we are looking at a top speed of about 290 kilometers per hour. Want me to go on?"

Lorenzo gave her a look of grudging respect. Pam pulled a tissue from her purse and lightly dabbed the corners of his lips. "Looks like you are drooling there, sugar. But don't be too embarrassed, you're not the first boy to underestimate me, and I am sure you won't be the last."

"Okay, I guess I had that coming. One should never underestimate an opponent."

"Oh, I'm an *opponent* now? Is that an improvement over virgin, or am I losing ground?"

"No, sorry. You will have to pardon my phrasing." He forced an embarrassed smile.

Pam studied his face for a few seconds, then she leaned back in the seat as she ran fingers through her hair. "It's okay, Lorenzo, it's okay. Just drive, pal. Just drive."

* * *

The assistant investigator knocked, then he quietly stepped into Special Agent Novikov's office. If not for the piece of paper he had just printed from his computer, he would not dare to go in. Ever since the American woman's escape, the special agent had been in a horrible temper—shouting at subordinates, throwing things, and generally very unpleasant to be around.

"Special Agent Novikov?"

Novikov glared, his finger holding his place on the report he had been studying. "What is it? I'm working, Orlov, as you can see."

"Yes, sir. I knew you'd want to see this." The assistant investigator handed Novikov the printout; he had highlighted the pertinent information in yellow.

Novikov's eyes scanned the page. "So she is in Barcelona, and she purchases an airline ticket for Brussels. Very well. Thank you, Orlov."

"Shall I notify the Interior Ministry that we will retrieve the boy?"

Novikov shook his head, giving his subordinate a look of pure disgust. "I could not possibly care less about the snot-nosed brat, Orlov. I wish that she had taken an even dozen orphans with her—the fewer street rats to clutter our alleys. The Graham woman is a co-conspirator with those traitors, the Andreyev brothers. She is a danger to Russian security, and the sooner I have her in my interrogation room, the better. Now stop asking me stupid questions and go book for me the soonest possible flight to Brussels."

"Yes, Special Agent."

CHAPTER 17

The Brussels tour with Lorenzo proved to be nothing less than spectacular. The areas he guided her through allowed her to see the true beauty of Belgium's capital city, and as he pointed out key locations and historical sites, Pam could hear the admiration in his voice.

Some places in Brussels reminded Pam of a medieval city frozen in an elapsed era. She loved the old buildings like St. Michael's cathedral. As she had done during her year living in Spain, she reflected how being surrounded by such timeless architecture was like living inside a history book. And popular tourist sites like La Grand-Place and Sablon exemplified Brussels' exquisiteness. At certain moments, Pam could almost imagine she had journeyed back in time.

The Ferrari raced along the small cobblestone streets until they parked in front of a line of antique shops. After hearing the ravings from Lorenzo, Pam could not wait to see one particular shop. Once the car was parked, Pam made a beeline for Pierre Marcolini, an exclusive chocolatier. Once inside, she inhaled slowly, allowing the rich, mouthwatering aroma of the chocolate to fill her from top to bottom. When he walked in behind her, Lorenzo closed his eyes, breathing in deeply and taking in the sweet smell. "The smell in here is like the city—a timeless aphrodisiac."

Pam arched an eyebrow at him. "An aphrodisiac, huh?"

Lorenzo opened one eye and looked at her. "I did not mean to insult."

"Oh, don't work yourself up, hon. If you insult me, I'll let you know."

He gave her an approving nod. "You are quite the lady."

"When I need to be."

"And when you don't?"

"Oh, you don't want to walk down that path, honey, trust me," she smiled.

"But when you say it with that look in your eyes, I think I want to walk that path very much, indeed."

"Fair enough. Just don't say I didn't warn you."

Lorenzo laughed. "You have a great sense of humor. I like that. I really needed a laugh; the week of the race is always very stressful."

Pam bought them both a bag of dark chocolates. She put one in her mouth and closed her eyes, savoring the smoky, slightly bitter taste of the dark chocolate. When she opened her eyes, Lorenzo was looking at her with an amused expression.

"What?" she said.

"Your face. You have an expression that one would normally associate with . . . a different experience than eating chocolate."

Pam gave him a mischievous grin. "Well, if I look like that when eating chocolate, you probably can't even imagine what I look like in that other situation."

"I should be so fortunate as to find out."

Pam held his eyes for several seconds. She could see the vein in his neck pulsing quicker as their thoughts entwined.

"Hey, let's do some shop hopping!" he said, breaking off the moment.

"If you're waiting on me, you're backing up."

His brow furrowed. "Excuse me? I don't quite understand."

"That's Texan, Lorenzo. It means, 'what are we waiting for?'"

They left Pierre Marcolini and walked along the narrow street, looking at the other shops. Pam felt a soaring sense of inner bliss. She wondered if it was the chocolate or Lorenzo. Both warranted a taste, she thought.

The stores in the Antoine Dansaert area pleasantly surprised Pamela.

On Avenue Louise and Rue de Namur she discovered the same shops that she would have found in New York.

"Surely you understand that a girl from North Dallas can't see places like this and not try on a few things, Lorenzo."

"If you are waiting on me, you are backing up," he said, grinning. They went inside. Lorenzo sat on one of the silk-upholstered couches in front of the dressing rooms, sipping complimentary champagne and smiling with approval as Pam tried on an endless number of outfits.

The evening dark fell all too fast across the city. After the dreary and apprehensive time she had spent in Russia, Brussels, so far, seemed to Pam like a golden paradise. Time galloped by, partly due to the enjoyable company, and mostly because of her appreciation of the city itself. The taste of the Marcolini chocolate lingered on her palate as they walked to the car. Pam arrived ahead of Lorenzo then turned to face him. "Thank you for the tour."

"Oh, the pleasure was mine, Pamela."

"Well, it did me a world of good, I promise you. Can you believe that I still can taste the chocolate we had, hours ago?"

"Really?"

"Yes, let me show you."

Pam leaned in and kissed him. He started to pull back in surprise, but then she felt his lips relax and melt into hers. His hands encircled her waist and he pulled her into him; her body responded easily to his touch. Pam cradled the back of his head with one hand; without her conscious intent, her leg rose up to caress his calf, beckoning Lorenzo's body to an even closer embrace.

The kiss ended with their faces scant millimeters apart, their eyes drinking deeply from each other's gaze. Pam gave him a warm smile. "Take me home, cowboy."

Within five minutes they were back at the Warwick Barsey hotel. Lorenzo pointed to the front of the Warwick as they passed by to enter the valet parking area around the side of the building. "Your home while you are in Brussels."

"And where are you staying?" Pam asked.

Lorenzo lifted his room key from his pocket. "I am here also."

"How convenient."

"Formula 1 has an agreement with the hotel, so this is where all the employees normally stay when we are in Brussels. They will have a room waiting for you."

Pam took the card key from Lorenzo's hand. "I see."

Across the top of the hotel's entrance the raised lettering stood out across the black door frame. THE WARWICK HOTEL, written in gold Old English font, brought to Pam's mind the classic silver-screen era of Hollywood, the time when class was king and the rats ran in packs.

The lobby's décor was warm, inviting, and classic. Pam walked across the highly polished floor, past the dark mahogany check-in desk. The opulent foyer, with its subdued lighting, made Pam think of a sixteenth-century palace.

"Pamela! Pamela!" Lorenzo called from behind her. She turned to see him standing at the front desk. Pam turned and continued on, making her way toward the elevators. Lorenzo called again. This time, he was pointing at the desk. He made a signing gesture, telling her she needed to sign in and get her room key.

In reply, Pamela held Lorenzo's room key above her head, then continued toward the elevators. She didn't look back but knew he was on the way. Plenty of time remained to check in to her room. Right now, she wanted to check into Lorenzo. *New beginnings, Pamela. Starting now.*

By the time the door closed behind Lorenzo, he was already reaching for her. Hands plunged beneath clothing that had suddenly become an intolerable obstacle. Their mouths clung hungrily to each other, their lungs feeding on each other's air even as their hands explored each contour of the other's body and the urge to join completely became an insistent, irresistible compulsion.

Pam fell backward onto the bed with Lorenzo's body pressing her down. He looked down at her, smiling open-mouthed as his eyes devoured her form, from top to bottom. "Brussels will never be the same for either of us, I think."

She placed her lips next to his ear, her breath warm against the side of his neck. "Just drive, Lorenzo," she whispered. "Just drive."

* * *

There was a quiet knock as the door opened, and the director of the CIA looked up to see his administrative assistant, holding a folder.

"What is it, Jill?"

"Sir, these just came in from the bureau chief in Spain, marked 'Urgent—DCIA Only.'"

"Okay. Bring it here."

She laid the sealed envelope on his desk. "He asks that you contact him as soon as you view the documents, sir."

The director nodded as Jill went out and quietly closed the door. He zipped off the perforated opening in the padded shipping envelope and slid out a plastic sleeve containing several 8½-by-11 color photographs.

The images showed Joseph Pierce standing in front of a house, talking to three other people. The director didn't recognize anyone in the shot except Pierce, but he now knew for a fact what the agency had suspected: Pierce had attempted to drop out of sight by going to his mother's house in Barcelona, rather than attending the supposed conference in Tokyo. The director was still pissed at the thought that it had taken them five precious days to recognize that Pierce wasn't where the ticket he bought with his credit card said he should be. What the hell good was it to be the chief of the world's most powerful intelligence agency if your people couldn't keep track of one rogue businessman?

Remembering the bureau chief's request, the director picked up his phone and dialed the access number for his secure international line. When he heard the "ready" tone, he dialed the number for the phone that rang on the desk of his bureau chief in Spain. As the call went through, he glanced at his wristwatch and calculated the time difference. Three in the morning in Madrid. *Oh well. He told me to call.*

The Spanish bureau chief picked up on the first ring. "Director, thank you for calling."

"I've seen the pictures. What's up?"

"Well, Pierce—"

"Is in Barcelona at his mother's house. Yes, I can read. Why am I talking to you?"

"The young woman in the sixth and seventh pictures."

The director shuffled the prints until he had the ones in front of him that the bureau chief had referred to. "Okay. What about her?"

"She's a U.S. citizen, Pamela Graham, from Dallas."

"And that means what to me, precisely?"

"Well, it turns out that she's wanted in Russia for kidnapping. Apparently, she grabbed a ten-year-old boy from an orphanage there and fled the country."

"What a shame. But I'm still waiting for the part where I care about any of this except Pierce's whereabouts."

"Well, sir, the chatter is that while she was in Russia, she made contact with one Viktor Andreyev. As you may recall—"

"Andreyev. Jesus. Is he related to—"

"Brother, sir. Yes."

"So the FSS wants her?"

"That isn't clear, sir. But I thought you'd want to know. It seems highly suggestive that she would be in contact with both Andreyev and Pierce . . . especially at this particular time."

"No shit. All right. Anything else?"

"No, sir. I just thought you should know."

"Yes. I appreciate it. Thanks."

The director hung up his phone and stared at the photo of Pierce and the Graham girl.

Holy shit. First Jones loses control of the distribution program, and now this Graham bitch is carrying messages to Pierce from the goddamn Russian underground. This is rapidly becoming the most screwed pooch in the civilized world.

The director thought for a few minutes. How could he stop the rapidly proliferating loose ends before the rug unraveled beneath his feet?

He picked up his phone again. "Jill, get me on the secure line to POTUS." He waited, feeling the tingle that he always felt on these calls. It was foolish, he knew, and he berated himself for not being accustomed to the experience by now . . . but the tingle was there; he couldn't deny it, no matter how he tried.

The call connected; the director heard the other party pick up, but pro-tocol for this communication demanded that, contrary to usual practice, the one who had initiated the call would speak first.

"Mr. President," the director said, "a situation is developing that I think you should know about . . . "

CHAPTER 18

Dr. Lee Jones felt hopelessly out of his element as he stood in the Oval Office. He had not been in this room since the day he was appointed head of the CDC, and right now he was about as comfortable as an acrophobe at the top of the Eiffel Tower.

He had been waiting for at least twenty minutes. He slipped a finger inside his shirt collar, which felt like it was getting tighter by the minute. Even in the regulated temperature of perhaps the most recognized house in the world, he could feel perspiration leaking out of the skin of his forehead and beneath his arms. The circular room seemed as if it were closing in around him.

A guard came in and escorted the doctor to an adjoining room. In sharp contrast to the Oval Office, the room's gray walls contained no decorations and no furnishings except a desk and a small table that held a phone, flanked by two chairs. He remained there alone for another ten minutes.

His awareness of the way things worked in D.C. told him that a personal meeting in this location was unlikely to be pleasant. No one in this town—especially at the level represented by these premises—had time for social calls. If an epidemic had been raging or government researchers had just made an amazing health breakthrough, then the director of the CDC might very well be called to the White House for photo ops and the obligatory hand-shaking and inspiring words from POTUS. But there was no such situation in the landscape, as far as Jones knew, which meant that he was probably here because of the vaccine distribution initiative.

And everything related to the vaccine distribution was out of control at this particular moment. Sensible assumptions dictated that his superiors were not pleased with the lack of progress. Pierce had gone underground, the distribution was at a standstill, and apparently, some very powerful people were very nervous about the whole situation. Jones hadn't been able to put the pieces together yet with regard to how the vaccine distribution was connected to all this, but he knew enough to realize that his failure to inspire Pierce to immediate action was not being received as glad tidings anywhere near the Potomac.

Waiting and sweating in the small, gray room, Jones second- and third-guessed his tactics. A personal appearance at Pierce's home may have been a better route. A face-to-face might have been more effective at putting the fear of God in him, inspiring prompt compliance. But now Pierce had vanished, as far as Jones could tell.

The door to the small room swung open. Jones was actually relieved that, rather than POTUS, Speaker of the House Steven Fraser entered the room. Still, everyone knew that Fraser was, for all practical purposes, the voice of the president. Jones could safely assume that whatever directive or ass-chewing he was about to receive from Fraser might just as well be coming from POTUS himself.

The Speaker sat down at the small table as Jones remained standing. Fraser flipped through the manila folder he had carried in. He glanced up. "Have a seat, doctor. This will be brief."

Fraser's eyes flickered back and forth as he read whatever was in the file. A distant part of Jones's mind reflected that Fraser looked a lot shorter in person than he did on television.

Fraser spoke, his eyes still on the contents of the folder. "We have been told that the H1N1 distribution has not been going as well as we hoped."

It was not remotely a question, so Jones kept his mouth shut and waited. Any attempt to bullshit someone who probably already knew more than Jones could ever imagine would be especially ill-advised. Jones held no false illusions; everyone was expendable. So he kept quiet.

The Speaker closed the file and got out of the chair, seating himself on the corner of the desk—allowing him to look down on the seated Jones.

Jones could now feel the moisture on his skin trickling down his back.

"Dr. Jones, we wanted you to come up here so we could make sure everyone is focused on the same page. I am sure we all agree that we don't want this thing to get out of hand."

"We" meaning you, POTUS, and possibly the NSA. But mostly POTUS. "Yes, sir, that is correct."

The Speaker pressed a button on the phone centered on the table. "Susan, get Langley on the line, please."

In a few seconds, the voice on the speakerphone said, "We have DCIA on the line now, sir. Go ahead."

"So you have him there now?" said a male voice.

"Yes, he is seated right next to me," Fraser said.

"The line?" the voice responded.

"Secure," Fraser assured.

Fraser turned back to Dr. Jones. His perch on the edge of the desk placed him mere inches from where Jones was seated. The proximity was a little too close as far as Jones was concerned, but he knew it was a calculated placement. In this world, everything was calculated and all motives were ulterior.

"Dr. Jones," the voice on the speaker said, "tell me what you think you know about Joseph Pierce."

Here we go. First the humiliation, then the real fun. "Well, sir, I'm aware that he has headed research and development at MMMI for several years, has been regarded as a decisive and motivated leader, and has the reputation for being a bit stubborn about his opinions."

"Uh-huh. And which part of this assessment, do you think, is responsible for his foot-dragging with regard to compliance with the H1N1 distribution directive?"

"Well . . . I—"

"Let me rephrase my question, Dr. Jones," the voice said. "How do you think you might approach persuading Pierce to do what he and his institution have been contracted by the government to do?"

"I . . . I suppose I should go and see him . . . personally."

"I see." There was a silence that lasted perhaps seven seconds. "Well, Dr. Jones, that's going to be a little more complicated now than it would have been back a little while ago. Are you aware why?"

Jones swallowed. "No, sir."

"Because the son of a bitch is in Spain at his mother's house, Jones, that's why! And would you like to know what he's doing while he's on his little visit?"

Another non-question. Jones waited.

"He's talking to people, Dr. Jones. Whatever idiotic notions Joseph Pierce is entertaining that are preventing him from doing as ordered, he's sharing these notions with various persons, some of whom are known troublemakers."

"I . . . I wasn't aware of that, sir."

"Hell, no, you weren't aware. Why the fuck do you think we're having this little talk, Jones? So I can air out my gums? Now, the Speaker and the President have made clear how important this effort is, correct?"

"Yes, sir."

"So the only thing I want to know, Dr. Jones, is whether, in your capacity as head of the Centers for Disease Control, you believe you can exert some control over this situation and get the vaccine headed to where it's supposed to be."

"I believe I can, sir." *Damn, I hope that sounded more convincing than I feel . . .*

"I hope so, Jones; this thing should have already been done."

"I realize that."

"Do you, now? So what does Pierce actually know? I mean, other than what he needs to know?"

"I haven't been able to determine that when I've spoken to him."

A sigh came over the speaker. "All right. Here's what we're going to do, Dr. Jones. My people are in the process of gathering up Mr. Pierce and transporting his ass back where it belongs. When that takes place, Dr. Jones, you will use whatever means necessary—" The director allowed the phrase to hang in the air for a moment. "—to see that MMMI accomplishes the job they've been given by the United States government. Is that clear?"

"Perfectly, sir."

Fraser leaned in and pressed the button to end the call. He turned to Jones. "That will be all for now. We will contact you if we need to discuss anything further."

The side door opened at the same time Fraser stood from the desk. Two men wearing dark suits waited outside. Dr. Jones watched as the door slowly closed, both men following Fraser into the Oval Office.

The door opened again and a uniformed man entered. "Dr. Jones, I will be taking you back to the airport for your flight to Atlanta."

Walking behind the guard, Jones pondered what it was about this vaccine initiative that was creating such volatility in every person connected with it. And, as quickly as the thought arose, he quelled it. The fact was, he really didn't want to know.

It was no secret to anyone familiar with the circumstances of Jones's appointment that POTUS had chosen him because he had a reputation for being an effective, creative, and unquestioning administrator of whatever policies were in force at any given time. He was unfailingly persistent—ruthless, even—in seeing that whatever directive he was given was carried out. It was his chief virtue, as far as his superiors were concerned. Because of it, he had risen to a position in the leadership structure that afforded him many of the prerogatives of power. And the one thing Jones knew about power was that it was better to be the one wielding it than the one submitting to it.

He had gotten this far by figuring out how to make things happen that people above him wanted to have happen. And he was too high up now to think of going back down. Indeed, Jones knew that after you'd reached a certain altitude, there was no such thing as a good landing.

So, even though at times he felt trapped by what he knew and what he didn't know, Jones knew that he would ask no questions, seek no clarification. The concept of "need-to-know" was stamped in his very fiber. When those who didn't have the need to know started asking questions, the tapestry of control and order had a tendency to unravel. Threads that are coming loose, Jones knew, were always easier to cut loose than to sew back into the fabric.

Jones's eyes fell on the holstered weapon carried by the escorting officer. The officer appeared like most such individuals who worked at the
White House; his expression remained unreadable—blank. Like Jones, he
would likely carry out his orders without question . . . even if those orders
involved giving Jones the last ride he would take on this earth—the cutting
away of a loose thread.

* * *

The director moved quickly across the glossy floor, striding over one of
the most recognizable emblems in the world: a sixteen-foot-diameter version of the eagle, shield, and sixteen-point star of the Central Intelligence
Agency.

His cell phone vibrated. "Yes?"

"Sir, we are meeting in the Hoover Room in five minutes."

"I am already on my way. Make sure we have POTUS on a secure line
listening to this."

"We have him already set to go, sir."

The director took the private elevator down into the underground
confines of the Hoover Room. He walked across a short hallway and then
opened the four-inch-thick steel door. The circular, soundproof room mea-
sured thirty-two feet in diameter. The director took his seat at the head of
the small, circular marble table, and he was flanked by two CIA agents. The
speaker placed in the center of the table was solely for POTUS to hear the
meeting held in the secret room—a constant reminder that a fourth set of
ears was listening, even if the president's presence was never acknowledged
verbally. If things went as usual, POTUS would listen but never speak.

The director waited for the red indicator to illuminate on the speaker.
This signified that the line was hot and that POTUS was on the other end.

"Okay, gentlemen, we have a hot line now so let's get started," said the
CIA director. "You know what I am already aware of, so just fill me in on
any new concerns."

"Sir, we have been unsuccessful in locating the Sudario woman," the
first agent said. "Apparently, she has gone into deep cover. She has not contacted her family in the Philippines, and no other evidence has surfaced."

"Understood," the director said.

"We have added Pamela Graham to our surveillance list, as instructed," the other agent said.

"All right. Where are we with Joseph Pierce?" the director said.

"Our repatriation team is almost in place. We have continued our phone surveillance, and we have noted that Pierce seems to be getting more cautious in his conversations."

"Sounds like somebody trying to guard what he knows," the director said in a low voice.

"Not sure, but it seems to be a possibility. If he does know something damaging, he hasn't said anything to anyone so far—that we can determine."

"I know that I don't need to tell you that we need to secure this before it gets out of control," the director said. "We don't need any more stray people getting wind of what we are trying to accomplish."

"I agree, sir."

"Speaking of which, what else do we have on this Pamela Graham person?"

The agent on the director's left opened his locked briefcase and pulled out a file, placing it open on the table. He slid a photo from the file toward the director. "You've already seen this photograph, sir, provided to you by the Spanish bureau chief. A copy has also been provided to—" The agent nodded toward the speaker. "As you know, sir, Ms. Graham's passport has been stamped in Russia, Spain, and Belgium, all in a short period of time. There was no exit stamp from Russia; apparently, she left that country using false identification."

"What's she doing in Belgium?" the director said.

"She now works for Formula 1. As you know, she apparently smuggled a child out of Russia and is now wanted there on kidnapping charges. We are in contact with one of the officers in Saint Petersburg who was involved with the case. We believe he is en route to or already in Belgium to seek her out."

"Have we established the FSS's concerns about her ties with the Andreyevs?" the director said, glancing nervously at the speaker.

"No, sir, that is inconclusive at this time."

"Okay, I need you to get me that Russian officer's information, and I need to talk to him yesterday, before he does something with a U.S. citizen that puts us in a reactive mode."

The agent on his right nodded and scribbled a note on a legal pad.

"So, let me see if I've got this right . . . This Pamela Graham goes to Russia, smuggles out a kid past the Russian immigration officials, shows up in Spain chatting with Joseph Pierce, and works for Formula 1, which basically gives her a license to trot all over Europe and mingle with the high and mighty? Is that about it?"

The two agents sat very still.

"Does anybody other than me see a problem here?" the director said.

Silence.

"Come on, guys! This is not Japanese geometry here! Why in the hell was she not dealt with?"

"Well, we've been unable so far to get an accurate read on her. We're still trying to see what she actually knows before we make a move."

"Hell, from what you guys are telling me, she sounds like someone we need to recruit."

The two agents looked at one another nervously. The one on the director's left silently produced a document, first giving the director a meaningful look, then glancing pointedly at the speaker, then shaking his head slowly while looking again at the director.

The director took the document, realizing that there would be no discussion of its contents in POTUS's hearing. Whatever this was, it would be kept in-house—for now.

CHAPTER 19

The director extracted a set of glasses from his jacket and began to review the text within the document. As he began reading, he circled an index finger in the air. *Keep talking, boys. We don't want POTUS to wonder if he's missing something.*

"Sir, the intelligence we've been able to gather on Graham so far indicates that in addition to Joseph Pierce, she has also been in frequent contact with Lorenzo Gatti, also an employee of Formula 1."

"What is our interest in Gatti?"

"Purely his relationship with Graham at this time, sir. Since she showed up on our radar, he is one of the few contacts she has made."

"So we don't think Gatti is involved in anything harmful to our plans?"

"Not from what we can determine, sir. Graham's interest in Gatti seems to be purely business . . . well, and they are apparently, um, dating, to some extent."

The director permitted himself a smile. "Oh, I'll just bet they are."

The document in the director's hands was drafted beneath the byline of the Director of National Intelligence. It was "eyes-only," an authorization for surveillance on Pamela Graham. *Well, since we've been photographing her and listening in while she screws one of her coworkers in her hotel room, I guess it's about time for this.*

"We've also been performing electronic and phone surveillance on the other people in the picture with Graham and Pierce," the other agent said. "They are Javier and Pilar Garcin, Spanish citizens. Apparently, Graham lived in their home when she was on a foreign study program a few years ago, during college. It also appears that they are harboring the child Graham took from Russia."

"Are they, now? Very interesting, and potentially useful," the director said, still reading. He had reached the paragraph in the document that dealt with the seizure of Pamela Graham. The DNI was authorizing all agencies under his direction—including the CIA—to take Pamela Graham into custody when he believed it to be necessary, to "terminate with extreme prejudice." The orders specified that agency personnel were not to make any direct moves to arrest or eliminate her without direct orders from the DNI.

The director slid the DNI document back to his agent. He had no need to know—indeed, not even any curiosity about—why he was not informed about the DNI's plans. He knew better than anyone that the system operated at a level of complexity that was best left unquestioned . . . especially if you wanted to remain as a part of the system, rather than becoming a casualty of it. Every piece of information the director received, including the way it was presented and the reasons for that presentation, was strictly need-to-know.

Just as the director prepared to summarize the discussion and dismiss the meeting, the room fell into a lifeless hush. All three men stared at the red indicator light as it blinked twice, paused, then blinked twice again. The voice on the other end of the speaker was going to break the code of silence. POTUS was about to speak. That had not happened in this room since the Nixon administration.

"Gentlemen, if you will excuse us, I need to talk to the director alone," the president said. The two agents promptly stood and exited the room. The director remained in his seat, staring at the speaker.

The solid steel door closed behind the two agents. "We're alone, sir," the director said.

"We are going to have to take this up a notch, Director. A big notch."

"Yes, sir, I agree," the director said.

"So what do you suggest?"

The director contemplated the DNI memo he had just read. He thought about the implications of the CIA potentially silencing two U.S. citizens; the Graham woman seemed a huge potential liability, and Pierce, it seemed, knew far more than had ever been intended. *Time for an insurance policy? Hell, the DNI has already as good as authorized it . . .*

"Sir, I think it is time to begin eliminating some of the loose sources of information floating around out there."

"I understand that, but I want this done without causing a total halt in what we are trying to accomplish. If we get sloppy, too many eyes will begin looking into the situation and we will have a political mess on our hands. We can't afford that."

"That is true, sir. That's why I think we need to start from the outside and work our way in."

"Okay. Let's hear what you're thinking."

"Sir, we are pretty sure that Pierce may be stalling because he has figured out what we were trying to get done. We also have reason to believe that his employee, Zia Sudario, knew enough to feel threatened and has gone to ground somewhere. We've been unable to locate her, of course, so this is unverified. Outside of this circle we have only one other person: Pamela Graham."

"Yes, you've already briefed me on her. I will let you in on some inside information about Pamela Graham. She has a good friend in Dallas—some entertainment reporter or something like that—but according to our surveillance, she has left her friend out of the loop."

Who the hell is doing phone taps on reporters in Dallas without me knowing about it? The director shoved the thought aside; POTUS was still speaking.

"Her father is fairly well known and is a semi-acquaintance of mine, but I will manage him if it comes down to that. So . . . you should carefully consider the ramifications of any actions you take toward Ms. Graham."

The director felt the hair rising on the back of his neck. *It's like he was reading my mail! What the hell?*

"Yes, sir, that makes perfect sense. But please consider . . . the idea I have will have to begin with Pamela Graham. We have to start with her since she may be the last one informed about what we are trying to do. I wanted to work our way from the outside in, leaving Pierce as the last one on the list since he is the nucleolus to all of this. Sir, I think it is the only way to be done—and we may be able to exert leverage to assure her cooperation without resorting to . . . the ultimate option. In fact, I am presently developing some plans toward that end.

"We can put more pressure on Jones at the CDC to have Pierce get things moving at MMMI. Recall that the CDC is still in the dark about this, so if anything sensitive does get out, they can be held accountable for anything that might be . . . objectionable to the public. That should keep you clear of any fallout. And, by the time Pierce has the ball rolling, we can end the bleeding with him. The others will already be gone—or cooperating, as I mentioned."

The intercom stayed silent for a long moment. The director wasn't sure if this was good or bad.

"I favor the smallest possible amount of collateral damage, Director," POTUS said, finally. "You do understand that, don't you?"

"Absolutely, sir. As it should be."

"So tell me, Director, can we roll this up quickly and move ahead with our plan?"

"I believe so. I can personally take over and have this thing under control in . . . less than one week."

"Well . . . that's encouraging. Because the longer things float along as they are, the greater our risk of the sort of attention we can't afford."

"Yes, sir, I understand. But we do have surveillance already set up in Barcelona and Brussels, so with just one call, I can get this rolling."

There was another long pause. "All right," POTUS said at last, and the director felt the thrill of adrenaline twanging his sinews. "From this point on, your team will have the lead on this, Director. As you know, we really need to get some answers and regain our momentum with the operation CDC is running. But never forget, Director, that every possible consideration should be given to accomplishing our goals without raising any concerns from the people in Graham and Pierce's spheres of influence."

"Understood, sir. I will make sure we get this done properly."

"Thank you, Director. On a personal note . . . if you can manage this situation efficiently and quickly, and if we can accomplish our ultimate plan, I think it would be appropriate for me to invite you to an upcoming event we have planned at Bonham Grove."

The director's jaw dropped. He continued staring at the speaker, hardly daring to believe he had heard accurately.

"Director?"

"Oh, yes, sir. I was just . . . what an honor, sir. I deeply appreciate the consideration."

"Well, we're not there yet, so let's not get ahead of ourselves. And . . . one more thing, Director, just so we're clear. I personally don't want Ms. Graham eliminated, but if it must be done and only after I personally approve it, make sure it doesn't happen on American soil."

The speaker made an audible click then a static hum. The red indicator light went dark. The conversation was now officially over.

Everything the director had discussed and heard since arriving in the Hoover Room awhile ago paled in his mind next to POTUS's tantalizing intimation. Might he really earn an invitation to a gathering at Bonham Grove?

An invitation to Bonham Grove symbolized the golden ticket; it constituted acceptance into the most exclusive and elite club in the world. His predecessor had been invited to join, but the one before that had not. The right to be included in the gatherings of the powerful and successful at Bonham Grove was anything but a perk; it was the ultimate laurel, given only to those who had truly made themselves indispensable to society as a whole.

Bonham Grove had existed for well over one hundred years, and for all that time the club had managed to withhold its members' names, activities, and true purpose from public view. Members—all males—were known to be from various nations of the world and included artists, industrialists, thinkers, scientists, and, of course, statesmen. Bonham Grove gatherings had led to many of the world's most momentous events. It was whispered that the Manhattan Project had originated from a Grove session. In all likelihood, the current vaccine project had been spawned at the same location. It made poetic sense to the director that the project's success would be his ticket to entry into the company of the gods. *Any price paid to get invited to the Grove is a small one.*

But first he had to make things happen as POTUS and others wanted. Obstacles cluttered his path, but now they also impeded his path to Bonham Grove, and that couldn't be tolerated. Joseph Pierce would have to be spared . . . for now.

CHAPTER 20

Pam stretched and arched her back, assembling her thoughts. The soft mattress and warm blankets tugged at her to remain in bed, but she couldn't accept the temptation. There was far too much to do, and procrastination was not her friend.

Pam rolled out of bed and wrapped her robe around her, padding barefoot across the carpet to her in-room coffeemaker. Once she had a pot brewing, she powered on her PDA and looked up phone numbers. The first call took several rings before it was answered. "Hello?"

"Hey, Mama Pili! This is Pam!"

"Hola, Pam! How are you? How are things in Belgium?"

"Going well; I really love working for Formula 1, and Brussels is such a beautiful city. The people I work with are great." *Especially Lorenzo, who is actually magnificent . . .* "How are you guys doing? How is Alex?"

There was an odd click and a faint hiss on the line that partially obscured part of Pilar's response, but Pam heard " . . . and Javier have become inseparable. He is such a delightful boy, Pam."

"Oh, Pili, that sounds wonderful! But it makes me miss him so much! Is he around?" There was another click, and a low hum. "Pili? You still there?"

"Yes, I'm here."

"It sounds like we don't have a very good connection."

"Yes, you're right, Pam. I can hear you fine now, though."

"Well, is Alex close by? I want to speak with him. By the way, did you receive the funds I sent to help with his expenses?"

"Oh, yes. You don't have to bother, but we got the money, and there is no need to send so much."

"Oh, not at all. I didn't know when I would get my first check from Formula 1, so I wanted to be sure you guys had enough until I am able to send more."

"Well, don't go out of your way, we will be just fine. And I'm so sorry, Pam, but Alex and Javier just left to go to the store. Really, we are doing just fine here."

"I can't thank you guys enough for this. Please tell Alex I called, and tell him I'm coming to see him as soon as we get a break in the races here."

"I'll tell him. He is doing fine, Pam, but I can tell he misses you."

"Oh, I miss him, too! Tell him I'll bring him some new books when I come."

"He will love that."

As Pam and Pilar were saying good-bye, there were more odd phone clicks. Shaking her head in confusion, Pam disconnected the call and dialed the international code for the United States, followed by Roxy's number.

Roxy answered on the first ring.

"Hey, Rox."

"Pam? What the hell? I didn't know where you were! So why did you leave Russia?"

Click. *There it is again—weird noises on the phone.*

"Long story. I will have to tell you that over a few drinks, when I bring your passport back to you. You left it in my purse, you goof."

"Oh, yeah, sorry. So when can we have those drinks? I'm pretty sure I can fit you into my calendar."

No kidding. If opportunity knocks and you don't answer, Rox, it's only because you're already waiting in the car.

"Well, no time soon, I'm afraid, unless you plan on flying to Belgium."

"Belgium? That sounds so awesome, Pam! Have you met any cute European guys?"

"All I need."

"Oooh, girl, do tell! Formula 1, huh? You think you can set me up with an interview with Dernhart or somebody?

"That would be a no, hon."

"Why?"

"Well, first of all it's Earnhardt—Dale Earnhardt Junior, to be precise—and secondly, he races stock cars, not Formula 1."

"Oh yeah, right. Anyway, hook me up with somebody, okay?"

"I'll get right on it, Rox." *Not!*

Pam heard what sounded exactly like the antique grandfather clock in her apartment chiming in the background. "Hey, are you in my apartment, Rox?"

"No."

Pam knew it was a lie, but she wasn't in the mood to call her on it. Confirming Pam's assessment, Roxy began chattering at high speed about the latest gossip from their circle of acquaintances in Dallas. And even over Roxy's babbling, Pam could hear more clicks and static on the line.

Someone had bugged her phone at home, Pam decided, and possibly Pilar and Javier's, too. *Who would want to listen in on my conversations? The Russian police?*

The thought froze Pam's blood. *Alex! They're going to come take him away from me!*

Roxy was still talking, but Pam suddenly had much more urgent business. "Well, I better get going, Rox, but I will give you a call in the next few days." She ended the call and immediately placed a call to the airline. She had to get to Barcelona!

* * *

Roxy stared at the phone in surprise. Pam had sure gotten off the line quickly!

She posed in front of the full-length mirror in Pam's bedroom, admiring the look and perfect fit of Pam's brand-new Manolo Blahnik shoes. She was pretty sure she hadn't given away the fact that she was doing a little more than just checking Pam's mail. Besides, Pam wouldn't care if Roxy wore a few of her clothes while she was in Europe, right? After all, Pam was busy living the glamorous life associated with those expensive cars, socializing with the wealthy and famous people who collected them and the sexy European men who drove them. And they were—although never formally acknowledged—best friends, after all . . .

Roxy imagined herself standing in front of the Cowboys' corporate headquarters at Las Colinas, wearing the Manolos and, in her fantasy, suddenly spotting Tony Romo headed for the parking lot. She took a few running steps across the room. The heel of one of the Manolos caught on the thick white carpet and snapped at its base.

"Shit!"

Now what? If Pam came home and found her Manolos broken, Roxy would be so busted. Worse, it would be a cold day in hell before Pam ever let her borrow anything. She searched Pam's apartment and found a tube of superglue. She reattached the broken heel, then she eyed it critically from every angle.

Good as new. No problem.

* * *

"Director, I have Mr. Chernikov on the secure line."

"Thank you, Jill." He picked up the phone. "Privet, Mr. Chernikov. Thank you for taking the time to speak with me today."

"Of course, Mr. Director. I am happy to be of assistance. As you mentioned before, our interests are very much aligned in this sensitive matter."

"Indeed they are, sir. I am hoping, in fact, that you may be able to put me in touch with your man—" The director peered at the note he had scribbled from his agents' briefing. "—Special Agent Novikov, I believe? We have reason to believe he is attempting to locate a U.S. citizen, a woman named Pamela Graham who is accused of abducting a Russian child from an orphanage?"

There was a pause. "I may have heard something about this, Mr. Director, but—"

"Yes, sir, I know you're very busy, as are we all. But more to the point of our shared interests, our sources indicate that Ms. Graham may have contacted a Viktor Andreyev while she was in your country. If it should happen to be that this is the reason for Special Agent Novikov's interest in her, I would very much like to speak to him."

"I see."

The director considered himself a master at portraying the role of an ally when it benefited his own purposes. "Sir, we are aware that your country may be attempting to take a bold step—one that would likely be grossly misunderstood by the public at large, if it were brought to light in the wrong ways. Please believe me, Mr. Chernikov, if Ms. Graham is in any position to jeopardize what your nation is trying to accomplish, no one has a greater interest than I in seeing that she is prevented from doing so. To the extent that we can aid your special agent's efforts, it seems to me we ought to be working together. Don't you agree, sir?"

After a pause, Chernikov said, "You make a very good point, Mr. Director. I will instruct Special Agent Novikov to expect to be contacted."

"Thank you, Mr. Chernikov, thank you very much. If I may, sir, where is Special Agent Novikov now?"

"I believe he is in Brussels."

"I thought so. Would it be too much to ask, sir, to request that he suspend his operation with regard to Ms. Graham until we have had an opportunity to exchange all available information? I think we could save both our agencies some time and trouble."

"Very well, Mr. Director. I will so instruct Special Agent Novikov."

The director hung up the phone, then leaned back in his chair and stared out the window at the Virginia landscape. He had a feeling, deep in his gut, that Pamela Graham represented a leak that needed to be plugged—permanently. POTUS, of course, couldn't come right out and say that a U.S. citizen needed to be killed, but the director knew that sometimes hard decisions had to be made in the interest of the greater good.

And if Novikov could be the one who pulled the trigger, the director maintained plausible deniability. *Hell, we can probably off Novikov, once he's taken care of Graham, and tie the whole package up with a bowknot.*

He nodded his head, still staring out the window. Sometimes, you had to make the tough calls. If he had a cigar he would have lit it right then. A dark smile crept across his squared jaw.

CHAPTER 21

B y the time the wheels of the Iberia 747 touched down in Barcelona, Pam felt like pushing on the seat in front of her to hurry the aircraft along. The jet taxied to the gate and Pam fidgeted, thinking that it was taking entirely too long for the cabin door to open and for her fellow passengers to get their asses out of their seats and off the plane.

She hailed the first cab she saw upon exiting the terminal and tersely gave the driver Javier and Pilar's address. "Y treinta euros más si se puede llegar en menos de veinte minutos," she told him, flashing the bills at the driver. He nodded and grinned, and they took off like a hellhound was on their trail.

Precisely eighteen minutes later, Pam flung into the front seat the fare and the thirty-euro tip she had promised the driver and raced toward the front gate of Javier and Pilar's house. "Alex! Alex, where are you, buddy? I'm here."

There was no response; the house was as still as if it were abandoned. Pam's heart leaped up into her throat. She bounded up the front steps and pounded on the door. "Mama Pili? Papa Javier? Alex?" She banged on the door again, but there was no response.

Trying to suppress her panic, Pam strode around the side of the house and scrabbled at the gate latch. She went into the backyard and stared around.

Alex and Javier were on their knees in the garden, spreading mulch around a plot of winter cabbage. Pili was at the far edge of the yard, pruning branches from a tree.

"Alex!"

His head spun around. He saw her, and his eyes went wide. "Pam!" He jumped up and raced toward her, his hands grubby and stained with mulch.

Pam didn't care. She went to her knees and her arms welcomed him; she buried her face in his neck.

"Oh, Alex, buddy! I missed you so much!"

"Me too, Pam! I miss you very much."

Papa Javier walked up, smiling from ear to ear. "Pamela! We didn't know you were coming!"

She looked up at him. "I didn't know either, Papa Javier. But I just couldn't stand it any longer without seeing this guy here." She looked at Alex, drinking in the sight of him. "I got a weekend off from work, and here I am."

Pilar was there by now. Pam stood up and embraced her, then Javier.

"Pam, listen to this," Alex said. "Me llamo Alex. Yo tengo diez años. Yo soy muy guapo."

The three adults roared with laughter. "Yes, you are ten years old," Pam said, ruffling Alex's hair, "and you are certainly very handsome. And I think you've been listening to Papa Javier a little too much."

Javier grinned and shrugged. "The boy must learn the most important words first."

"Come inside," Pilar said, scooping Alex and Pam ahead of her like someone shooing chickens. "I have some hot cocoa and fresh coffee. And Alex has just helped me bake magdalenas."

Pam beamed at Alex. "Well, I can see that your education is getting an important boost while you're here."

"I like Mama Pilar and Papa Javier a lot," Alex said. "But are you taking me back with you, Pam? I want to live in Brussels with you."

Pam thought her heart might break, right there in the doorway to

Pilar's kitchen. "I'm working on it, buddy, but I'm not even sure where I'm going to be based yet. I'm in Brussels for two more weeks, then I've got to go to Monaco for the next race."

Alex's face fell. Pilar's hand rested on his head as she passed. "Come and sit down, Pamela. You must tell us all about Brussels and your new job." Pilar went to the counter and retrieved a plate of the small, sweet cakes that had quickly become Pam's favorite dessert when she had lived with Javier and Pilar.

As they sat at the kitchen table, a knock came on the front door. Javier went to see who it was, and soon he came back with Joseph Pierce.

"So, Pam, Javier tells me you've been living the high life with Formula 1 in Brussels," Pierce said, accepting a cup of *café con leche* from Pilar. He selected a magdalena from the plate and leaned against the kitchen counter, listening as Pam recounted her adventures while learning the ropes in her new job.

Pam noticed how Alex's eyes lit up when Pierce came in; apparently they had been spending time together while she had been in Brussels. Alex came up to Pierce and pretended to punch him in the stomach.

"Oooh you are killing me, kid!" Pierce said, doubling over in mock pain. "You been working out or something? Your punches are getting harder every day! Let me see that bicep of yours." Alex beamed at Pam as he let Pierce squeeze the scrawny area of his arm where his muscles had yet to develop.

"Okay, Javier, you are going to have to stop letting this kid work with you in that garden! He is getting way too strong for his age!" Pierce winked at Pamela.

* * *

A bit later, Pierce invited Pam to come next door and say hello to his mother. "She's been asking about you ever since that evening you came for dinner," he said. "If she finds out you're here and didn't come see her, she'd never forgive either one of us."

Pam hesitated at first; she had just gotten there and wanted to spend every moment with Alex. She then caught Alex staring at her from the other side of the room, smiling and nodding eagerly. It was obvious that he approved of Pierce.

"You sure your mother isn't going to get on you for bringing a stray blonde over?" she said.

He laughed. "Oh, you really don't know my mother. Trust me, she'll be trying to talk you into having her grandkids before you've been there an hour."

They approached the freshly painted wooden steps that led to a porch extending across the entire front of Joseph's mother's house. As they started up the steps, Joseph paused, staring for several seconds at a car parked down the street.

"Anything wrong, Mr. Pierce?" Pam said.

He looked at her and smiled. "Oh, no, just . . . nothing. And Joseph sounds a whole lot better to me than Mr. Pierce, if you don't mind."

Pam nodded. "You got it, Joseph."

They went inside. The crooning voice of Julio Iglesias pealed from a stereo, so loud it was almost painful. Pierce went to the stereo and twisted the volume knob to a lower setting. He gave Pam an apologetic smile. "Mom loves her Julio," he said. "Mom!" he called toward the back of the house. "I'm back and I brought a guest over!"

Pam heard her footsteps coming down the hall. Pierce's mother rounded the corner then stopped in her tracks. "Pamela!"

The petite woman looked to weigh no more than ninety pounds. Her aged face maintained a beauty that the years had been unable to vanquish. She moved quickly toward Pam and wrapped her in a hug of greeting. Then she playfully slapped Joseph across the shoulder. "Why didn't you tell me you were bringing your lady friend over? I could have made dinner!"

"Mom, for heaven's sake . . . "

"So, Pamela, how long have you been in Barcelona? How long will you be able to stay?"

As Joseph's mother led her to the sofa, Pam began filling her in on everything she had just shared with Javier, Pilar, Alex, and Joseph. "I was a little surprised your son was still here," Pam said. "I got the impression he was just here for a short visit." She looked at Joseph, who looked away.

"Sort of a . . . working vacation," he said. He stood and walked to the window and peered down the street for a few seconds, then returned to his seat in the armchair beside the sofa.

Joseph's mother gazed at him fondly. "He was accepted to MIT, you know, and was only fifteen years old at the time. Isn't that something?"

"Quite impressive, actually," Pam said. Joseph shook his head and sighed. "Mom, Pam doesn't care about ancient history." His mother was still smiling at him. "He is such a good boy, but I tell him he works too much."

"You know, I used to live next door to you," Pam said, "when I attended the university. I lived with Javier and Pilar for a whole year."

Joseph's mother stared carefully into Pam's face. A spark of recognition flashed across her eyes. "The little girl who wore the blonde ponytail?"

Pam laughed. "Yes, ma'am, that was me, all right. I was always too tired to do much else with my hair back then."

"I knew you looked familiar, the first time I saw you!" the older woman said. "That explains it. Oh, I used to watch you walk by all the time. I didn't get out much then, since my husband was so ill. He passed on, you know, after a long battle with cancer."

"I am so sorry to hear that."

"Oh, dear, it's fine, we had a long life together. There were a lot of good memories, so for that I am grateful. Some people never get that, you know."

"Say, Pam, what would you say to going with me for a drink?" Joseph said, suddenly. "I know a great place on Passatge Banca, just off the waterfront. It's kind of a local attraction, actually. Very unique atmosphere."

"Sure, sounds great. Just let me go next door and let Alex know what we're doing."

His mother's eyes twinkled. "I think that's a wonderful idea. You two kids go on and have a nice time."

Pam smiled. Joseph was easily in his late fifties, old enough to be her father. But if his mom wanted to think her baby boy was putting the moves on a twenty-something, who was she to burst the bubble?

As Pam exited the house and turned to go next door, she happened to glance down the street and noticed that the same car that had apparently attracted Joseph's interest was still there. At this distance, she couldn't tell if anyone was in the vehicle or not. She decided not to alarm Javier and Pilar.

Obviously, they were relaxed and happy; it was probably just Pam's overactive imagination.

But a few minutes later, as Joseph Pierce opened the passenger door to his BMW E93 convertible for her to get in, his jacket gaped open just enough for Pam to see the holster tucked under his arm and the blunt-looking pistol grip resting inside. And by that time, it was too late to change her mind . . .

CHAPTER 22

The convertible wheeled out of the alley behind the Garcins' house, but instead of turning right onto the street that ran in front of the two houses, as Pam expected, Pierce steered left, accelerating briskly and shifting smoothly as they motored down the narrow residential street. One thing was for sure: Joseph Pierce knew his way around cars. Pam relished the smooth roar of the BMW's turbo inline-6 engine and the way it seemed to be stuck to the roadway, as if it were caught in a vacuum.

"Nice car."

"Thanks," Pierce said, but he sounded distracted. Pam glanced over at him, and he was intently studying his rearview mirror. Pam looked out her side mirror—nothing.

"So, who do you think might be following us?" Pam said.

He gave her a sharp look. "Why do you ask that?"

"You looked pretty worried, back there at your mom's house, when you saw that car down the street, and right now you're spending about as much time looking backward as forward."

He stared at her for a second, then he smiled. "Yeah, sorry. Not sure what's gotten into me lately. Guess I need more vacation and less work?"

Pam gave him a smile, but it was clear that Joseph Pierce had certain people he was anxious to avoid meeting. Oh, well . . . one more thing they had in common. Just as long as that piece he was carrying stayed in its holster.

They turned onto a main road and Pam leaned back, enjoying the wind in her hair, despite the chill in the early evening air. "So, tell me about this place we're going," she said. "What makes it such a local hot spot?"

"Well, the Bar Bosc de les Fades is kind of like—shit!"

"Sounds wonderful," Pam said, then she noticed Pierce's intent gaze in his rearview mirror. She looked back.

The car that had been parked on the street near the house was behind them.

"Guess they were watching the alley," Pam said. "What do we do now?"

Instead of answering, Pierce swerved suddenly onto a side street and then swerved again, this time down an alley that looked about two inches too narrow for the BMW. Pam gripped the handle of the door, pressing her feet hard against the floorboard—but the brake her leg muscles were wishing for wasn't there, of course.

The car raced out of the alley into the path of a beat-up, ancient Ape, its bed loaded with spare engine parts. Pierce swerved and gunned the engine out of the oncoming vehicle's path, while the three-wheeled Ape skidded and tilted dangerously, dumping most of its cargo into the street before righting itself. The driver leaped out of the cab and stood in the street, shaking his fist and swearing at them as they raced away.

"Sorry about that," Pierce said, giving Pam a remorseful look as she released her white-knuckled grip on the dashboard.

"Hey, don't worry about it; I've been known to have a lead foot myself. Besides, I think you lost them. Nice driving."

Pierce stared at her, and Pam thought she detected a hint of suspicion in his expression. "You seem pretty calm for someone who was nearly in a wreck."

"I work around fast cars, remember? And I'd learned how to perform a controlled 360-degree skid by the time I was seventeen. My dad's a big race car buff, too."

He held her eyes a second longer, then he looked back at the road.

"So . . . about that drink at that bar?" she said.

Pierce shrugged. "Sure. Why not?"

He made a turn off La Rambla onto the smaller Passatge de la Banca. They glided to a stop almost across the street from their destination, easily discernible by its well-lit sign, lettered in fanciful characters reminiscent of a book of fantasy stories. "Bosc de les Fades . . . Fairy Woods?" Pam translated.

"That's pretty close," Pierce said.

Pam could already taste the salt and lime on the rim of the margarita glass. She looked around them as they parked, and as far as she could tell, the car that had been following them was nowhere in sight. But as they got out of the car, Pierce was still looking at her as if she were a piece of moldy cheese.

A light evening crowd was scattered through the restaurant. The scents of perfectly cured ham and garlic floated throughout the interior. They sat in a booth in the back corner of the establishment. The fairy-tale theme was cleverly carried throughout the popular eatery: floor-to-ceiling trees made of plaster were molded with vaguely human features, like the talking trees in *The Wizard of Oz* or the Ents from *The Lord of the Rings*; replicas of antique lamps hung from chains, casting a candlelit ambience that was amplified by artificial ferns, overhanging, leafy boughs, and wall paintings that gave the place the look and feel of an enchanted forest. From time to time, the rumble of recorded thunder deepened the illusion of dining and drinking outdoors in a sylvan wonderland. Pam half expected Tinkerbell to flit from table to table, taking drink orders.

Pierce seated himself with his back against the far wall. The drinks they ordered were quickly delivered to the table, and the tension headache Pam had felt looming began to ease away as she downed her first margarita.

"You like tequila?" Joseph asked, watching her drink. Pam set down her glass and nodded. "How about a couple of Patrón shots?" he said. Pam nodded again, more appreciatively.

The waitress brought the shot glasses and a decanter of the light amber-colored tequila. Joseph poured them each a shot, and they tapped the glass rims together.

"To new friends?" Pam said.

Joseph studied her for a few seconds, then he nodded like someone who had come to a decision. They tossed back the Patrón. Pam felt the liquid fire gliding down her throat with a pleasant burn. Joseph picked up the decanter with a questioning look. Pam nodded toward her glass and said, "Hit me."

Soon, Pam's insides glowed pleasantly and Joseph appeared to be loosening up, at least a little bit.

"Mr. Pierce—excuse me, Joseph—I think you needed this time worse than I did."

"You think? I was that uptight, was I?"

"Hell yeah, you were! For a few minutes back there in the car, you were turning into a—pardon the Spanish—cabeza del dick."

He sprayed a mouthful of Patrón off to the side of the table and roared with laughter. "You've got to warn me before you say stuff like that!" He wiped his mouth and laughed into the table napkin.

"Hell, Joseph, if I could, I would. Sometimes I even surprise myself, hon."

His phone emitted a high-pitched ring. He checked the caller ID, frowned, and put the phone back in his pocket.

"Somebody you'd rather not talk to?"

He wouldn't look at her.

"Mind if I see your phone?" she asked. He hesitated an instant, then he passed the phone to Pam. She keyed in her name and number and handed the phone back to him. "Here you go, Joseph. We are gonna have to stay in touch."

He looked at the number, then at her. "Maybe."

"Well, hell, Joseph, there you go again! Looking at me like I'm contagious. Not reassuring from a guy who's packing heat."

His eyes shot open and his hand moved toward the inside of his jacket. "Why would you say that?"

Shit! He's reaching for his gun! "Say what, Joseph? Which part?"

"Contagious. Why did you say that?"

His hand was barely inside his jacket and motionless, but his eyes on her were intense, like someone standing at the edge of a chasm and trying to decide whether to jump.

"Just a figure of speech, Joseph . . . I didn't mean anything . . . "

Contagious. The word hung in her head as her mind flashed back to

Saint Petersburg, and her cab ride with Viktor Andreyev. *Do not take vac-cine, Pamela Graham . . . never take . . .*

"Wow." Pam said, staring blankly ahead.

"What is it?"

She told him about the vodka-breathing cabbie in Saint Petersburg and the story he had related about his brother. "Your reaction just now . . . it made a connection, I guess. Do you think it means something?"

Now it was Pierce's turn to look shocked. His hand fell away from his jacket and he slumped in his seat. "Good God. What you just said makes a lot of sense. Too much, in fact. Looks like Russia may be . . . God help us."

Pam felt her buzz washing away on a tide of adrenaline and apprehen-sion. *Damn. I was really starting to enjoy myself . . .* "Joseph, I don't know what you're thinking, but I am getting seriously freaked out here."

He leaned forward, his elbows on the table. "Okay, listen, I am about to take a big gamble."

His face had as serious an appearance as Pam could imagine. She gave him a careful look. "A gamble? Okay, what's on your mind, Joseph?"

His eyes darted around the room as he leaned even closer. His words, when he spoke, fell just above a whisper.

"Pam, I am in a very strange situation. I work—well, I run the place, actually—at the Maxwell Morris Medical Institute in Maryland. Being there has exposed me to some very sensitive information, and for the last few weeks, I've been looking over my shoulder like some prison escapee."

"Hey, look, Joseph, I am a hell of a listener, but you don't have to tell me anything that you're not comfortable with."

"For some reason, I believe that. But, to show you just how paranoid I've become, when we walked in here tonight, I thought maybe you were one of them."

"And who is 'them,' exactly?"

His eyes never leaving hers, he reached beneath his jacket; this time, his hand didn't pause.

Pam's eyes went wide; her pulse flared in her temples. "What the hell are you doing, Joseph?"

Keeping his hands below the table, he said, "Take this . . . please." His eyes shifted around wildly, scanning the restaurant.

Pam felt something hard bumping against her knee. Her hand slid across the checkered, rubberized grip of the pistol. *What in the hell is going on here?* "If this is supposed to be reassuring, Joseph, it's not working."

"Please, it's okay. Take it and put it in your purse."

She discreetly followed his instructions but confusion swam in circles in her mind. *Well, at least he handed it to me butt-first. I guess he could just have easily pulled the trigger.* "Okay, it's in my purse now. I am guessing you have one hell of an explanation to go along with this, right?"

"Oh, you have no idea. But first—do you know how to use it? The gun?"

"I have seen it done."

Joseph waited for a bar patron to pass by before he spoke again. "To be honest, I am thinking that you won't even have to use it. I really hope things don't get that serious. But better safe than sorry."

"Well, I have to say, Joseph, all things being equal, if the proverbial shit starts to hit the fan, I'd rather be holding a piece than not."

He gave her a little grin. "There's that wit again."

She shrugged and smiled hesitantly. "So . . . I'm listening."

He began speaking in a voice that carried across the table but was still quiet enough to be masked by the eighties and nineties pop music that oozed constantly from the restaurant's sound system. A distant corner of Pam's mind registered that a Pet Shop Boys song she had loved as a kid was playing. But as Joseph's words continued, every thought left her except her growing horror at what he was telling her.

He said that he believed the U.S. government was planning to do something terrible, and now, based on what she'd just told him, that Russia, and perhaps other governments, was involved as well. He said that the H1N1 vaccine his company was manufacturing for national distribution had been contaminated.

"Contaminated by what?"

He stared at her. "Biological weapons."

Her mouth sagged open.

"Cholera, polio, smallpox . . . at least, that's what I've seen so far."

"You're kidding, right? That just doesn't make sense. I mean, I can see them shipping to places that they consider enemies, but why would they issue that stuff in the U.S.?"

He made a quieting motion. "Keep it down, Pam. Who knows who might be in here?" His eyes flickered around the room.

"But . . . why?" She shook her head, still unable to make any sense of what he was telling her.

He shook his head slowly. "That's what I can't work out, exactly. That's partly why I came to Spain—to try to buy some time, put more of the pieces together. I was able to document some of it, but not everything."

He told her about the tests he had personally performed, the other information he had gathered. As he spoke, the Pet Shop Boys' words wove in and out, their meaning taking on a weird symbolism for the image of her native country Pierce's words were painting.

I thought I loved you but I'm not sure now / I've seen you look at strangers too many times . . .

But now I know you play a different game / I've watched you dance with danger, still wanting more . . .

"Pam, the grip of the pistol I gave you will slide back to reveal a hidden compartment. Inside is a flash drive that contains files documenting everything I've just told you. Okay, now listen carefully. There's an Australian journalist who has contacted me. His name is Giles Girard. I think that I am being watched too closely, so I want you to get in touch with him and get these files to him."

"A journalist? But how do you know—"

"I trust him, Pam. He has the confidence of the only other person at MMMI who also realized what the government was planning, and she's the one who put him in contact with me. Until I spoke to him, in fact, I wasn't even sure where she was or if she was still alive. Get these files to him; he'll know what to do with them."

"So, I just, like, e-mail them or something?"

"No! Sending them over the Internet is too dangerous. The Department of Homeland Security has sophisticated snooper programs that can pick up on transmissions containing certain keywords. For all I know, DHS is in on this, too. No, you've got to physically hand him the flash drive."

Reflecting on the irony of a department that was purportedly dedicated to keeping people safe being involved in something that was sounding more and more like genocide, Pam said, "Okay, then . . . what am I supposed to do?"

"Get in touch with him. He's setting up a whistle-blower network, and that's the only way to stop this thing—with massive publicity. The only thing governments fear is the outrage of the masses."

"True that," Pam said. "How do I get his contact information?"

"It's on the flash drive inside the pistol grip," Joseph said.

Pam locked eyes with him. "Joseph, why me?"

"Because they're not watching you. Because your job demands that you move around a lot and stay in large population centers where it's easier to stay anonymous. Because I think I can trust you. Because I like the way you drink your Patrón. Because you were right when you called me a cabeza del dick."

Pam had to smile. The Pet Shop Boys song was still playing, its final chorus fading:

All day, all day . . . watch them all fall down . . .

Pam looked around the bar at the people laughing, smiling, drinking, eating. She imagined them diminishing one by one as she helplessly watched them dropping like dominoes.

"Pam. Get your purse and walk to the restroom. Now."

She looked at him; his eyes were fixed on a location over her shoulder. "Don't turn around," he said. "Three of them. They just came in. Now, go ahead. I'll meet you at the car in five minutes."

Her face freezing with apprehension, Pam put her purse strap over her shoulder and scooted out of the booth. She walked toward the dark hallway where the restrooms were located.

CHAPTER 23

A s Pam walked away, Joseph maintained a visual of the three men who had entered the bar. They all wore dark suits, white shirts, and black ties. One of them looked up as Pam went to the restroom, then he quickly looked away; all three of them appeared to be trying just a little too hard to avoid looking in Joseph's direction. They sat in a booth just a few feet away, but they took no menus and none of them ordered drinks. To Joseph, they were about as inconspicuous as giraffes in a parking lot.

Joseph moved to a booth on the left side of the bar. He moved casually and the men pretended not to notice. His new location permitted him to sit just outside their vantage point. On his far right, a metallic wall divided a section of the bar. In it he could see the reflection of the three dark-suited men, but they could not use it in the same way to see him.

Pam emerged from the restrooms and walked past the booth where they had been sitting. She never paused or looked around. *Good girl, Pam!* She never noticed Joseph in his new location, but moved on through the area, disappearing around the corner as she made her way to the front door. If she noticed the three suited men, she gave no indication.

The men's heads turned in her direction after she passed their table; their eyes followed her until she went out of view. As they did, Joseph moved quickly to the restroom door and down the short hallway, entering the women's restroom.

He wondered briefly if he had miscalculated; the way the three had watched Pam made it seem almost as if they were observing her, not him. Too late for that now, though.

Like its counterpart for the men, the women's restroom had a window above the hand-washing area. Hoping the three watchers had not yet missed him, he unlatched the window and quickly scrambled through the window and dropped down into the unlit area located in the back of the restaurant. He hugged the wall of the building and moved to the corner, then cautiously peered around.

The three men were already standing outside, several feet away, with their backs to him. They were side by side and Joseph couldn't see what, if anything, was in front of them. Then one of the men reached into his jacket to pull out a phone; he moved slightly away from the others to take the call, allowing an opening. Pam stood there, talking with the other two.

Shit!

He reached into his pocket and highlighted the number Pam had keyed in earlier. He keyed in a text message. *Just stay cool, Pam, just stay cool . . .*

* * *

Pam saw the faint outline of Joseph's shadow at the corner of the building, but she avoided staring at him or acknowledging his presence.

"So, I'm sorry, but I never caught your name," she said to the one who was obviously the leader of the three.

He flashed a badge. "Kevin Elgreen, Ms. Graham, and we are from the Central Intelligence Agency."

"My goodness," she said in her best dumb Texas blonde inflection, "the CIA! What in the world do y'all need with me?"

Elgreen gave her what she supposed passed for his smile. "Well, Ms. Graham, that man you were seated with inside, Joseph Pierce? He is a very dangerous individual whom we've been investigating for some time now. He is very intelligent, but we believe he is delusional and is involved in a plot to harm the interests of the United States. But don't worry; we are here to help you." He leaned in, his brow furrowing with apparent concern. "Ms. Graham, he hasn't threatened you in any way or told you some wild conspiracy nonsense, has he?"

Mr. Elgreen, I'm going to pretend that I don't think you're an ass and also that you don't annoy the hell out of me. She gave him a wild-eyed look and shook her head. "No, sir, I sure didn't hear anything like that at all. He was just giving me a ride to my hotel and we stopped for drinks on the way."

All three of them, even the one talking in a low voice on his phone, were constantly looking all around them. Each time someone exited the Bosc de les Fades, all three of them would snap to for a quick inspection. *Waiting for Joseph.*

She felt her phone vibrating, inside her purse. "Excuse me, please," she said to the two men who were still engaged with her, "I need to take this." Elgreen nodded.

It was a text message from Pierce. Careful to shield the screen from the men's view, she read, "Get away NOW. Say u need restroom. Go to men's. I will distract." She thumbed off the screen.

She turned back toward them, rolling her eyes. "Boyfriends . . . I swear." She waited a few minutes then started dancing in place. "Mr. Elgreen, I'm so sorry, but I really need to go to the little girls' room. Those margaritas do it to me every time." She gave him a sorority-girl smile and started mincing back toward the main entrance.

"Sure, no problem," Elgreen said. "I'll have Agent Cutler come with you . . . you know, to make sure you're okay." Cutler stepped forward and took her elbow as if they were walking out onto the dance floor. *Son of a bitch is probably planning to kidnap me as soon as they can get me away from here. Think, Pam, think!*

As they went inside, a waiter with a tray full of drinks collided with her, scattering liquid, ice, glasses, and the tray all across the waiting area. In the ensuing confusion, Pam hurried toward the back of the restaurant, leaving Agent Cutler in the foyer with liquor soaking his dark suit. In the confusion she also dropped her cell phone.

Dammit! But I can't go back there now! She half-ran toward the hallway where the restrooms were.

Behind her, Cutler retrieved her cell phone from the debris. He keyed the screen on and read the last message she had received, the message sent by Joseph Pierce. He sprinted toward the back of the restaurant, scattering patrons and waitstaff in his wake, speaking into the microphone of his personal communication device. "She's with Pierce! They're working together. In pursuit."

Pam slammed into the door of the men's restroom, ignoring the surprised cries of the men standing at the urinals. She made straight for the window above the sinks, unlatching it and diving through. She hit the ground outside, taking the impact on her shoulder and rolling with it.

Just seconds later, Agent Cutler burst into the men's room, his Glock 30 in his hand. He immediately saw the open window above the sink. Followed by the astonished stares of the room's other occupants, he sprinted for the window and dove through.

As he sailed outside, he looked down to choose his landing place and realized that it was already occupied by the Graham woman, lying on her back with a weapon trained on his face as he flew above her. It was the last thing he ever saw.

* * *

In front of the restaurant, Elgreen and the remaining agent stood with a handcuffed Pierce. They reacted to the gunshot by sharing a smile. Elgreen spoke under his breath, "Numb nuts should have used his silencer."

Joseph Pierce lowered his head as tears began to form in his eyes.

Agent Elgreen paced a few steps away from Pierce and the other agent as he pulled out his cell phone. He pressed a single digit; the director answered on the first ring. "Yes?"

"She tried to run, sir. We were forced to terminate. And we have Pierce in custody."

* * *

Pam rolled to her feet, the dead agent's blood spattered on her. Panting and trembling, she held the gun with both hands and pointed it at the inert body; he wasn't moving. *Oh, God, Pamela! Oh God oh God oh God oh God . . .*

His weapon was still in his hand; Pam reasoned that if she hadn't shot him, she would likely now be the one lying dead behind a Spanish restaurant. But that didn't calm her down.

She frantically fumbled with the grip of the pistol Joseph had given her. Finally, it swung open, and the flash drive fell into her hand.

"Cutler! Agent Cutler, where are you?"

Elgreen's voice, coming this way. Dropping the weapon, Pam sprinted down the alley, away from the sound of Elgreen's approach. Now her only hope lay with a journalist named Giles that neither she nor Joseph had ever met.

* * *

"Cutler! Where the hell are you?" Elgreen stepped down the dark alley. He paused, seeing a dark form lying on the ground. *Okay, there's the target; now where's my agent?* He came closer, and as he neared the form, his eyes widened in disbelief. This wasn't the Graham woman—it was Cutler!

Pulling his gun and staring all around him in the dark, he raced to the form and placed his hand beneath Cutler's jawline, searching for a pulse. But even as he probed, the dark, spreading pool beneath Cutler told Elgreen that, no matter how bizarre it might seem, his agent had been killed by the bimbo he was supposed to be guarding. Cutler had his weapon drawn; somehow she had simply gotten the drop on him. How was this possible?

Elgreen looked around and saw another gun lying on the ground nearby. He grabbed a handkerchief from his pocket and picked up the pistol. He sniffed the muzzle—freshly fired. One side of the grip was swiveled aside to reveal a hollow compartment in the handle. *What the hell . . . ?*

Elgreen stared at the hollow space. What could be important enough to make Graham, who had just killed a federal agent, open up the handle of the pistol, then drop a weapon that was apparently in good working order and just run away? Something small . . . something she considered supremely important . . . *Oh, shit.*

Elgreen stood, wrapping his handkerchief around the abandoned pistol and pocketing it. He snapped open his phone and speed-dialed the director.

CHAPTER 24

Pam stood in an unfamiliar section of Barcelona. It was night, she was scared, and her mind was turning backflips trying to form an idea about what to do next. Vacant shops surrounded her on all sides. The lack of lighting made it difficult to distinguish one building from the other. A faint illumination remained visible just on the opposite side of the buildings. *But how far away was that?*

She took a moment to catch her breath. Her leg muscles ached and she had a stitch in her side. She was unsure how long she had been running through the back streets of Barcelona. Forty minutes? An hour? Who knew?

So now the CIA was after her. The agency did not seem to work under any rules. With the Russian police, the worst-case scenario would have been losing Alex, some jail time, and deportation. But if Agent Cutler had had his way, someone would be reading the latest version of her will to her father when he came to identify her body.

Again and again the scene behind the restaurant played on a loop in her mind. As she saw the traces of Cutler's blood on her, she felt sick to her stomach. Right or wrong, a life was taken. Someone's friend, someone's husband, someone's father . . . gone.

Pretty impressive, Pamela. In just a few months you've gone from wide-eyed college grad to International Enemy Number One. She was probably at the top of the karma shit list.

The smart thing to do would be to get out of Spain on the very first flight possible. She remembered Joseph's words: " . . . your job demands that you move around a lot and stay in large population centers where it's easier to stay anonymous . . . " She guessed it was time to put that advantage to the test. The next race was in Monaco . . .

In the dim light of a street lamp, she dug through her purse. She had quite a bit of cash—a good thing—and her credit cards—useless to her, unless she wanted to telegraph her location to the CIA, Interpol, and whoever the hell else was looking for her by now. She also still had Roxy's passport. And she had the flash drive Joseph had given her. It lay there in her purse like the One Ring in Frodo's palm, a grim reminder of the responsibility she now carried. The only way to save herself and Joseph—not to mention an unsuspecting portion of the U.S. population, apparently—was to somehow get this thing to Giles Girard. And the only way to find Girard was by accessing the information on the flash drive. So, she needed to get to a computer . . . not her laptop, back at the Garcins'; there were probably fifty CIA agents there by now. *Oh God, poor Javier and Pilar . . . and Alex!*

Okay, so she needed to find an Internet café . . . and she needed to get some clothes that didn't have Cutler's blood on them. Too bad all the shops were closed . . . or not.

Pam walked until she came to a street with shops. Sure enough, there was a little boutique with some cute items in the window. Any other time, Pam would have been eager for morning to come, so she could go inside and try on everything that struck her fancy. But tonight she didn't have time to wait.

She eyed the displays in the windows until she had narrowed her choices to what she would need and what she was reasonably sure would fit; on this little excursion, there wouldn't be time to change her mind or to mix and match. She found a brick in an alley and hefted it. Standing in front of the shop window, she took a few deep breaths.

Okay, Pamela. Hell, you've already got a dead federal agent on your rap sheet; what's a little smash-and-grab?

She hurled the brick, shattering the shop window. An alarm whooped. Pam scooped the clothing she had chosen and ran for the nearest dark place. In a darkened doorway, she stripped off the bloodied clothing, leaving it in a pile in the alley after turning it inside-out and using it to clean Cutler's blood off her face, neck, hands, and ankles. She put on the stolen garments, then she started walking. Somewhere in a city the size of Barcelona, there had to be a pay phone and an open Internet café. She needed both. Within a half-hour, she had found the phone.

Pam placed a call to Roxy, calculating that it was still early evening in Dallas. After the third ring, Pam knew that the call would not be answered. Roxy's far-too-chipper voice message ended, and Pam left a message. Remembering that her calls might be bugged, she waited for the beep, then said, "Hey, Rox! This is me—on the go again. Surprise, surprise, right? This time I'm headed for Monaco, can you believe it? That's where the next race is. Anyway, would you be a dear and send me the luggage bag that I left packed in the bedroom closet? A lady named Helen from Formula 1 is going to call to give you the address. Can't wait to hit the clubs there in my new shoes! Overnight it, because I'm out of clothes. Thanks, hon! I'll call you when I get to Monaco. There's a lot going on, gotta run!" *Good . . . enough info to get my stuff but no real details. They—whoever the hell they are—were sure to know that I was headed to Monaco anyway.*

* * *

Roxy came out of Pam's bathroom, just missing the call. She picked up her cell phone and listened to Pam's message. "Oh, great," Roxy said, tapping her palm against her forehead.

The luggage bag in the bedroom closet contained only one pair of shoes, the olive-green Manolos—one of them with a broken heel. Roxy peered down at the shoes, sitting right where she had left them. The left shoe sat upright in front of the luggage bag. The right shoe, with its heel superglued, lay on its side. It would be okay; it would have to be . . .

* * *

"Cyber NOW!" the sign exclaimed. The fluorescent light from the Internet café had a greasy, tired look—or maybe it was Pam who was greasy and tired, and everything looked that way to her. It was well after midnight and the adrenaline current that had been keeping her going was beginning to ebb. But she had to find out how to get in touch with Giles Girard, and then she had to get to the airport—preferably without crossing the paths of any law enforcement or national security authorities, U.S. or otherwise.

The street was deserted, and there looked to be only a handful of customers in the café, most of them sad, tired, and greasy-looking. *Nope, it's definitely me.* She went inside, found an unoccupied terminal, and began to slide in her credit card.

No! Stupid, stupid, stupid . . .

She found the attendant, a tired, greasy-looking man who appeared to be far more interested in the paperback novel he was reading than in helping her. "Por favor, señor, no tengo carta de crédito. Puedo pagar con efectivo?"

He gave her a tired, greasy look. "Que estación?"

"Dieciocho."

"Cuánto tiempo?"

She paid for two hours on station eighteen. The attendant keyed a few strokes on his keyboard, and when Pam returned to her terminal, there was a Google page, in Spanish, ready to go. She inserted the flash drive into the USB port on the front of the CPU, then she double-clicked its icon when it appeared on her desktop.

Fifteen minutes later, she dragged her eyes away from the documents she had been reading and began scrolling through the files, looking for Giles Girard's contact information.

Pam couldn't believe what she had read. Everything Joseph had told her was backed up by the documents: the tainted vaccine, its origin from government sources, the escalating pressure in the communications Pierce had received from the CDC . . . There was even indication that some government agency was trying to negotiate the purchase of Amtrak in order to facilitate the quick distribution of the vaccines, then use Amtrak for "post purposes," whatever the hell that meant. It was sickening.

She saw a file named "Girard" and double-clicked it. Apparently, their super-journalist was Australian. But even better, it appeared that he had begun setting up his network in a way to keep it off the government's radar as much as possible; there was an e-mail address that the document described as being dedicated to a secure server in Sweden. Pam high-lighted the address and opened her Internet e-mail application. She pasted Girard's server address in the "to" field, keyed "URGENT" into the subject field, and began typing her message.

* * *

"What the fuck do you mean, you are not sure?" The director slammed his fist on his desk. "What the hell is going on here, Elgreen? Have we really dug into the background of this woman? She is either not who we think she is, or she has one hell of an uncanny lucky streak going!"

"As far as we were able to find out, sir, she is fresh out of college with a background clean enough to eat off of."

"Find her, Elgreen! Immediately!" He slammed his phone into its cra-dle, shoved himself up from his desk, and paced the floor. This was a fuck-ing nightmare.

"Is there a problem, then, Director?" asked Special Agent Nikolai Novikov, seated in front of the director's desk.

"You bet your ass there's a problem," the director said. "This little col-lege girl that you allowed to slip through your fingers in Saint Petersburg is about to piss all over my government and yours." The director wanted to say more about what Elgreen had just told him, but that was "need to know" information. *Novikov is a pawn, not a player. Keep it together.*

The director looked at Novikov for a moment, realizing that the Rus-sian likely had his own agenda. There was probably a way to play this to the director's advantage.

"What do you suggest?"

"I suggest, sir, that you get your ass to Barcelona and take care of what you should have done when you had Pamela Graham on your own soil. I've given you a full briefing on the case and I've described the parameters under which we're willing to operate. The woman has stepped on some serious toes. Is there anything else you *need* to know, Mr. Novikov?"

"No, Director. I believe you have covered everything quite satisfactorily."

"I'm glad to hear it."

Novikov got up, nodded to the director with a tiny smirk, and left.

The director stared after him. *Go find her and take care of her, you Russian prick. And then we'll take care of you.*

* * *

Pamela leaned forward to check the cab's meter. She reached into her purse and passed the driver twice the amount that the total fare would have ended up costing her. He looked down at the generous amount and smiled. "Gracias tanto!"

She tapped him on his shoulder. "Le daré la misma cantidad si usted me puede conseguir al aeropuerto en quince minutos."

The driver held up two fingers and gave her a questioning look. Pam nodded and returned her signature Southern smile. *Yes, friend, I'm gonna pay you twice to get me there in fifteen minutes.*

He jammed the gas pedal to the floor. Pam flew backward into the rear seat. Eleven minutes later the cab pulled in front of the airport. Pam tossed the extra money over the seat, never so happy to overpay for a cab.

"Uh oh . . . " The taxi driver's body stiffened as he lifted a hand, pointing to the image in the rearview mirror. Pam looked through the back window to see the alternating blue flashing lights of the police car pulling behind them.

"Shit!"

"Sí . . . no es bueno."

Pam's desire to leap from the cab and run was overwhelming. El policía approached on the right side, next to the curb. Pam slid her body to the left side of the car.

The driver was already out of the car, moving in the officer's direction with animated gestures. He met the policeman at the rear of the car; their voices rose as they argued. The policeman looked over at Pam, who was still seated in the rear of the car.

Dammit! Are they looking for me?

Another officer stepped out of the police car and made his way to the taxi. A small crowd had gathered around the two vehicles. The defiant voice of the driver rose even louder as the second officer made an effort to move the crowd back.

But more onlookers gathered. The first officer took out his club in an attempt to intimidate the crowd, who began flinging insults at the officers. The second officer moved to the taxi and looked inside. He spotted Pam seated in the backseat, but he wheeled back toward the crowd when a crumpled coffee cup sailed from the group toward his colleague.

The second officer approached the cabdriver. Pam could see him pointing at the taxi, speaking about her. More people gathered. The two officers tried to ignore the crowd and moved to flank the cabdriver.

The driver pumped his fist to incite the crowd. One of the policemen made another attempt to quiet the group. After that failed, both officers moved toward the crowd with their hands raised. "Calmate, por favor. Movimiento, por favor!"

The crowd ignored the orders to move along. Pam saw one of the officers pointing toward her as he spoke to his colleague.

They tried to get the driver to help them calm the crowd. The driver leaned against the car with his arms folded. "Esta es su problema, no es mío!" he said.

A small scuffle broke out between two of the onlookers. Pam reached over and lowered the right-side car window. The policemen managed to move the crowd back, then talked some more with each other.

The group of onlookers once again drifted closer to the curb. The policemen walked over to the driver, close enough for Pam to hear and translate every word. "We are going to let you go this time. We need to take the lady away in our car and question her."

The driver displayed a slight smile, relieved that there was not an issued ticket. He disguised his relief with more defiance. "I don't care. I stand here all evening with you for nothing; I am just losing money!"

One of the policemen moved to the street, guiding the oncoming traffic around the two parked cars. The other policeman followed the cabbie as he made his way back to the driver's seat. The officer then walked around the back of the taxi and opened the rear left car door.

"Favor paso fuera del coche, Señorita?" he said, without looking inside.

He waited, but no one stepped out of the car. He leaned down to look inside. The right rear door was open wide. He stood up quickly, peering over the top of the taxi.

The crowd was just closing from the path they opened for the lady to vanish through. Many were laughing and pointing at him. One of the onlookers reached over and closed the right-side rear door.

The cabbie started up his car and put it in gear. The officer slapped the roof of the taxi as it pulled away.

CHAPTER 25

At an office on the coast of the Baltic Sea in a suburb of Stockholm, Garey Allen sorted through the countless number of messages sent to the company's website that day. The late hour and the length of time he had already put in staring at the monitor had begun to take their toll on him. He slid his fingers behind the lenses of his frameless glasses to rub his eyes. He looked at the on-screen clock and thought again about calling it quits for the night and going home. He still wasn't used to the Scandinavian winters; it had been dark since about 4:30 p.m., and psychologically he felt as if he'd been pulling an all-nighter. But as his clock conclusively demonstrated, it was only about 10:00. He had put in plenty of later nights during his undergrad days at MIT.

But Giles had been clear: check all new incoming data every day. WebLeaks was going to be built on two principles—rapid response time and zero censorship. That meant that the information scoop had to be wide open, every single day, so that no credible lead was ignored and no critical reaction was deferred.

Garey believed in Giles's vision and the mission of the newly organized network. It was especially exhilarating to feel that he was doing his part to counteract the repression and deception practiced by most, if not all, national governments. The Internet, in Garey's vision, was about freedom, openness, and instant access. WebLeaks was dedicated to all three.

He had written most of the code for the programs WebLeaks used to screen incoming data for topics deemed strategically important. It was the only way a limited number of personnel could efficiently sort through the tidal wave of data that began pouring into WebLeaks' servers, almost from the moment they went online. Based on a set of criteria that could be altered or modified according to need—usually, when Giles was onto something— the incoming data was screened logarithmically, then rescreened using special logic programs designed to measure the likelihood that a given piece of data had high relevance to the current set of criteria.

Today had been a little slow, all things considered. The highest relevance any incoming data had achieved so far had been 68 percent on a majority of the strategic criteria. Garey, though dedicated, was, frankly, a little bored right now, on top of being tired. He might be a foot soldier on the front line of the information war, but right now he felt as if he were an actuary at an insurance company—a tired one.

Then, as he highlighted the header line of an incoming data packet, the screen program buried the needle—100 percent relevance on every single criterion. Was that even possible?

The data signature indicated this was in the form of an e-mail, as well over 90 percent of the incoming data was. Garey selected the header line and dragged it to the icon for his e-mail client.

The sender was listed as PamelaGraham@me.com. He scanned the body of the e-mail and felt the hair standing up on the back of his neck. If this information had a credible source—and the screening program gave it the maximum possible number of thumbs-ups—this was mind-boggling. Very few messages involved the need to forward the information directly to Giles. Garey was one of the few people at WebLeaks who had direct access to the founder of the network. He didn't take that privilege lightly, but he was quickly coming to believe that failure to forward this message would constitute gross negligence.

He reread the message four more times. He shook his head and gave a low whistle. Then he forwarded Pamela Graham's message directly to Giles's private phone. No matter where on the face of the globe he happened to be at this moment, the message from PamelaGraham@me.com would already be there too.

* * *

"So let me see if I understand you, Dr. Jones," the director said, barely able to control his voice. "You have been on the premises at Maxwell Morris Medical Institute for forty-eight hours, and we still have not shipped a single vial of vaccine? Did I hear you correctly?"

Jones sat in front of the director's desk and his eyes never wavered from those of the other man. This was another one of those questions that wasn't really a question, and anything he said would only make things worse. So he waited, trying not to wince at what he knew was coming. But when the director spoke, his voice was still surprisingly quiet.

"I assume there's a goddamn good reason."

Jones gave the barest of nods. "Pierce is a long way from being an idiot, Director. Before he took off for Spain, he programmed lockdown codes on the processing equipment at MMMI. Triple-encrypted codes. We've tried every password-bypass program we've got access to, and we haven't made a dent. We can't run the equipment to process the vaccine until we have access, and without the passwords, we don't have access."

The director pivoted his desk chair away from Jones and stared out the window. "Son of a bitch."

"Any progress on finding out how much he knows?"

The director shook his head without turning around. "He knows his value declines dramatically when we know what he put in the files now presumably in the possession of Pamela Graham, so he's not exactly talkative. And now you're telling me he had a backup insurance policy."

"It looks that way, yes."

The director swiveled back to face Jones. "Any ideas, Doctor? I am very goddamn interested to hear your thoughts."

Jones took a deep breath. "If you've got any better decryption programs and personnel than I have access to, I'd appreciate you sending them to me at MMMI."

"Done. What else?"

"Well . . . we really need—"

At that moment, the director's door flew open and an agent with flushed cheeks came in, huffing like someone who had just run up several flights of stairs. She approached, holding a piece of paper. "Sorry, sir," she panted. "Agent Lewis, from Web surveillance. This just came across, and I knew you'd want to see it right away, sir."

The director reached out and took the paper. He scanned it, then dropped it on his desk and put his face in his hands. "Thank you, Agent Lewis."

"Yes, sir." She started to leave, but the director said, "Agent Lewis?"

"Sir?"

"I assume your people are already pulling everything we have on this Giles Girard?"

"Yes, sir."

"I want it on my desk before anybody on your floor so much as goes to the restroom."

"Yes, sir." She left, closing the door quietly.

After waiting a few seconds with no movement or word from the director, Jones leaned forward and picked up the paper. He read the e-mail from PamelaGraham@me.com and placed it back on the director's desk.

"Guess it's a good thing she used her own e-mail account," Jones said. "She gave you a break, there."

The director looked up. He stared at the air above Jones's head, a thoughtful expression on his face. "I'll be damned. Of course. Why didn't I think of it sooner?"

"Was there anything else, Director?"

The director pulled his eyes back to Jones as if he'd momentarily forgotten he had another person in his office. "Oh. No, we're done. Speak to my administrative assistant on your way out; she'll set up everything for the decryption assistance you requested."

Jones got up and walked out as the director was dialing a number on his phone. "Elgreen?" he heard him say as he neared the door. "The boy she brought out of Russia—he's still in Barcelona, right?"

* * *

Novikov's phone vibrated just as his flight to Brussels was called for boarding. He glanced at the screen; it was his assistant in the Saint Petersburg office. He snapped the phone open. "Da?"

"Special Agent Novikov, we have just received some information, and I was instructed to relay it to you immediately," the assistant said in Russian.

"I'm listening."

"An American named Roxy Reynolds just purchased a ticket to fly from Barcelona to Monaco. She lands there in four hours."

"Yes, I understand. Thank you. I will make the necessary arrangements to get to Monaco as soon as possible."

"Shall I inform the American liaison? Will you want to coordinate efforts there with them?"

"No, that will not be necessary. I don't want the Americans involved at this time."

"Very well."

Novikov closed his phone and strode toward the nearest ticket counter.

CHAPTER 26

Aéroport Nice Côte d'Azur was crowded—not surprising, given the upcoming races in Monaco. Pam did her best to stay in the middle of the crowds, constantly checking to see if any particular individuals seemed to be consistently in her vicinity. Paranoia played a cruel game; it filled her with unreasonable suspicion and made everyone she saw appear as possible enemies. Distant shadows appeared and disappeared; every blind corner she approached seemed ominous with potential threat. And the guilt of Agent Cutler's death was still like a lead weight on her conscience.

What if I have to live this way for the rest of my life? Always worried about who's watching, never knowing whether to trust anybody . . . Pam began to worry that she might lose her mind. Well, there was only one way to lighten the load. Pam needed to shift the weight onto a person who was—as far as she knew, anyway—far more accustomed to carrying the weight of sensitive, life-and-death information. She had to find Giles Girard.

In the e-mail she had sent to the address on the flash drive, she had told him that she would be in Monaco for the Formula 1 race. Rather than suggest a specific place and time for meeting, however, she had left it up to him to get in touch with her. It seemed a little safer that way, despite the increased uncertainty. For all she knew, he might be here in the airport with her. She scanned the passing sea of faces, although she had no idea what Girard looked like, or if he would even decide to meet her in person, initially.

As she was walking down the concourse toward the ground transportation area, an arm reached from an alcove and grabbed her wrist, dragging her aside. "Hello, Pam," a male voice said.

With one hand, she scrabbled in her purse for her can of mace, while with the other she shoved blindly against the man's chest, trying to get free.

"Hey, Pam, Pam! It's me! Look at me, Pam!"

She spun around and realized she was looking into the face of Lorenzo Gatti.

"Jesus, Lorenzo," she said, releasing the mace can and sagging against the wall of the alcove. "You scared the living shit out of me."

"Sorry, Pam." He folded her in his arms and she allowed herself to relax into his strong chest for a few seconds. He held her away from him, peering into her face. "Are you okay?"

"Oh, God, Lorenzo, where to start?" she said, staring into the air beside his face.

"Well, you could begin, perhaps, by helping me understand why, right after you left Brussels, I was visited by some goons who work for the CIA. And shortly thereafter, a Russian who works for whatever they're calling the KGB these days. And I think someone is listening to my phone calls."

Pam closed her eyes. "Lorenzo, I'm so sorry. I had no idea that I had gotten you mixed up in something that . . . " She gave him a sudden, wide-eyed look. "A Russian, you said? What did he want to know?"

"Just where you were, how I knew you, when you would be back. He gave me some crazy story about you stealing a child from Russia. I didn't tell him anything." He gave her a curious look. "Pam?"

She looked at him like someone coming out of a trance. "It's a very long story, Lorenzo, and assuming I get the chance, I'll tell you the whole thing. But for right now, can I please ask you to believe me when I say that I actually saved a child's life by bringing him out of Russia? And that I am more grateful than I can express that you didn't tell him anything?"

Lorenzo smiled. "It was easy. I didn't know anything. And it's starting to sound like it needs to stay that way."

She gave him a weak smile. "You're here for the races, I guess."

"Yes. And you too, I assume?"

"Yeah, kind of. Where are we staying?"

"Most of us—you and me included—are at the Hotel Miramar in Monte Carlo; that's the main hotel for Formula 1. But the town is packed, so some of us are at the Palais Joséphine. It's still close by."

Pam's body ached with the craving to stretch across a hotel bed and stay there for about a week. But if Formula 1 had a room reserved in her name at the Miramar, that was the last place she needed to go. And she couldn't just move in with Lorenzo; he was under surveillance, too. "Lorenzo? Do you know anyone I could share a room with? Or even swap with? Someone who works for the company who might like to stay at the Miramar? There are some people I'd rather not run into, and I'm guessing the Miramar is about the first place they'll look."

His brow furrowed in thought. "Well . . . Justine Dumont. I heard her telling someone she was bummed about not getting a room at the Miramar. I could talk to her for you." His eyes warmed as he looked at her. "But I have to say I'm deeply saddened that you can't just stay with me. Brussels was incredible."

She laid her hand on his cheek. "You got that right, buddy boy. And maybe someday we'll be able to arrange a repeat performance. But I don't think you want to hang around with me so much right now. Might not be healthy."

His face creased with concern. "Pam, this is very serious, isn't it? Should we call the authorities? Somebody?"

She sighed and shook her head. "The authorities are the last people we need to call right now." She gave him a quick look. "But there is someone I need to get in touch with, and maybe you can help me."

"Anything, Pam."

She told him about Giles Girard, that he was expecting some information from her and that he knew she was in Monaco for the races. "I'm guessing he'll leave a message for me, maybe at the Miramar," she said. "If you could figure out a way to get that to me, it would be awesome."

He nodded. "I'll make it happen."

"And one other thing. I've got some luggage that my friend in the U.S.

shipped here for me. I imagine it'll be at the Miramar, too. I'm getting really tired of wearing this same outfit."

He laughed. "I will make your luggage my first concern. After the message, of course."

Pam hugged him. Lorenzo's arms went around her, and the sensation of being embraced by someone, of feeling protected and safe, if only for a few seconds, was almost enough to break her heart in half. She released him and stood back. "Okay. Here I go. The Palais Joséphine, you said?"

He nodded. "It's on Avenue du Général de Gaulle, in Beausoleil, just across Boulevard du Général Leclerc from Monte Carlo, proper. Very close by."

"All right. Lorenzo . . . " She grabbed his hand.

"I know. And it's okay. Now get going, you international woman of mystery."

She followed the signs toward the rental cars, but got distracted by a poster advertising the services of Heli Air Monaco. Suddenly, renting a car seemed much less interesting; Heli Air Monaco sounded just too enticing to pass up.

About twenty minutes later she was in a helicopter, rising above Nice en route to Monaco. For a few minutes, the sight of the sun-washed Mediterranean coastline, its pastel-painted buildings climbing the steep slopes of the Maritime Alps, washed the fatigue and anxiety from her body; the sight of the Provençal landscape took her breath away. The helicopter pilot saw her expression and winked, and she gave him a big grin.

* * *

John David Boone poured his third scotch of the morning as he stared out the window of his sixty-foot yacht, docked in the harbor in the deep waters of Port d'Hercule in Monaco. He poured two fingers into another tumbler and handed it to Giles Girard, who sat in a corner that shielded him from the view of anyone on shore or aboard a vessel anchored nearby who might be studying the yacht.

The walls of the lounge in which he sat were of smooth, glazed redwood with a rich grain. Deer antlers hung over an artificial fireplace. Boone kept looking out the window as he spoke to Girard. "Hellfire, Giles, take a drink and relax, boy! You look as nervous as a cow with a bucktoothed calf."

Giles's mood called for a lot of things, but having a drink was not one of them. Still, he relented and accepted the scotch after turning down J. D.'s first two offers. "Well, I certainly don't want to be rude, now, do I? Okay, J. D. I'll take one—but just one."

"Attaboy. And don't ask for no goddamn mixers; this shit is too good to spoil it with anything except maybe a little water. Hell, just drink it straight, the way I do. Like the real cowboys use to drink it."

"Yes, sir." Giles took a long sip.

"All right, now tell me where we are with this thing. Your last e-mail said the fella at the Morris outfit—Pierce, that's his name?"

Giles nodded.

"You said he had some stuff that tied the CDC to this bad vaccine, and that he was gonna try and get it to you."

"Right. But from what I was told, the CIA took him into custody. Right now they're probably trying to find out what he knows, to see how badly compromised their operation is."

"Damn. I hate to hear that."

"Yes, but Pierce was able to hand the information off to an American, a woman named Pamela Graham. Apparently she's a Texan, like you."

"Graham . . . Graham . . . " Boone mused, his bushy white eyebrows drawing close together. "Seems like maybe . . . Ah, hell, it don't matter. So she's a Texas gal. That sounds pretty good."

"Yeah, she contacted my network from some place in Spain, said she had the files from Pierce and was going to try to come here. Seems maybe she's associated with the races, or with Formula 1, or something."

"Texas women and fast cars. Shit, this is sounding better all the time," Boone said with a grin.

"Well, wait until you hear what I'm about to tell you," Giles said. "My people did some background on Ms. Graham, and she seems to be in one hell of a mess."

Boone gave Giles a questioning look.

"She abducted a child from a Russian orphanage, fled the country using false ID, and from what I can tell, she killed a CIA agent in Barcelona."

"No shit? Hell, this gal sounds like she can kick ass, if she needs to."

"Yeah, well, right now the last thing I want is the kind of attention she apparently has on her. From the CIA and the Russians, no less."

Boone nodded. "Do we know why she killed the CIA agent?"

Giles shook his head. "Nothing for certain. But from what we've been able to put together by snooping around, it looks like they were trying to take her into custody, like they did with Pierce. In fact, Pierce might have given himself up to give her a chance to get away with the data." Giles tilted his head toward the miniature Ferrari replica sitting on the small table next to him. "You know, J. D., sometimes I wonder if it is all worth it. It's like a fast drive on an open road, you know? I mean, I love to drive fast as much as the next bloke. But I never expected that I would be forced to press the pedal to the floor the entire time."

"Oh, hell, Giles, you ain't gonna have to do all this ducking and dodging for the rest of your life."

"Yeah? Well, that is what I thought months ago. Now . . . well, now I am just not so sure, mate." Giles stared thoughtfully into his glass. "I think the U.S. is up to something really big. Maybe Russia, too, from what Pamela Graham said in her e-mail, but I am missing just a small part of the puzzle to put it all together. The odd thing is, it seems like the closer I get, the more nervous I seem to make the American government."

"Well, hell, you can't pull back on the reins now! I say shove it right in their fucking faces. It's a hell of a lot harder to make you vanish when you're out in the open, raising hell for all the world to see and hear. Once this is all out in the open, there'll be too many eyes on you for them to just make you disappear, see? Safety in numbers. 'Course, if they can't make you disappear, they'll try to discredit you."

"You may be right, J. D."

"Damn right I am! I didn't fall off a turnip truck, son. I made my money running with some pretty tough old boys, remember."

"But what if I am onto something they can't discredit? What if the only way to make it go away is to make me go away—make *us* go away?"

J. D. held Giles's eyes for a long time. "Look, son, I never ask you to tell me anything. I just wanted to help . . . but are you telling me that this is that big? Air-to-ground-missile big?"

Giles nodded slowly. "It's looking that way, J. D. And if what I am hearing is true, then killing me, you, Pamela Graham, and anyone else who knows too much will be what they will feel like they will have to do."

Boone shook his head slowly. "Damn, boy. I sure as hell hope you know what you're doing." He drained his glass, then he poured himself the fourth scotch of the morning.

* * *

The door splintered with a loud crack and the extraction team rushed into the Garcins' house. Their LED headlamps flickered this way and that as they fanned out, two of them taking a position in front of Javier and Pilar's bedroom door, two more heading quickly for the back room where the boy was sleeping. Alex was sitting up in his bed, staring at the door, when they burst in. Before he could speak, one of them clamped a gloved hand over his mouth, then quickly wrapped two strips of duct tape around his face, one completely covering his mouth and the other his eyes. After binding his wrists and ankles with zip strips, they carried him toward the front door.

The two men securing the door of the other bedroom backed out behind the others. From inside the room, the house's adult occupants were pounding on the door and yelling, but the clamp the team had placed on the door ensured that they never saw who had broken into their home.

The team crossed the dark front yard to the waiting minivan. They laid the boy in the middle seat. Two of them climbed into the back, one in the middle beside the boy, and one got in the front passenger seat. He nodded to the driver, and the minivan drove away as the door slid closed.

The man in the front passenger seat removed the black ski mask from his face and flipped open his satellite phone. He pressed a single button and waited.

"Yes?"

"Target secured, Director. We are now transporting the boy to a safe location."

CHAPTER 27

The knock on the door dragged Pam out of a deep sleep. She looked at her bedside clock and groggily calculated that she had had something like eighteen hours of sleep, but she still felt as if she had not slept for weeks.

She went to the door. "Oui? Qui est là?"

"Hi, Pam. It's Justine Dumont," said a voice with a slight French accent. "Lorenzo told me to bring your things?"

God bless you, Lorenzo. After a quick inspection through the peephole to ensure that there wasn't some armed guerrilla waiting behind Justine, Pam slid back the bolts and unchained the door.

Justine had a slender, athletic build much like Pam's, but her short hair was a lustrous, chestnut brown, and her olive complexion and dark eyes, along with her accent, indicated that she was a native of Provence, maybe even the Riviera. She gave a little grunt as she heaved Pam's large suitcase over the threshold.

"Sorry it's so heavy, but thank you so much for bringing it over," Pam said.

"No problem," Justine said, straightening. "Lorenzo also said I should give you this. It was waiting at the front desk of the Miramar. And here's the schedule for the day." She handed Pam two envelopes, one of them printed with the Formula 1 logo and the other on Hotel Miramar stationery. "And I thank you for switching rooms with me. I've lived here all my life, but I've never stayed at the Miramar. It's quite lovely."

"You are more than welcome, Justine," Pam said. "Thank you for being flexible."

Justine left, and Pam scooted her suitcase over to the bed and hoisted it up. *Rox actually came through—hard to believe.* She unlatched it and laid it open, feasting her eyes on the treasure trove of clothing inside. You never appreciated what was already in your closet until you didn't have access to it, she decided. The first things she reached for were her new Manolo Blahniks. Pam couldn't wait to have a chance to wear them. But first, she probably needed to see what she was supposed to do today. A less fashionable but more comfortable choice of footwear might be in order.

She called for room service and then sat down on the edge of her bed, first tearing open the Formula 1 envelope. According to the company schedule, she was supposed to be at the Formula 1 booth at 9:00 a.m. to meet and greet some of the sponsors and guests. She looked at her clock again: 7:23 . . . just enough time remaining to eat, get dressed, and get going.

Next, she opened the Miramar envelope. Inside was a handwritten note in clear, block letters—a journalist's writing, for sure, she thought.

> *Dear Pamela,*
>
> *Meet me at the Japanese Garden; any taxi driver will know where it is. There is a small footbridge with red side rails crossing a small pond. I'll be there at noon today. Be careful. –G. G.*
>
> *PS: I advise against using your personal e-mail account again, at least until all this is over. Set up another account using a different name that will be harder to track back to you.*

Damn! The e-mail she'd sent from the Internet café in Barcelona had informed Girard she was coming to Monaco. So that meant that maybe the CIA . . . Oh well, too late to do anything about that now.

Pamela arrived at the booth just a little before nine. As soon as they saw her company badge, many of the hotel guests walked up to her to get more information about the race. One couple requesting race tickets approached with their five-year-old in tow, a little boy dressed in a red Ferrari jumpsuit with matching red tennis shoes. He shied away from Pam, holding on tight to his father's leg.

Pam bent over to get at eye level with the little boy. "Now who is this handsome race car driver?"

The little boy pulled away, but smiled from the safe position behind his father. Pam reached below the counter of the booth to withdraw an oversized lollipop with a picture of one of the Disney characters driving a Formula 1 car. "I bet you would like one of these, right?"

The little boy's eyes got bigger, then he looked up to his father for approval. The father smiled warmly and nudged him toward Pamela.

"Come on now, son, you're not gonna let the pretty lady eat that by herself, huh?"

The mother arched an eyebrow and gave a half smile. "Hmm, race tickets *and* candy? I think both of my men would leave me for you right about now."

The little boy ran over and grabbed the lollipop, then ran back to latch on to his father's leg. The dad placed an arm around his son and pointed to Pam. "Now, what are we going to say to the pretty lady?"

"Thank you!" the youngster said as he was tearing off the wrapper. He then surprised Pam by reaching in his pocket and holding out an item toward her.

"Well now, is this for me, sweetheart?" she said.

He gave Pam a proud smile and nodded. Pam walked over and took it from him; it was about the size of a wide bookmark folded in half. Pam unfolded the item and found a mirror decal with a picture of a car drawn in crayon.

The mother raised both eyebrows, giving her husband a surprised look.

"Oh, he really likes you," the man explained, smiling. "He has this thing for mirrors, so I bought these mirrored decals for him. He loves them and drew a picture on one during the flight here. He takes it everywhere. So I guess he wants you to have it now."

Pam kneeled down and kissed the little boy on the forehead. "Well, thank you, darlin'! I will keep it forever, I promise."

Pam fought back tears as they walked away. She missed Alex terribly. Would she ever be able to see him again? She hoped he was doing okay with Javier and Pilar, and that he didn't think he'd been abandoned once again.

* * *

From across the lobby, Novikov observed the American family as they walked away from Pamela Graham. He looked at his watch. As soon as she stepped away from the booth, he would be waiting for the first opportunity that presented itself.

He would extract from her the information he needed, and if it was possible, he would retrieve the data Pierce had given her. Either way, Pamela Graham would cease being a threat before the day was out.

* * *

The morning seemed to crawl by for Pam, despite the fact that the booth was probably the busiest place in the crowded lobby of the Miramar. The hotel was almost directly across Avenue d'Ostende from the starting line for the races, which was why it was Formula 1's base of operations in Monaco. Nevertheless, the festive, busy atmosphere was increasingly lost on Pam. The hands of her Movado watch barely seemed to move; was noon ever going to get here?

Finally it was a quarter of twelve. Pam turned to the girl who was working the booth with her. "Monica, I have to meet somebody for lunch. I'm going to take off a little early, okay?"

"No problem."

Slinging her day pack on one shoulder, Pam joined a large group of Japanese tourists who were making their way toward the exit. She walked outside, hailed a cab, and told the driver she wanted to go to the Japanese Garden. He gave her a quizzical look but then he nodded quickly. Soon, she figured out why he looked at her strangely; the garden was almost directly behind the Miramar—she could have walked there easily enough. No visitors lingered at the entrance, but the gates were wide open. The front sign displayed the park's hours of operation; the gardens were free and open from sunrise to sunset.

Pam checked the clock on her phone. Eight minutes before noon. She walked toward the front gate and went inside. The sculpted landscaping and the sound of gently falling water greeted her. She stepped quickly along the footpath.

An outcropping of pale lavender flowers caught her eye and she quickly stooped to breathe in their scent. When she did, a bullet ricocheted off a boulder with a *smack!* and a loud whir—exactly where her head had been, half a second before.

Pam reacted instantly, diving off the footpath and behind a low stone wall. She ran, crouched over, even as three more slugs sliced through the air near her.

It was very strange—even though most of her brain was screaming in panic because someone was trying to kill her, another part of her mind was registering the fact that the gunshots were making no sound. Obviously, her attacker had a silencer.

She lost her bearing in the twisted maze, zigzagging through the garden and leaping over the artfully placed stones, rambling walls, and trees with trunks that looked like modern sculpture. As she did, she could hear bullets pinging off stones and splintering the wood of the trees. As she scurried past a stone lantern, a bullet smacked into it, knocking a huge chunk out of the ornate top. She leaped across a small wooden bridge in two strides.

There was another low bridge up ahead—not the one where she was supposed to meet Girard. She barrel-rolled down the slope beside the bridge and scrambled beneath it, then crept into a space between some boulders that buttressed the bridge on its left side. She wedged herself as deeply into the cleft as she could and tried to breathe absolutely silently.

For a long time she heard nothing. Then, her ears picked up the sound of slow, cautious footsteps, crunching along the pea gravel of the footpath.

She allowed her hand to feel around in the tiny space of her hiding place. If only she'd taken the can of mace out of her day pack before she got out of the taxi! On the other hand, this situation was likely not one the can of mace would get her out of. Not that it mattered; the only way she could get to her day pack involved leaving her concealment in the rocks beside the bridge.

She felt something—a smooth rock the size of an orange. It fit perfectly in her palm. She hefted it and then readied herself. It wasn't much against a firearm wielded by a professional killer, but it was all she had.

Was I set up? She wondered if Girard may have had a hand in this; he was the only person who knew she was supposed to be in the Japanese Garden right now.

The footsteps on the path had stopped. Then, from the narrow vantage available to her, she saw a shadow cast by the flawless light of the Mediterranean sun; the attacker was stooping low to get a ground-level scan of the area. He was standing on the grass to the left of the bridge. If he took two or three more steps down the slope toward the small, man-made pool spanned by the bridge, Pam calculated he would be almost directly in front of her hiding place.

The only way out of there was to run directly into him. Pam felt her body tightening with rage—a welcome relief from the paralyzing fear she had been battling moments before. She felt like a sitting duck in the Japanese Garden, and it was starting to really piss her off.

He was moving again. Slowly, the silencer of his gun came into view, followed by his arm. He was moving very quietly and cautiously. She saw his shoulder . . . now his face. Pam stared hard at him, trying to remember where she had seen him before . . . And then she had it: the airport in Saint Petersburg. This was the man who led the crowd of police into the terminal as Pam watched from the safety of her flight to Barcelona. So, the Russians really were trying to kill her, just as they had probably already killed Viktor Andreyev and his brother.

He eased forward a bit more, staring into the shadows beneath the bridge. He knew she had concealed herself somewhere nearby; it was only a matter of time until he probed the space between the boulders where she hid.

By now she had the hand gripping the stone fully extended behind her, like a center fielder who had just fielded a short-hopper and was preparing to wing the ball toward second base. His head began to rotate in her direction.

In one swift motion, fueled by all the anger and adrenaline in her body, Pam launched the stone at his face; it connected just above his right eye with a sickening, meaty thump. The impact snapped his head backward;

his arm jerked skyward as his finger convulsed on the trigger. The silencer spat, but the projectile went into the air over her head as he fell backward onto the grass. His body slid down toward the pond; his left shoulder and part of his face went into the water. A large, purple knot was already swelling above his eye, and blood sheeted over his face from the gash the stone made when it crashed into his forehead.

Pam grabbed the stone from the ground and stood over him, ready to pound him again. He did not move. After a few seconds she grabbed the gun from his motionless hand and flung it into the pond. Then she ran, the only thought in her mind that of getting away as far as possible from all the people who wanted to hurt her.

Right this second, Giles Girard was the furthest thing from her thoughts.

CHAPTER 28

Avoiding the main roads, Pam walked around and through several sections of Monaco, trying to make her way back to the Palais Joséphine before finally realizing she was in an area that was unfamiliar to her. She crossed over two major roads, then she moved along the outside perimeter of a large building that took up most of a city block. As she rounded the corner, the restaurant La Coupole appeared in the near distance.

The landmark eatery told her where she was in the city. The chic establishment had been the talk of all her Formula 1 colleagues ever since she had arrived in Monaco. Owned by celebrities, La Coupole was the go-to hot spot if you wanted to catch a star. But the only star Pam wanted to see at that moment was the one she could make a wish on, a wish that would put her somewhere safe in Texas.

She moved from the shadows with caution, making her way toward the restaurant. She had her passports and some money in her day pack, and she had the flash drive, of course, but most of her cash was still in the luggage she had left at the hotel. She needed to get that stuff, but at this point, she felt as if any time she stepped into the open, somebody was putting crosshairs on her chest.

Okay, think, Pamela. What to do next? Luxury automobiles pulled up to the entry of the restaurant, one by one. The valets rushed to the cars to move the vehicles into the private parking lot behind the building. She continued to draw a blank on what to do next.

Then, a small commotion swirled around the restaurant's entry as a silver Ferrari 612 Scaglietti pulled along the curved drive toward the front doors. Valets and customers jostled each other for a view of the sleek automobile. The door swung open and the driver stepped out, preoccupied by keying a text message into his cell phone. Meanwhile, the valets discreetly pushed and shoved one another as they jockeyed to get into position to receive the keys.

Pam could not believe her green eyes. It was Lorenzo.

Whispering a prayer of thanks, she strode quickly toward him. He looked up and saw her. "Pam! How are you doing? So good to see—"

She shoved him back into the driver's seat and ran around to the other side to get in. Sliding into the seat, she nervously looked behind her. "Drive, Lorenzo. Just go—I'll tell you where while we're going."

He grinned at her. "I remember the last time you told me to drive."

"Go, goddammit!" she said.

With a shocked expression on his face, he yanked the car into first and peeled out. Just as they pulled away from the disappointed valets, Pam saw a black Mercedes pulling out of the parking lot across the street from the restaurant. It pulled into the street behind them, accelerating rapidly.

"Shit! Somebody made us," she said.

Lorenzo's eyes flickered to the rearview mirror. "The black Mercedes?"

Pam nodded.

"I've noticed it a couple of times since I've been here. You think those are some of the people who are following me?"

"Hoping you'll lead them to me," Pam said, her jaw clenched. "Looks like it worked."

"Pam, I'm sorry."

"My fault, not yours. Can you lose them?"

"For a while, probably. This *is* a Ferrari."

Lorenzo made several turns onto narrow streets at very high speed. He pulled a 180-degree power skid onto the Boulevard des Moulins and the Ferrari screamed southwest, the needle quivering near the 150-kilometer-per-hour mark.

Pam gripped the tan leather of the door handle with both hands. Her back pressed against the sleek soft leather seats as her wide eyes alternated between staring at the road ahead of them and looking behind for any sign of the black Mercedes. Pam started to relax slightly, allowing the 540-horsepower engine to do its work. Looking across at Lorenzo, she could see that he was in a tense silence as he drove.

Six minutes later they pulled up in front of the hotel. "Wait here," Pam said, "I'll go up and get my stuff and be right back."

She dashed through the lobby, ignoring the many stares, and, not bothering with the elevator, she sprinted up the stairs to the third floor, where her room was located. She raced inside, slammed her suitcase closed without attempting to make any decisions about what to take and what to leave behind, and hurried back downstairs, barely noticing the heavy luggage dragging at her arm. She ran back through the lobby, vaguely hearing the desk clerk's protest. If she arrived in Dallas alive, she'd make sure to square things with Formula 1 and the Palais Joséphine.

She went through the front doors at a dead run and looked up just in time to see a man in a dark suit standing on the passenger side of the Ferrari, pointing a gun at Lorenzo.

Pam never broke stride. She put the suitcase in front of her like the blade of a bulldozer and ran straight at the gunman. He looked around just in time to see the suitcase collide with his face, knocking him in a sprawl to the pavement. Pam flung her bag into the Ferrari's small rear seating area. Lorenzo hit the gas pedal while she was still sliding into the seat.

Lorenzo glanced in the rearview mirror as they roared down the drive of the Palais Joséphine. "Oh my God, Pam, that was great! You totally laid that guy out!"

Good Lord. Now I'm turning Lorenzo into a criminal, just like me. "Hey, Lorenzo, I am really—"

"Wait, Pam. You are not about to apologize, are you? Come on now, I'm a big boy. Do you really think that I regret—any of this?"

Pam sighed. "Well . . . okay. Then drive, Lorenzo. Just drive. Like a bat out of hell, preferably."

"That's my girl."

The great thing about being in the second-smallest country in the world was that you were always close to the border. In no less than forty minutes they would be in France, on their way to Aéroport Nice Côte d'Azur.

But their problems weren't over, Pam realized, when the black Mercedes swerved onto the D6098 highway behind them. "Dammit. I cannot catch a break here, Lorenzo." She looked over at him. "Is your cell phone still on?"

He nodded.

"Turn it off. They're tracking you with GPS from your cell phone."

He glanced at her. "How do you know that?"

"I saw it on TV. Just do it."

He fished the phone out of his jacket and handed it to her; Pam flung it out the window.

They passed a sign that was directing traffic toward the Parc Paysager de Fontvieille. Pam suddenly had an idea. "Lorenzo, go there," she said, pointing. "Try and lose them, first."

Lorenzo nodded. He executed several quick turns before heading for the park, to buy them a little time.

"Lorenzo, pull over here at the next building," she said when they neared the park. "I'll bail out and lie low. You keep driving until you've taken them all the way to the airport or they give up, whichever comes first. Once they figure out I'm not with you anymore, they'll lose interest."

"I hope you're right about that part," Lorenzo said. "But it sounds like a good plan to me."

He screeched to a halt and Pam yanked her bag out of the back of the sports car.

"You gonna be okay?" he said, looking up at her.

"I'll be fine. Lorenzo, I am gonna make this up to you, I promise." Pam leaned inside the car and kissed Lorenzo softly on the lips.

"Was that a preview?" he smiled.

"You bet your ass it was," Pam said with a wink.

Lorenzo spun the tires as the car shot back on the road. Pam grabbed her bag and dashed toward the park, throwing herself behind a hedge. Less than a minute later, the black Mercedes flashed past. Pam surfaced from her hiding place and walked toward the building across the street from the park, toward the coastline. The sign on the front of the building read

"Heliport de Monaco." Close to it was a smaller sign that displayed the bright red-and-gray logo of Heli Air Monaco.

The front desk clerk stood to assist her as soon as she walked through the door. "Bonjour, mademoiselle. Peux-je vous aider?"

"Oui . . . un moment, s'il vous plaît," Pam said. She set down her suitcase and dug through her day pack, looking for the scrap of paper on which she'd scribbled the name of the pilot who had brought her here from the airport in Nice. Ah, there it was. She looked at the clerk and said, "Alain Harp? Il est ici?"

"Ah, oui," the clerk said, smiling. He turned toward a small break area to the left of the front desk. "Alain! Tu as une amie; elle te demande."

A pilot stood and Pam recognized him immediately. "Hi, Alain," she said with a big smile. "Remember me?"

His eyes lit up with instant recognition. "Eh, bien! Well look here, it is my favorite passenger," he said in a thick French accent. "So you are headed back to the U.S. already?"

"Something like that," Pam smiled.

"Who is flying you?"

"Well, that's where I was hoping you could help me out. I am leaving kind of on the spur of the moment."

He gave her a confused look.

"Really quick-like. Immédiatement," she said, finally remembering the French word.

Alain nodded in understanding, then he massaged his chin. "I wish I could help you, Miss, but it must be prebooked through my company. And . . . to fly you at the last minute, it is très cher—very expensive." He gave her a Gallic shrug.

Pam noticed that he had a signed picture of Indy driver Michael Schumacher sitting on his desk. She reached into her organizer and retrieved two Formula 1 event tickets. She dangled the tickets in his face.

"Well, mon ami, since I will be stuck here, I guess I will just have to use these lower grandstand seats myself. Now, if someone could just fly me over to Nice, well, I guess I wouldn't need them."

He stared at the tickets for a full ten seconds, then snatched them out of her hand, flashing her a big grin. "Mademoiselle, I have wanted tickets to one of these races for years! Wait right here, I am going fly you myself, right now."

"Right now works for me," Pam said, smiling.

* * *

Novikov opened his eyes onto a bright blue sky. His head was splitting open with pain and the side of his face seemed to be wet and sticky.

He sat up, groaning aloud as a bolt of agony lanced his skull. Gingerly he put a hand to the throbbing area just above his right eye. There was a huge, tender knot there, and his fingertips had rusty smudges of dried blood when he pulled them back. He looked around him; his gun was gone.

Cursing under his breath—which was as loud as he could manage without making the pain worse—he slowly got to his feet. He stood for a moment with his palms braced against his knees, then slowly raised himself upright. A wave of dizziness hit him, but he somehow stayed on his feet long enough for it to pass.

He had to get back to his room and clean himself up, and then he had to put an ice pack on his throbbing head. And then, when he was able to move again, he had to find the Graham bitch and kill her—preferably, very slowly.

It had now become personal.

CHAPTER 29

By the time Alain came back inside from his preflight check to tell her they could leave as soon as she was ready, Pam was leading the way to the chopper. She tossed her suitcase in the back of the helicopter and climbed in. *Okay, Texas, here I come. I think that I have had enough of Europe for now.*

Alex's face rose up in her mind then. As soon as she got home, she would send for him, and she promised herself that she would never leave him, ever again.

Upon arriving at Aéroport Nice Côte d'Azur, the first thing Pam did was to go to a store in the airport and purchase a prepaid cell phone. The second thing she did was to place a call to her father's private number. He answered on the third ring. *Thank God!*

"Daddy? It's Pamela. Daddy, don't ask me any questions right now, but I'm in a little bit of trouble, and I need to get home as quickly as possible."

After a short pause, he asked her, in his quick, gruff voice where she was. When she told him, he said, "Okay, then. Call this number . . . " Pam wrote it down. "Tell the person who answers that Ben Graham would regard it as a personal favor if he would provide transportation for you, direct to DFW International, and that I will compensate him in the usual manner. Got that?"

"Yes, sir."

"You need any money?"

"No, I don't think so."

"All right, then. We can talk when you get home. Whatever kind of spot you're in, I'll do whatever I can."

"Okay. Daddy?"

"Yes?"

"Thank you."

"Just take care of yourself, Pamela. I can't have anything happening to you—you know that."

"Yes, sir."

And he was gone. As usual.

Pam dialed the number he gave her; a man answered. "Allô, c'est Germond."

"Germond? I'm calling for Ben Graham, and—"

"Benjamin? From Texas, yes? Is this the little girl that comes to the races with her papa?"

Of course! Germond was her dad's friend and sometime business partner, though Pam had never been quite certain what sort of business they would be doing that consisted entirely of flying to various unnamed places in one of Mr. Germond's private jets. Pam remembered him from the jaunts to the Grand Prix races that she and her father took. Germond was a small, wiry man with coal-back hair and eyes that never stopped moving.

"Yes, Monsieur Germond, it's Pamela; I'm Ben Graham's daughter."

"Parfait! How may I assist the child of my good friend?"

"Well, before we get to that, Monsieur Germond, can I ask if you have an office here at the airport somewhere—one with a computer and Internet access? There's somebody here I need to get a message to before I leave . . . "

* * *

Agent Bates was tired and bored and generally pissed off that once again, she was left out of the action. She had been sitting in the airport at Nice for three days now, sleeping in snatches and still wearing the same clothes in which she had stepped off the CIA charter onto French soil, all on the off chance that this Pamela Graham everyone was so worked up about might happen to stroll through on her way to cause more trouble. It was a pain in the ass, that's what it was, and certainly not what Bates had thought she was signing on for when she became a field operative. Hell, the rest of the team was probably getting drunk or laid or both over in Monaco amid all the Grand Prix hype, and she was sitting on her numb butt in an airport, watching overweight Americans walk back and forth. She had half a mind to open a sex discrimination file.

And then, in an instant, everything changed.

When the young, slender, blonde woman walked past, laughing and talking with a short, wiry, older French man, she thought her fatigue was combining with her irritated state of mind to play tricks on her eyes. But she took another look and then surreptitiously compared the woman with the blown-up passport photograph she had been carrying around, and there was no question.

Let's dance! A chance to actually do some fieldwork!

Bates allowed the pair to proceed for about thirty paces beyond her position, then she got up and strolled after them, being careful to maintain a casual attitude and avoid any sort of eye contact.

They walked out of the main terminal and got into a waiting Citroën. The vehicle had the words "Aero Excellence" painted on the door, along with a wing logo and a local phone number. Bates memorized the number, waited a few seconds, and then hailed a cab.

"Suivez cette voiture," she said, pointing at the departing Citroën.

The Citroën drove to the charter hangar. Agent Bates paid the cabbie and got out, finding a spot across the road where she could observe the hangar without being easily seen.

But she didn't need to worry, apparently. The Citroën stopped in front of a Gulfstream G650 with the identical logo as the Citroën. Bates jotted down the aircraft number and watched as the Graham woman and her companion walked up the steps and into the aircraft. The man was carrying a suitcase. Apparently someone, at least, was packed for a trip.

A bit later, the Gulfstream's engines whined to life, and soon after that the aircraft taxied out to the runway.

Bates took out her satellite phone and dialed the number of the team leader. She told him what she had seen and gave him the aircraft ID number, reading it twice, slowly, as he repeated the number back to her.

Bates smiled. Wherever Pamela Graham was headed, the Company would soon know her destination, based on the flight plan filed by the pilot of the Gulfstream. And it was all because of Agent Bates's hard work.

* * *

Roxy took the elevator up to Pam's apartment. She dug in her purse frantically one more time; where were those damned earrings? She had to find them, or Pam would kill her. Nope, not in her purse. She sighed, staring at the floor indicator light as it slowly ticked higher. Roxy prayed that the earrings had fallen out while she was still in Pam's apartment. But a nagging voice in the back of her mind said that they could be lying on the sidewalk, on the street, or almost anywhere else along the route from her place to Pam's high-rise.

The elevator opened to the tenth floor. Roxy walked down the hall, now digging in her purse for Pam's apartment key. She located the key at the same moment she saw her compact. Looping her purse over her shoulder, she stuck the key in the lock with one hand while performing her habitual beauty self-check with her compact mirror, held in the other hand. *Hell, I look a mess!*

Suddenly, she realized that the mirror revealed two men in sunglasses, standing behind her in the hallway. "Ms. Reynolds?"

Roxy spun around, and the thought that immediately flashed into her mind was "government." "Yes, I am Roxy Reynolds, how can I help you gentlemen? And if this is about my missing passport—"

One of the men smiled and shook his head. "Not exactly, Ms. Reynolds. He pulled out a badge. "My name is Special Agent Elgreen, and this is my partner. We think we may need your assistance on an urgent matter."

Roxy began to spin the possibilities in her imagination. Was this a special request to do a big story? She'd heard of reporters being approached to break news items, so maybe she was about to get a scoop bigger than entertainment news. She smiled broadly. "Hey, I will do whatever I can do to help you, gentlemen."

"That's great, ma'am. We're here in the interest of your friend, Pamela Graham," he said.

"Pam?" *Damn. Of course; it's always about Pam . . .*

"Yes, ma'am. Although I am not at liberty to go into detail, we think that she may be in trouble."

Roxy exhaled loudly, allowing the purse to fall to her side. "Okay, what do you need from me?"

"We anticipate that she will be returning to Dallas soon. If she contacts you, have her meet you at this location." Elgreen passed Roxy a card with the address on it.

Roxy stared at the address on the card, then at the two men. Elgreen stepped forward and placed a hand on Roxy's bare shoulder. "We want to draw her away from her apartment for security reasons, Ms. Reynolds, and place her in the safest environment possible. Again, I'm not at liberty to explain much more than that. Also, if you could, please contact us as soon as you hear from her; my number is on the back of the card. We don't want to alarm her, so just tell her you need to talk to her at that location. From that point we can debrief her on what is going on and get this all taken care of safely. Can we count on you with this, Ms. Reynolds?" He gave her a sad little smile that seemed to say, "Whaddya say? Can you help a guy out here?"

Roxy placed the card in her purse and shrugged. "Sure, why not," she said.

"Thank you, Ms. Reynolds. Believe me, you'll be doing your friend a tremendous service. Not to mention, your country."

"Okay, well . . . always glad to help out," she said. *As far as the service for my country, I think that week I spent partying on the army base in California should have covered that.*

The two agents walked away, down the hallway. Roxy watched them go, then sighed, unlocking Pam's apartment. *Yep, always about Pam. Now, where are those damned earrings . . .*

* * *

Joseph Pierce slumped in the chair. "I don't know what you're talking about, Director." His head fell back against the back of the chair and his eyes sagged closed. The nausea from the drugs was wearing off, but that only meant that the fatigue from being kept awake for seventy-two hours straight was coming back into focus. "Listen . . . I can't tell you what you want to know."

"All in good time, Mr. Pierce," the director said. "But here's the thing. You're standing in the way of a very important national security initiative. I can't allow your stubborn, unpatriotic attitude to derail something so important."

"And I can't allow your bullshit to go unchallenged," Pierce said without opening his eyes. "If this were about patriotism, you wouldn't be violating everything the United States stands for in order to carry out your plan."

"While I deeply admire your frank attitude," the director said in a bored voice, "I'm afraid we're out of time. So here's what's going to happen next. You will either go to the Maxwell Morris Medical Institute and enter the codes necessary to restart the manufacture of the vaccine—"

"You mean the poison?"

"—or I will instruct my team that is standing by in Barcelona to go to your mother's house and let her test the vaccine for us. And while they're at it, I'll have them pay a visit to her next-door neighbors, the Garcins. Hell, while we're at it, we might as well plug that little kid we're holding. You know, the one Pamela Graham kidnapped from Russia."

Pierce was tired and his mind was beginning to play tricks on him. And it was only a matter of time before the Agency's decryption masters broke the code he'd used to lock down the equipment at MMMI. He had been playing for time all along, trying to get the information into the hands of Giles Girard, but it seemed that things had just about reached the end of the line. With nothing else to lose, he decided to ask the question he most yearned to have answered. What was the worst that could happen? He opened his eyes and wearily raised his head to look the director in the eye. "Okay. I'll do it. But . . . why? Just tell me that one thing, Director. Why is the government of the United States conspiring to infect its population with deadly diseases?"

The director looked at him for a long time. Perhaps sensing that he had won, he smiled slowly. "You really want to know, Pierce? Okay, why not? But you've probably already done the math and figured it out for yourself; you just don't want to admit it.

"There are about thirty million reasons why this plan is good for the

U.S., Pierce. You know your history, right? Tell me something: did you ever notice how the economy always gets much better after a world war? It's because you've just eliminated a lot of people who have been a drag on the economy and using up the country's natural resources. Unproductive elements, Pierce. The sort of people who won't be missed.

"Maybe you don't read the newspapers, but we've got budget problems in this country, Pierce. And can you guess what one of the biggest drains on the budget is? Yep, entitlement programs and social security—huge sums of money that go primarily to benefit those who aren't contributing anything to the economy anymore, if they ever were. Get rid of those people, Pierce, and you get rid of the expense of their care and feeding. Do that, and you've given the national budget a huge nudge in a positive direction. And remember what they said a few years ago when they were busy voting out the first President Bush, 'it's the economy!' Of course, that's just the U.S. perspective on the matter. The Russians are even hip to it. As far as they are concerned, they may just want to wipe out a bunch of Chechens. But that's not really any of my business."

The director paused, looking at him. "We've got to work together on this, Pierce; this really isn't anything new. Think about it. It will start to make sense, I promise you." *Take the bait, you moron; we are on the same team here.*

Since it appeared that the director was on a verbal roll, Pierce took another jab at a question that had been bugging him. He decided to probe indirectly. "So you know that Amtrak is really not going to be able to get the vaccine out any faster than we already can, right?"

The director shook his head. "You're not quite as sharp as I thought, Pierce. We didn't need the trains to ship the vaccine in. We need the trains to ship the infected people out."

Pierce felt every ounce of his remaining strength exiting his body. It was clear that the director was certain that the plan would make perfect sense to any intelligent person and that he thought Pierce was smart enough to understand. Pierce's head hung between his shoulders; he was utterly defeated, out of any more stalling tactics. "Yeah . . . yeah, it makes sense."

"Of course it does." The director got up and walked over to the door of the bare room. He opened it. "Come on in and help Mr. Pierce out to the car, gentlemen. He has decided to cooperate, after all."

CHAPTER 30

The sound of his phone ringing caused his head to begin throbbing again. Special Agent Novikov swore mightily as he fumbled across the nightstand, feeling for the phone. He finally located it and thumbed the button to answer the call and halt the infernal racket.

"Novikov."

"Special Agent Novikov, you asked to be kept informed about anything we learned regarding the U.S. investigation of Pamela Graham?"

"Yes, that's correct."

"Our sources indicate that they have pulled their team out of the region where you are presently located."

"I see. And do we have any information on Graham's whereabouts?"

"We have intercepted a transmission from one of their agents to the effect that she left Nice sometime this afternoon on a private aircraft."

Novikov waited, but the caller said nothing. "And? Do you require me to lead you by the nose, you idiot? Where was she bound?"

"The flight plan was filed for Dallas/Fort Worth International Airport, in Texas."

Novikov raised himself to a sitting position. "I will need immediate transportation."

"Yes, Special Agent. The request has already been submitted. A car is waiting for you downstairs; it will transport you to the airport."

Good. They do know a few things on their own, it would seem.

* * *

Dr. Jones sat in Joseph Pierce's office at MMMI, contemplating his next move. DCIA had just called to inform him that Pierce would be here tomorrow to unlock the processing equipment. The H1N1 vaccine would begin shipping out two days later, with Jones overseeing every aspect of the process and insuring that the plan was carried out to the letter. In fact, if Pierce had caved in, it meant that either the director had broken him, or that he had made some threat that Pierce feared more than being forced to participate in genocide.

Which meant that this was Jones's last opportunity to question just how much his moral considerations meant to him. Either he got on board all the way, or he jumped off the boat. He knew the waters were shark-infested, and that he had no life jacket.

The phone on Pierce's desk rang. "This is Dr. Jones."

"Jones, we have you on a three-way conference call with POTUS," the director said. Jones took a deep breath, then he let it go slowly. *Here we go.*

The calls from POTUS had been thrilling at first but had now lost their appeal; most of them tended to end up as pretty much the same conversation. The director did most of the talking and already knew most of the answers to the questions he asked, while POTUS remained silent for security purposes.

"So is everything ready for Pierce's arrival tomorrow?"

"Yes, sir. Should be ready to ship two days later." *And you already know all of this, asshole; we just talked about it.* Jones was beyond weary of the scripted lines of questioning.

"Outstanding, Doctor," the director responded. "So here is the next move. Pierce will arrive first thing tomorrow morning, escorted by my people. He will unlock the equipment, and you'll take it from there.

"Hell of a job you've done, Doctor, to keep this thing moving as much as possible. All the promotion and publicity is well in place; the transportation logistics are assured. Once the product begins leaving the shipping dock at MMMI, successful completion of the initiative is just a few steps away."

Was there any way to stall the shipment? Probably not, but Jones decided to try. "Were you able to take care of that other situation? The woman who has been in contact with Pierce and others?"

The pause that preceded the director's reply made it clear that he disapproved of this departure from the script. Right now, Jones didn't give a shit.

"Let me bring you up to date there, Doctor. Pamela Graham has been linked to a journalist named Giles Girard, who, from what we can tell, is attempting to gather and release sensitive information that would be harmful to government interests, both our own and certain of our allies."

I wasn't aware that the Russians were thought of as our allies. Partners in crime, I guess . . .

"So, there are still a number of uncertainties, Doctor, which make it more important than ever that we take advantage of this window of opportunity to get the vaccine out now and have it all out by the end of the week. From there, matters should proceed to the desired strategic conclusion. And we owe much of the success to you. Welcome to the inside, Dr. Jones." The call disconnected.

The small radio on Pierce's office desk turned on automatically—some sort of preset alarm, Jones guessed. Maybe Pierce needed a reminder that it was time to leave the office. For some reason, the radio was set to a Hispanic station. A mix of Tejano and salsa played until a commercial break.

The commercial was one of the PSAs that Jones had approved for the vaccine program. In Spanish, the announcer urged all the listeners to get the H1N1 inoculation that would soon be available at no cost, courtesy of the kind and caring folks of the "gobierno federal de los Estados Unidos y los Centros de Control de Enfermedades." Dr. Jones lowered his head on to the desk. He did not consciously do it, but it was done. For the first time in his entire life he said a prayer. The prayer consisted of just three words. *God help us.*

* * *

Walking on the glossy floor tile inside DFW airport felt to Pam like stepping into comfortable shoes; she wanted to kiss the Texas soil. Even the unseasonable heat, this early in spring, was a reminder of home and familiar surroundings. She retrieved her luggage from the baggage carousel and set it down with a sigh of relief, then made her first call.

"Rox! Hey, honey, guess what? I am in Dallas now."

"What? No way!"

"Yes way. So, you gonna come and pick me up or what?"

Roxy took a moment to think.

"Rox? You still there?"

"Oh yeah, I am here! Sorry about that; I got distracted. Hey, can you take a cab to the Shops at Legacy? Can I meet you there? I am about finished getting my hair done here."

"Tell you what, I can just meet you at my place later. I am beat."

More silence followed. *What is going on with Roxy?* "Rox? Are you okay? I thought the line went dead."

"No, I'm okay, but, um . . . yeah, I do have something kind of important to tell you, so can you just meet me here before you go to your apartment?"

Pam took a look at her watch. *Roxy, you are nothing but trouble, girl.* "Okay, it's about 6:40 now, so I'll give my dad's limo service a call and have them bring me there." She could see the skies already beginning to darken outside the airport glass. "With the traffic, it might be dark before I get there, but I'm on the way."

"Okay, great! See you in a bit!"

* * *

As soon as she disconnected from speaking with Pam, Roxy dialed the number on the back of the business card.

"Elgreen."

"Hello, Agent Elgreen? This is Roxy Reynolds, Pamela Graham's friend?"

"Oh yes, how are you?"

"I am super. I was calling to let you know that I just got a call from Pam and she is on her way from the airport to meet me at the Shops at Legacy, just like you said."

Elgreen turned to his two assistants and twirled an index finger in the air to signal that the operation was under way. "That is perfect, Ms. Reynolds. We'll meet you there and get everything taken care of, so you just relax. Your friend is in good hands."

"Okay, no problem, glad I could help."

"Oh, before you go, are you at the location now?"

"No, I am actually at Pam's apartment right now. Should I stay here?"

Elgreen nodded at his assistants, giving them a thumbs-up. "Yeah, perfect, you stay right there, and we will come and get you when everything is clear."

"Okay, gotcha!" Roxy said. She ended the call and then hurried through the apartment, trying to put everything back in place before Pam returned home.

* * *

In the air somewhere above central Arkansas, Giles Girard could hardly sit still. J. D. was looking at him as if his hair was on fire, but Girard couldn't help it.

Ever since he had gotten the message Pamela Graham had sent from the heliport in Monaco, he had been, by turns, exhilarated and fearful. On the one hand, he knew he was about to finally get the piece he needed to finish the puzzle; if the flash drive had half the documentation on it that Graham had described in her first e-mail, this story would be bigger than Watergate and 9/11 combined—in fact, it combined elements of both. Getting this out in public view would feel like a vindication of everything he had ever believed in and fought for as a journalist. And to be this close but not yet able to finish the job was maddening—like having the Hope Diamond right in front of you, but not being able to grasp it.

So he paced up and down the aisle of the jet J. D. had chartered, wishing he could somehow will it onto the ground in Dallas and himself into the physical presence of the elusive and tantalizing Pamela Graham. He had already alerted his staff that a big story was in the works. Everything was ready—he just needed that bloody flash drive.

"Hellfire, boy, you better put your ass in a chair for a minute or two, hadn't you?" J. D. said. "You ain't speeding this plane up a damn bit with all your pacing." Boone poured a healthy swig of scotch into one glass, then he repeated with another glass, which he offered to Giles. His face registered surprise when Giles accepted it and tossed the liquor down without hesitation. Then he sat down in a chair across the aisle from J. D. The two men stared at each other for a few seconds. "You're afraid it ain't gonna work, ain't you?" Boone said.

Giles nodded. "There are so many ways things can still go wrong, J. D. She could get scared and back out, or they could somehow get to her before we do, or hell, they could just kill us all and be done with it. I hope our little plan works out."

"You sure you got the arrival time right, and all that?"

Giles nodded. "She's flying in a charter owned by a Frenchman, name of Germond. Friend of her father's, she said. I had one of my clever blokes retrieve the flight plan."

"Well, if she's where she's supposed to be when she's supposed to get there, my boys'll be ready."

"I hope it's enough," Giles said. "We're not going up against mall security here."

"We'll get there as quick as we can, son," Boone said. "Can't do no more than that."

They sat in silence for a few more moments. Boone stared out the window at the landscape crawling past, 25,000 feet below. "I still haven't figured out how something this flat-out evil got started in the United States," Boone said. "You ever give any thought to that, Giles? I mean, beyond the bare-ass facts, I keep asking myself, 'What the hell?' You know? How'd we get so far off track?"

Giles smiled. "One of the things I've always loved about you, J. D., is your bloody innocence."

"Me, innocent? Been called a lot of things but that's a new one!"

"I don't know anything conclusive, J. D., but I've got a few theories. Want to hear them?"

"If it'll keep you from wearing out the carpet in the aisle, yeah."

"Ever heard of Bonham Grove?"

"Well, yeah . . . Ain't that the good ole boys' club that was started back some time ago? It's private, all men, and has members who are the global big shits. Hell, I even heard tell that Ronald Reagan was a member. Rumor has it that the Bonham Grovers make the decisions that make this old blue dot spin."

Giles gave him an impressed nod. "Actually, you are more up on the club than most. Bonham Grove was formed in the late 1800s, and I assure you that they are still a thriving force."

"No shit? Well, I never took the stories I heard too serious."

"Most do not, and that is what they bank on. The reality is that they control more than we will ever know, J. D. In fact, the entire concept of the atomic bomb was born during one of their northern California retreats. Now . . . well, now it seems they are linked with a new master plan, one that will supposedly rid society of elements the Grovers deem counterproductive to a healthy world economy. This is all theory, of course, but the more I have dug into it, the more I am subscribing to the notion."

Boone shook his head and stared off into space. "Lord a' mighty, Giles! This is some crazy shit." Now J. D. got up from his seat and began to pace in the aisle. "I mean—Jesus Christ! If that is true, how in the hell are they able to keep all this stuff under wraps?"

"Oh, that's the easy part, J. D. The people in control are fully aware that power lies in the media. Control the media, mate, and you control the world. Want to know the biggest illusion that the government has ever pulled off?" Giles opened his hands in the air, spreading his long, slender fingers apart like a magician. "They pretend that they do not control everything."

Boone stopped pacing and moved closer to Giles. With the most sober expression Giles had ever seen on J. D.'s face, Boone stabbed a finger toward Giles. "This is why we need a hell of a lot more people like you in the world."

Giles gave a humble shrug. "I'd like to think so."

John David Boone strode toward the pilot's cabin, then thought better of it and returned to his seat. "Hell, ain't this damn thing ever gonna land?" he growled.

Giles gave him a broad smile. "Sounds to me like you need a drink, J. D."

CHAPTER 31

As soon as she sat back in the Graham Publishing limo, Pam grabbed the Manolo Blahniks and slid them onto her feet. "Hello there, fellas! I've finally gotten a chance to put you on," she cooed to the shoes, wiggling her feet back and forth as she admired the fit. The shoes gave her the needed feeling of being back home—sweet normalcy. They were the only items she had gotten out of her suitcase when the limo arrived.

Still enjoying the look of the shoes, she pulled out her phone and dialed Javier and Pilar's number. It was a bit late in Spain, but she knew that often, like many Iberians, they dined late and might still be awake. She really hoped so; she was dying to hear Alex's voice and tell him that soon, they would be together. She waited impatiently for the international call to click through the various exchanges and finally begin ringing in Barcelona.

She heard someone pick up. "Hello? Mama Pili? Papa Javier? This is Pamela, I'm in the U.S. Is Alex there?"

"Pam . . . This is Pam? Oh, Pam, my God, Pam . . . " It was Pilar, and she was weeping on the phone.

Pam's heart leaped into her throat. What was wrong? "Mama Pili? What's the matter? Tell me, please! Is it Papa Javier? Is he okay?"

"Alex is gone," she finally said, through her sobs. "Some men came in the dead of the night, and they took him away. He is gone, Pam, oh, Madre de Dios, he is gone!"

Pam couldn't speak; for several seconds, she couldn't even breathe.

"We have been trying to reach you, Pamela, ever since . . . But your phone . . . All we could get was your voice message. We have even tried calling your father, thinking he might be able to reach you . . . "

The bastards have got Alex. The Russians? The CIA? It doesn't really matter. Someone got him, and I got him into this. Shit, shit, shit!

She ended the call without even realizing she had done it. The phone fell into the seat as her mind drifted uncertainly, trying to sort through a set of options too awful to consider—except that now she had no choice.

Maybe this was it; maybe she really was whipped this time. Maybe the best thing to do would be to simply give them the flash drive. Maybe if she did that, this whole nightmare would go away and Alex would be safe, and he would be with her. She could put the last few days behind her and begin living her life.

But there was no going back to the old Pam. She was a different person now. She was someone who had seen the pitiful squalor of a Russian orphanage. She had seen children living like rats in a sewer and learned that the government of her own country was perfectly capable and willing to murder its own citizens. The old Pam was indeed gone and that was okay. She had grown in ways she never could have achieved by remaining in the sheltered confines of Dallas.

The limo had stopped; the driver was stepping out to open her door. Pam peered out, uncomprehending. Oh, yeah. They were at the Shops at Legacy. She was back home, standing amid the upscale retail development that glowed with soft, tasteful lighting. Most of the shops were closed for the day, and as the sound of the limo drifted away she wished she had made the driver wait.

Pam walked along the vacant sidewalk, thinking of Alex. Her mind was clouded with all that had occurred. Then she had the thought, *Where in the hell is Roxy?* She pulled her cell phone from her purse and pressed the power button. The phone flickered to life then powered off. *Shit! Dead battery!*

* * *

The director's black SUV glided through the vacant streets. He had his driver park at a distance as he and his team of two watched Pamela Graham like sharks following a wounded fish. He was well aware of POTUS's instructions, but the hell with that, he had decided. It was past time to cut away this loose thread. He was already imagining the satisfaction of reporting to POTUS that everything was taken care of and all variables were accounted for. *Maybe not exactly in the manner POTUS wanted, but I can't make everyone happy.*

* * *

As much as Pam had frequented the Shops at Legacy, it was her first time there at night. Now all of the stores were shut down, displaying only a sample of their wares. In the distance, Pam noticed a few people moving in and out of the Fox Sports Grill; aside from that, hardly anyone remained in the area.

Pam gazed at the shops that lined the side street, hoping to spot Roxy emerging from one of the stores, pretending that she was on time. Really, though, Pam was more angry at herself than at Roxy. *Will I ever learn not to trust that girl to be on time?*

Specialty, gift, jewelry, and clothing stores stood side by side, giving the upscale shopping destination a "Main Street" look. Pam moved slowly, trying to remember the relief of being back home. She looked at her watch: 7:52 p.m. and there was still no sign of Roxy.

Crash! The sudden sound of breaking glass jarred Pam's nerves. Startled, she reflexively jumped to the left.

"Wonderful!" a woman said in frustration, not even noticing Pam. The slender redhead stood a few feet away, glaring down at the small broken glass figurine that she had just dropped on the pavement. The woman went back into the shop she had come from, holding a sheet of paper in one hand and a hairbrush in the other. She brushed the glass fragments onto the sheet of paper, then she angrily dumped the paper and the brush into an outside trash barrel.

She reentered the shop, then she exited again, slamming the door shut. Her face appeared unnaturally tight—a botched face-lift or an overuse of

Botox, Pam guessed. The woman locked the shop's door behind her and then walked into the darkness of an alley that connected to a separate parking area. Minutes later she pulled out of the parking area and drove away in a metallic blue Mercedes.

Pam could feel her body still shaking from the adrenaline rush caused by the sudden sound of the breaking glass. *Damn . . . chill out, girl, we're home now.* She shook her head, wondering at her hair-trigger nerves.

The dim streetlights spaced between the shops were not intended for practical purposes, apparently. Their faint glow was more for appearance than actual luminosity. Contemplating the lights, Pam questioned how much of her life was needing a stronger degree of illumination.

She turned on her cell phone, hoping that it would have enough power remaining to call Roxy. The Shops at Legacy area included just a few blocks but there was no sense in circling it again, especially on foot—and especially in her new Manolos. Pam also realized, suddenly, that as many times as she had visited the area, she could not ever recall seeing a hair salon. *Where in the hell is Roxy?*

The small window on her cell phone lit up as it came to life. Pam's foot tapped rapidly as she waited for the phone to complete its electronic rebirth. *Come on, come on!*

While looking down she noticed for the first time the scratch on the toe of her right shoe. The imperfection on the never-worn Manolo Blahniks did not sit well. Deductive thinking pointed to the single most likely culprit. *I'm gonna choke you, Roxy!*

And then, out of the quiet, hard footsteps approached behind her.

CHAPTER 32

At first, Pam ignored the approaching footsteps; she projected her concentration onto her cell phone that was finally coming to life. One power bar remained on the battery indicator. *Yes!* The incoming call light flashed in the center of the small phone screen. The call was coming from an unlisted number. *Giles? Dad, maybe?*

She tried to maintain focus, but the approaching footsteps distracted her attention. *Okay, okay . . . chill out, Pam; don't overreact again.* She needed to answer the call, but her thumb hovered over the button as she listened to the footsteps drawing nearer.

The heavy steps grew faster, coming directly at her. She spun around at the last second to find a masked figure just two feet away. He snatched the purse off her shoulder and then ran in the opposite direction. Her astonishment was overtaken by anger. "Get back here!" she shouted at the running figure. "I said get your ass back here!"

Without making a conscious decision, she was suddenly tearing after the purse snatcher. As she ran and her blood began to pound in her temples, it was as if life was flooding back into her body; everything she had been through seemed to somehow focus on this moment—the chase, her fury at the snatcher, at the CIA, at the people who had taken Alex, at the whole stinking mess the world had become, right at this moment. This son of a bitch had her purse, and he had the flash drive.

Her legs took on a life of their own, tearing after the masked man. She chased him past the brick walls that enclosed the parking lot. She could have sworn that she saw a silhouette moving out of the corner of her eye, but she shot past the shadow with her focus remaining locked on the man only a few feet away from her grasp.

Her body pressed forward; there was no way she was going to let him get away. The muscles in her calves bulged as they worked powerfully to maintain her balance and speed. She got closer, almost close enough to grab his collar and drag him to the ground.

Thoughts of her unfinished last will and testament popped into her head. More random thoughts surfaced: Alex, Pierce, Sofia . . . others flashed like visions from another life. She tried to think about what she would do if she was able to pull the snatcher down. *Maybe I can just snatch the purse back away from him?*

The gap between them closed to within a couple of feet. She could hear the labored breathing that accompanied his slowing stride. Their bodies were less than an arm's length apart.

Just as Pam reached out to grab him, the heel of her shoe snapped, throwing her headlong onto the pavement of the parking lot. At that same instant, she heard the all-too-familiar *crack!* of a gunshot. The snatcher cried out and fell to the parking lot, then lay still.

CHAPTER 33

Pam struggled to regain her equilibrium after the violent fall. Through a haze she could see a man stepping from the shadows. As he stood over her, the dim illumination from a distant security light fell across his face, and she recognized the man she had cold-cocked in the Japanese Garden, back in Monte Carlo. It was the Russian. A few blinks later, he was gone. *Am I seeing things now?*

* * *

Novikov took a half step forward. *Time to finish the job.* He stopped when he felt a hand grip his shoulder, pulling him back into the shadows. Next he felt a steel muzzle pressed into his back. Novikov lifted his hands, surrendering his weapon without a fight.

He spoke over his shoulder with his hands still raised in the air. "This is something you do not want to do. Aside from diplomatic immunity, I have very high connections here in your country."

The hand pushed Novikov forward, walking him back out through the alley. Novikov smiled once they reached the street. In the dim light he spotted the director leaning against an unmarked black SUV. Novikov twisted his head to the side to speak to the man behind him. "I know this man. Why don't you put that gun away before you get yourself in a bad situation?" Novikov nodded at the director, giving him a knowing smirk.

The director, apparently looking at the person behind Novikov, raised a finger and lowered it. There was a burst of pain at the back of Novikov's head—then nothing.

CHAPTER 34

The director watched impassively as Novikov's body fell limply to the parking lot. The Russian blinked twice, then his eyes glazed over.

The director was still struggling with POTUS's request to spare Pamela Graham. He nodded, agreeing with the conclusion that had just settled in his mind. *Hell, why not?* He looked up at Elgreen and his two men. "Go into the alley and make sure that no one leaves there alive but you three." As they turned to go, the private phone in his pocket vibrated with a call. *Shit. That'll be POTUS.*

"Yes, sir," he said into the phone.

"Director, I wanted to give you an update. I just had a very interesting conversation with Benjamin Graham. He is set on making sure my reelection campaign gets the financial backing needed."

The director held up a finger to signal his men to stop. "Financial backing, sir?" The director's voice was laced with confusion; he didn't like where this was headed.

"Yes, it seems that he now has a vested interest in seeing that I keep my position for a second term. Now I am sure that I don't have to tell you that his daughter's well-being is even more essential now. I mean . . . there is nothing worse than a tragedy in the family to throw key assistance right out the window. You following me, Director?"

"Yes, sir. But—"

"Listen closely, Director. If anything happened to Ms. Graham, I would be very disappointed. I will not be a happy campaigner if I discover that Benjamin Graham's donation somehow slides to the opposing party. Any other time I wouldn't care what happens, but this is not one of those times. I have an election coming up and there are certain entities that I do not want to disappoint. Understand?"

"Yes, sir," the director replied. His breathing shortened, and his jaw clenched like a vice.

"Okay, Director, we will discuss this more, later in the week. I just wanted to make sure that we were all on the same page."

The call disconnected and the director slammed the phone into the side of the black SUV. Agent Elgreen stood next to him. "Bad news, sir?"

"Not for us, agent. We are going along just as we planned. When this comes up, as far as anyone is concerned, including POTUS, Novikov got to her first." He handed Elgreen a pair of latex gloves. "Go get Novikov's weapon, then take care of Pamela Graham. That bitch has been a pain in my ass long enough."

The director watched as Elgreen and the other agent disappeared into the alley that led into the parking lot. They could finish this and be out of here before any witnesses gathered.

CHAPTER 35

The director got into the back of the SUV. *It shouldn't be long now.* He finally lit the Cuban cigar he had been saving, then he lowered the tinted window. He waited for the sound that would signal that the loose thread had been cut loose.

After two minutes he shifted uneasily in the leather seat, staring into the dark shadows of the alley.

Bang! Bang! Bang!

The three shots echoed through the night. Lights turned on from the inside of several of the apartments above the street-level shops. *Too much noise, guys; way too much noise. Now get your asses back here so we can leave before the good citizens get curious.*

But the pitch-black alley entrance revealed no movement. The director waited for the agents to emerge; time was ticking and they needed to be away from the scene. *What the hell?* His eyes strained into the dark in an effort to catch a glimpse of his men. *Come on, come on!*

And then the driver's door of the SUV suddenly opened. The director slid his hand toward his chest holster, just as a head leaned inside. The director stared in surprise.

"Dr. Jones? What the fuck are you doing here?"

"Undercover work."

"Undercover? Undercover for who?"

Dr. Jones held up his cell phone, pressing the side to turn on the speakerphone. The voice of POTUS spoke from the device.

"Director, I thought we had an understanding?"

The director looked at Dr. Jones and back at the phone. *Well I'll be damned; the lions are keeping watch on the wolves.* "Sir, we do. What do you mean?" The director shifted again in his seat.

"Is that right? Hey, it's okay, Director. We all can get a little off track sometimes. Dr. Jones, can you hear me okay?"

"Yes, sir, we both hear you fine. You are still on speakerphone, sir."

"Okay, good. Doctor . . . if you will."

The gun appeared in Jones's hand too fast for the director to react. The bullet entered just below the director's right eye, penetrating into his lower brain and exiting out the back of his skull. His body fell back against the seat. One eyeball bulged from its ruined socket and hung down his cheek. The other eye remained open; the director appeared observant even in death.

CHAPTER 36

"Pamela . . . Pam . . . Pamela."

The weak voice called out to her in the dark. Pam's state of shock engulfed her as she tried to make sense out of what had just occurred. First the Russian had disappeared, then Elgreen and two other men had come toward her, only to fall dead from shots that came out of nowhere. Now her name was being called by the person who had just taken her purse. *I think I'm totally losing it here . . .*

The voice called out again, between long, struggling draughts of air; each word sounded like a supreme effort. "Pam . . . can . . . you hear me?"

Pam dragged her body over closer to the figure, the voice of the injured man now groaning softly. Through the eye openings of the mask a set of grayish blue eyes looked up at her. She pulled the wool mask up to the top of his head. "Holy hell . . . Joseph?"

He looked into her eyes affectionately. "Pam, I am so sorry."

"But I don't get it. Why would—"

He reached up, gently placing his fingertips on her lips. "It's not what you think. I . . . " He coughed, and his head sagged weakly in her arms. "I played along so that they would let me go. When I . . . when I found out how serious they were about getting that information I passed to you, I had to do something." He tried to lift his head, wincing at the pain from the bullet still lodged in his shoulder. "I followed you here. I knew they were watching and that you had what they wanted."

"But how?"

"Got a call from Giles, he told me everything. He wanted to come himself, but knew that he would risk being spotted. I thought if they saw a masked guy grab your purse and take off with the information, then we both would be off the hook." He coughed some more. "Crazy, huh?"

Pam kissed him softly on the forehead. "Yeah, damn crazy, but I have done crazier, trust me."

"Hey, wanna hear something funny?"

"Okay."

"The day you met my mom and when we were about to leave for those drinks—" He was seized by another coughing fit. "When you were about to leave, she whispered to me that I'd better get in shape so I could keep up with you."

Pam laughed. "Damn, Joseph, that *is* funny!"

Pam heard murmuring and looked up, realizing for the first time that people were gathering, drawn by the sound of the gunshots. Sirens from approaching ambulances came from somewhere near the shops. Pam held Joseph Pierce in her arms, praying that he pulled through.

He was struggling to talk more. "Come on, Joseph," she said, "we can talk about this later. Save your strength."

Joseph coughed even harder this time. "No . . . no, you have to listen. While I was trailing you I noticed that someone else was doing the same thing. Middle-aged guy, official looking, dark suit, short, salt-and-pepper hair."

The description did not ring a bell. Then she spotted a man standing in the crowd that fit Joseph's description to the letter. When she spotted him, her body froze as their eyes locked. She had never seen the man but it was obvious that he knew her.

Joseph coughed hard; his body began to shiver. Some EMTs hustled up, pulling a gurney. When Pam looked up again, the man in the crowd was gone.

* * *

Lee Jones slipped out the back of the crowd as the EMTs bundled Joseph
Pierce off toward the ambulance. When he was certain he was out of earshot of anyone, he pulled a phone from his pocket and pressed a button.

"Mr. President, by the time I could get back to her, there were too many
people around. I was unable to retrieve the data. I recommend that we
withdraw the program and issue a blanket denial of responsibility. It's too
risky to proceed at this point, in my opinion."

"Understood, Doctor, and agreed. Good work. See you back here soon."

"Yes, sir."

Jones ended the call. He looked back toward the crowd, drawing a deep
breath. He felt relief, but he knew there would be a next time, and one after
that, and one after that . . .

CHAPTER 37

Pam left the elevator and walked down the hall toward her apartment, barefooted and wearily dragging her suitcase behind her. She looked up and realized that her apartment door was partly open. *Now what?* Quietly she slipped to the opening and peered inside.

Roxy was sprawled on her couch, her feet propped on Pam's coffee table, watching the flat-screen TV. Pam shook her head and smiled. *Some things never change. And one of them is Rox.*

Hearing her bump the door open, Roxy spun around and saw her. She squealed, jumping up from the couch and running over to give Pam a hug. "Welcome home, world traveler," she said. "Here, let me take your suitcase. Girl, why are you barefoot?"

"It's a long story, Rox."

"So . . . is everything . . . okay?" Roxy said. "No problems? Nothing unusual?"

"Well, yeah, but . . . " Pam collapsed onto the couch. "Before we get into that, where the hell were you? I walked all over the Shops at Legacy looking for you." Of course, Pam realized that if Roxy had been where she said she was going to be for once, it would have possibly gotten her killed. Still, she didn't feel like just letting her off the hook.

"I did it for you, you know, the CIA thing . . . "

Pam's look told Roxy that her friend didn't have a clue as to what she was talking about.

"You know, that Agent Elgreen guy? He told me to tell you all that. He said I wasn't supposed to say anything about him; he said it was for your safety, or something like that. Where is he, by the way?" Roxy said, walking to the door to peer down the hallway. "He was kind of cute. He said I was supposed to wait here, and he would come back when everything was taken care of."

Roxy, Roxy, Roxy. Where to begin? "Oh, yeah. Agent Elgreen . . . Well, it's all taken care of, for sure. He didn't need to come here, after all."

"You saw him, then? Everything is cool?"

"Oh, yeah. Everything is fine now."

Pam's words drifted into silence when she noticed the picture on her television. The Speaker of the House stood at the podium, offering his condolences for the untimely death of the director of the CIA. According to the report, the director had no known immediate family. The Speaker attributed the death to suicide. The Speaker also informed the press conference that "Until further notice, Dr. Lee Jones will serve as interim head of the CIA." Jones's picture filled the screen, and Pam gasped. He was the man in the crowd.

Pam waited for something to be said about the demise of the agents at the Shops at Legacy, but the topic was never mentioned. Apparently, the entire incident that occurred in the parking lot had miraculously slipped past the media. The deadly scene moved into the world's background as if the murders had never even happened.

* * *

"That motherfucker is as smooth as silk," John David Boone said, shaking his head as he watched the live newscast.

"He's a loyal soldier," Giles said. "And, you've got to admire how quickly they developed a response. Looks like they are going to brush the whole thing under the rug. Like I said, J. D., they're masters at puppeteering the media."

"They can play innocent all day long, but you can bet your ass they're pissed that vaccine ain't gonna get shipped."

Giles nodded. "Yeah, that bit is over with, for the time being anyway."

"That's what I'm afraid of," Boone said. "Next time, they'll just do a better job of covering their tracks."

"But we'll be watching, J. D.," Giles said with a tiny smile.

* * *

" . . . our offices learned of certain unauthorized communications between the office of the director of the Central Intelligence Agency and one of our government subcontractors," the Speaker was saying. "This situation resulted in the usual precautions not being taken to make sure that the vaccines were properly tested before authorizing the shipments to be sent to the public. Our investigation has indicated that the subcontractor was very close to distributing a tainted vaccine . . . "

Pam watched with one hand clasped over her mouth. The picture on the screen then shifted to another image. Pam felt her heart shift into a higher gear when the face of the Russian agent filled her television screen.

"From sources at the scene, we have also learned that a Russian operative, Nikolai Novikov, was found dead near the scene. We are cooperating fully with our Russian colleagues in a full investigation of Novikov's involvement."

Now Giles's picture was on the screen. The text crawl across the bottom announced that he was wanted by U.S. authorities. He was also wanted by Interpol, but on unrelated charges. *Of course. They've got to try and smear him with something. He's dangerous to them now.*

Pam couldn't stop wondering about Alex. She knew that she could not rest until she was able to find out exactly what happened to him. Whoever took him should have no reason to hold him now . . . or did they?

* * *

Giles remained tucked away out of sight until he was able to leave the country again without being noticed. His name remained on the U.S.

government's "public enemies" list along with the likes of Osama bin Laden and a host of others. But before he slipped out of Texas, his friend John David Boone arrived at Pam's door in person to pick up the memory stick containing the files with proof of the ties between the tainted H1N1 vaccine and the CIA. According to J. D., they planned on holding on to the files as insurance. Or, in J. D.'s words, "We gonna keep this info safe and hold them rotten bastards by the hairy balls." He gave Pam a quick hug and then left to fly Giles back to whatever undisclosed location he resided in that particular week.

* * *

Pam couldn't help but notice the time as she placed her watch on her wrist. She was formally dressed for a charity party Roxy had invited her to, and the watch was the last item she had to put on. The time on the watch, she discovered, was exactly nine hours off. She had not reset it since she had adjusted it in Russia. She was about to reset it, then she left it like it was; it was her way of holding on to another time for a little longer.

The doorbell rang. Pam opened the door and blocked the entry. "You are sooo late, Rox."

Roxy squeezed by with two bottles in her hands. "Oh, come on now. We don't want to be the first ones there." She made a beeline to the mirror to begin her ritual. *Some things never change.*

On the TV in the living room Pam overheard a news report that sparked her attention. The journalist was doing a live investigative report about a secret retreat in northern California. The "ultraprivate meeting," as he labeled it, involved the annual gathering located at Bonham Grove. *Uh oh. What's my dad up to now?*

The reporter displayed live film footage that he had shot from a hidden location outside the entry to the Grove. The footage, although sometimes out of focus, captured a number of the attendees arriving at the highly confidential gathering. The reporter's whispers gave voice-over narrative about the history of the Grove and who was entering the meeting.

At that particular moment a twelve-passenger limousine pulled up to the checkpoint at the entry. One of the tinted windows lowered as the passenger spoke to the guard who screened the members before allowing them to pass through the gates. The video went fuzzy and then slowly came back into focus as it zoomed in closer.

Once the picture came into focus, the remote fell from Pamela's hand. She saw her father as he smiled at the guard and extended his hand in greeting. But then another occupant of the backseat leaned into view.

It was Dr. Lee Jones, the current interim director of the CIA. The reporter's breathless whisper confirmed it.

Pam stared at the screen in absolute shock. As the tinted window raised and the car began to roll through the gate, she could see her father turn toward Jones, laughing at some shared jest.

Pam stared at the screen, now unseeing. *Daddy? Who are you?*

EPILOGUE

For the first few weeks she was back in Dallas, Pam did little else but sleep, except for the times when Roxy would drag her out, fearing that Pam was sinking into a depression. Gradually, though, as her emotional and physical exhaustion began to yield, she spent more and more time wondering about Alex. Javier and Pilar had still not seen or heard anything from him. Pam was beginning to worry that perhaps he had been taken back to Russia. Each time the thought would enter her mind, she would try to shove it away, but it kept coming back and bringing reinforcements.

She called her boss at Formula 1 and explained as much of the situation as she could, and he was surprisingly understanding. "Take the time off that you need," he told her. "But could you give Gatti a call so he will stop asking me about you?"

Pam laughed. "I'll give Lorenzo a ring." The next day, she spoke to him and asked him to settle things with the Palais Joséphine in Monaco for her. "You and I might want to stay there again sometime," she said, "and I don't want to burn that bridge."

"Promises, promises . . . but I'll handle it," Lorenzo said in the warm voice that had caught Pam's attention when they first met. "Come back to work, Pam. It's boring here without you; no one has shot at me or chased me down the highway in a whole week."

Pam threw her head back and laughed. "I'll be back; you can count on it," she said. She hung up the phone, feeling a warm glow.

When she had been home for almost a month, a letter arrived for her, postmarked from Saint Petersburg. It was hand addressed, and Pam was half afraid to open it. What if it was somehow connected with Alex—perhaps notification that he was back in the orphanage? Or that he had been found and that something had happened to him?

In an agony of uncertainty, Pam tore open the letter and began reading.

> *Dear Pamela,*
>
> *I hope you can read this; I don't get much practice writing with the Latin alphabet. But you have been on my mind a great deal lately, and I felt I needed to reach out to you somehow. Your address was still in my files from your passport—the real one! (haha)*
>
> *I was detained by the authorities for a day or two after you left Russia, and then they just let me go. I thought they would ask me about Alexander or that at least they would investigate the orphanage, but they did neither. It was almost as if they didn't really care, one way or the other, once they knew you were no longer in Russia. It was very strange, and I still don't understand it.*
>
> *Pamela, I know why you took Alexander, and a big part of me hopes you were successful in getting him to your home in the U.S. He is such a lovely boy, and I know that you will do all you can to give him opportunities he could never have in this country. Each day when I walk past the place where he used to sleep, I say a prayer to Saint Nicholas, asking him to be kept safe, wherever he may be. Somehow, I know in my heart that he is okay. If he is with you, I know that he is. At any rate, I wanted to let you know that I have no ill feelings toward you at all. You were following your heart and doing what you thought was best for Alexander. If you made a mistake, it was made in love, and such a mistake is not always a bad thing, I think.*
>
> *Yuliya is still here, and, believe it or not, she asks about*

you sometimes. She has a hard shell, but she truly loves the children, and I think she sensed that you did, too. She is just not very good with other people.

Pamela, if you should ever come back to Russia, I would count it an honor to see you again. I hope good things are happening in your life.

Your friend,
Sofia Lebedev

P.S. Sometimes a taxi driver named Viktor comes by, asking if we have heard from you. He will not give me his last name, but he says you will remember him.

Another piece of paper was inside the envelope. Pam unfolded it to find a picture inside. On the photo was a picture of her standing next to Alex. He was beaming up at her as her surprised look was frozen in the flash. Sofia's words floated in the air . . . *I like to get pictures of our new volunteers with the children before the craziness of this place drives them away.*

Pam held the picture and letter, sobbing uncontrollably. A confusing mix of emotions washed through her: relief that Sofia was not languishing in prison on her account; guilt for having put Sofia in a difficult position; anguish at the plight of all the thousands of children still in cheerless orphanages or, worse, living in the streets of Russian cities; nostalgia for the times—hard though they had been—when she gave her days and her energy to caring for the children in the Belarov Institute; and over it all, anxiety for what had become of Alex. Would she ever see him again?

As time went on, she continued to notice the peculiar noises on her phone, and finally came to accept it as her lot in life. She was officially on the government's radar screen now, she supposed, and it was what it was. Besides, if she wanted to have a conversation that she really didn't want overheard, there were pay phones and prepaid cell phones. She knew that now.

One day, as she was checking her e-mail, she noticed a letter from Giles Girard. She clicked on it and read Giles's note of appreciation for her great risks in getting the flash drive from Joseph Pierce to him.

"You started it all, Pam," he wrote. "Without the documentation you placed in our hands, WebLeaks could never have had enough on the government to force them to stay away from us. Things are crazy here, because there seems to always be something underhanded afoot in this world of ours, and the open invitation to expose the truth without fear of retaliation seems to have made WebLeaks a household word overnight. But we owe it all to you, Pam. I'll never forget what you've done."

He went on to tell her that he had heard from Joseph Pierce and also from Zia Sudario, a classmate of Giles's from back in the day who had originally tipped him off about the suspicious activities at Maxwell Morris Medical Institute.

Pam smiled. She thought about Zia Sudario—whoever that was—and had a feeling she knew a little bit of what Giles's friend had felt, carrying information that she didn't want to know and having no idea what to do with it. It was a burden not many would ever be called to bear, and Pam prayed that she would never have to bear it again.

Giles closed the letter with an odd message:

> *He was released to an undisclosed address, but I knew you'd want to know. Here is the address, Pam. Please be discreet. You're welcome,*
>
> *Giles*

The address was in La Moraleja, in the northern section of Madrid. *What in the hell does that mean?* She read the words over and over. *Here is the address . . . be discreet . . . You're welcome . . .*

After two days of pondering the message, Pam couldn't take it anymore. She called Roxy. "Rox, can you get away for a week?"

"Yeah, why? What's up?"

"We're going to Spain."

* * *

Pam arrived at the address with Roxy in tow; she triple-checked it against the one that Giles had sent to her. She and Roxy looked at one another and then back at the snow white, contemporary-style mansion that sat on the hill rising up from the street. Roxy shrugged her shoulders. "Should we try to knock on the door?"

"Hell, I don't know. I don't even know why I came here. Besides that, how in the world do we even get to the front door?"

Roxy pointed toward a path that led around the edge of the property and up the side of a steep hill. Pam nodded, and they made their way along the extended path, ignoring the "Prohibido el paso" signs, until they were a few yards from the elevated home. They then heard the sound of horses coming up the trail behind them. *Shit!*

Pam led the way off the trail as Roxy followed quickly. They ducked behind a row of trees, remaining out of view but peering through the branches. Two of the most beautiful Arabian horses Pam had ever seen galloped into her view.

"Muy bien! You won that race, but there will be others!" the man laughed as he dismounted.

Pam reacted with an audible gasp as the boy leaped from the second horse to the ground. It was Alex, standing next to the horse and smiling broadly as he stroked the horse's muscular withers.

Alex laughed, holding up three fingers to the man. He and the man were dressed in matching riding outfits. "But that's the third time now! Tercera vez!"

"Three? I don't remember three! One maybe, but not three," the man responded with a subdued grin.

Pam felt the tears streaming down her face. She was unable to speak, unable to move, unable to believe her eyes. Alex and the man mounted the horses and raced up the trail to the white mansion.

Pam felt Roxy's hand rest on her shoulder. "You okay, Pam?"

Pam looked at the mansion and the vast land that surrounded it. She recalled the pure joy she saw in Alex's smile, then wiped the tears off of her face. "Yeah, Rox, I'm fine." She looked back at Alex and the gentleman as they led the horses to the stables located behind the mansion.

"Yeah . . . yeah, I think that I'll be fine now. Let's head back to Dallas. And then . . . I've got to get back to work."

I am grateful and thank those who mentored and supported
this project from the heart.

CPSIA information can be obtained
at www.ICGtesting.com
Printed in the USA
BVHW031145290820
587372BV00006B/202